The Tomb
That Ruth Built

A Mickey Rawlings Mystery

Troy Soos

Praise for Troy Soos and the
Mickey Rawlings Baseball Mysteries

"Baseball and mystery team up for a winner."
— *USA Today* (on *Murder at Fenway Park*)

"Full of life." — *New York Times* (on *Hanging Curve*)

"An entertaining double play. . . The plot will appeal to mystery fans, baseball purists will appreciate Soos's attention to detail."
— *Orlando Sentinel* (on *Hunting a Detroit Tiger*)

"Well-judged period background (including a winsome role for Casey Stengel) enlivens a solid mystery."
— *Kirkus Reviews* (on *Murder at Ebbets Field*)

"A richly atmospheric journey through time."
— *Booklist*

"Soos deftly weaves fictional characters with legends."
— *Houston Chronicle*

"Troy Soos does a red-letter job of mixing the mystery into a period when all baseball was played on fields that had real grass." — *St. Louis Post-Dispatch*

"Tough and terrific." — *New York Daily News*

"A perfect marriage between baseball and mystery fiction."
— *Mystery Readers Journal*

"Equal parts baseball and mystery are the perfect proportion." — *Robert B. Parker*

Chapter One

I may only be a utility infielder, but I'm a *veteran* utility infielder with more than ten years in the big leagues playing for half a dozen teams. Although my role has been part-time and unsung, I've always played the game with pride and made the most of every chance I've had.

The only category in which I'd led any league was the number of backside splinters from warming dugout benches, but I have had some incredible moments in my career. Especially gratifying were those times when I managed to get the better of one of the game's all-time greats—like tagging out the ferocious Ty Cobb as he came sliding into second base with his spikes slashing, or the time I cracked a clean single off a Walter Johnson fastball. I even won a game by stealing home on Grover Cleveland Alexander.

That's one of the great things about baseball: Every now and then, a dead-armed pitcher can baffle opposing batters for a no-hitter, a weak-hitting second string catcher can loft three home runs in a single game, or a team in distant last place can beat the World's

Champions.

The problem was that these occasional moments of glory led me to believe that it might be possible to stretch a moment into a week, a week into a month, and a month into an entire season. I imagined myself fielding flawlessly in every game, batting .350, and capping off the year by playing in my first World Series. It was merely an illusion, of course, and it usually faded into reality around mid-April, but I always looked forward to those springtime fantasies. Baseball to me was about hope, about anticipating all the spectacular things that *might* happen rather than a dry statistical record of what actually did occur.

This year, however, the dream was already flickering out in March, thanks to my new ball club. When I signed a contract to play for the powerhouse New York Yankees, I had expected that 1923 would be the most promising season of my career. Yankees' management lacked my optimism, though, and gave no indication that they intended to make use of my diamond skills. Throughout the first weeks of spring training, they had thoroughly neglected the "player" part of my job description while taking full advantage of "utility."

That's why I was now trudging through New Orleans in the middle of a cold March night, sent to pick up a bush-leaguer who was getting a tryout with the team. Do they send Babe Ruth, or Jumpin' Joe Dugan, or Sad Sam Jones? Of course not. When somebody was needed to meet this kid at the train station, Mickey Rawlings got the call.

Walking along Canal Street, on the edge of the French Quarter, I became aware of the festive atmosphere around me. Most of the shops and restaurants that lined the street were closed and dark, but street lamps provided enough light for me to see that I was far from alone. A street car rolling through the central median transported a crowd of young people singing a bouncy blues tune in voices exuberantly off-pitch. An open touring car driving in the opposite direction was packed with double its advertised capacity; the laughing men and women who filled it appeared more than comfortable with the seating arrangement. Now and then, I had to walk around clusters of people holding impromptu parties in the middle of the sidewalk. Mardi Gras was a month ago, but this was a city where even the funerals were street festivals and there was no day of the week that didn't merit some kind of celebration. As I passed one group of revelers after another, I started to get the feeling that I was the only unhappy person in New Orleans.

Being sent on a midnight errand didn't bother me nearly as much as the fact that I could very well be en route to picking up my replacement. There were twenty-five players on a major-league roster and I was usually number twenty-five. That meant if this new kid made the team, I could be cut loose—again.

I arrived at Southern Railway Station, on the corner of Canal and Basin Streets, in plenty of time. Since the train was half an hour late, I restlessly paced the polished floor of the waiting area, admiring the architectural charms of the depot but growing less and less enamored of my task.

Finally, on what was now Monday morning, the train pulled in and I walked through a brick archway to meet the newcomer at Track Two. He'd better not expect me to carry his bags, I thought. Despite what the Yankees seemed to believe, there were limits to what a utility player should be asked to do.

With one look at the strapping young man who stepped onto the platform, I realized he wouldn't need my help carrying anything. Almost six feet tall, he had a powerful build that his serge suit couldn't hide. Even his stolid face looked muscular. A scarred leather suitcase was in one hand and a bulging canvas satchel in the other. Several bat handles stuck out of the bag, confirming that this was the man I'd been sent to meet.

I stepped up to him. "Haines?"

He nodded. "Yes, sir. Hinkey Haines. Thank you for meeting me." He put down his suitcase to proffer a handshake.

"Mickey Rawlings," I said. "I'll get you to the hotel. You must be tired after the trip."

"That's very kind of you, sir." He picked up his luggage again with no discernible effort. "Do you work for the team?"

Do I *work* for the team? My image has appeared on a Sweet Caporal tobacco card, *Rawlings, M* has been listed in a couple hundred box scores, and yet this kid doesn't know who I am. Maybe I should have shown up in my uniform and cap instead of a three piece suit and a high crown derby. I simply answered, "Yes."

As I led the way to the exit, I commented, "Looks like it won't take much to get you in shape." The primary reason for spring training was for ballplayers to work off the excesses of winter, but Haines already appeared perfectly fit.

"Oh, I've been playing some football."

I couldn't imagine why. Football seemed to me a pointless game for college boys and head-butting brutes. "Rough sport," I said. "Be careful you don't hurt yourself, or it could kill your baseball career."

He shrugged his beefy shoulders. "I already have a pretty good football career. Made All-American in college and I've been playing with a couple of pro teams around Philadelphia. Football is really my preferred sport."

I was having serious reservations about Hinkey Haines. Not only was his last sentence sacrilege as far as I was concerned, but I could be losing my job to somebody who didn't even care about baseball.

Outside the station, Haines' eyes widened and he looked around like a little kid who'd just walked into a carnival. His darkly handsome face broke into a broad grin as he noticed the attractions that abounded in the Crescent City. Even at this time of night the buildings and the people fairly glittered. The air was rich with the mingled scents of jasmine, French bread, jambalaya, and the Mississippi River. It also carried the wonderful sounds of jazz from the saloons and night clubs nearby.

"Hotel's this way," I prodded. When Haines resumed walking, I asked, "You play any pro baseball?"

"Yes, sir, with Reading in the International League last year. And Jersey City before that."

We'd walked a couple of blocks when a packed streetcar rolled by. Haines cast a wistful look at the trolley and his shoulders sagged slightly. It was the first sign that he was tired.

"Sorry," I said. "I should have thought to get a cab." I reached for his equipment bag and hoisted it up. "It's only a couple more blocks."

"Thanks."

Neither of us said much while we covered the next block, as Haines craned his neck this way and that, taking in the colorful sights of New Orleans. They would have been difficult to miss since this was a city that made no attempt to hide its charms, not even the illicit ones. After the fabled Storyville red light district was shut down by the Army during the Great War, the vice industry had simply spread throughout the rest of the city. Every variety of brothel, speakeasy, and gambling den was readily available to anyone in the market for such entertainments. To my mind, it was a ludicrous place to hold spring training—especially for a team like the Yankees that was known to enjoy the night life. Judging by the eager expression on his face, I feared that Haines would fit right in.

I brought his attention back to baseball when I mentioned, "We got a game tomorrow against the Pelicans."

"They any good?"

"Not bad for bushers." In fact, the city's minor league team had trounced us 13–0 in today's first exhibition contest of spring training. It didn't portend well that the American League champion New York Yankees could be so easily humiliated by a bush league club.

"I'm ready to play," Haines announced confidently. "Hope I get in the game."

I stifled a chuckle. He'd be lucky to get a chance at batting practice. Veterans are not known for their hospitality to newcomers. Besides, we'd need our best on the field to keep the Pelicans from routing us again. Unfortunately, that meant I probably wouldn't get to play, either.

Haines suddenly pulled up short, staring slack-jawed at two garish women of the night standing next to a street lamp. Behind them was a narrow clapboard building with a sign over the door that read *Creole Candy*. A lamp with a red shade glowed prominently in the store window. This sweet shop was not making its money from gumdrops.

One of the women, barely dressed in a low-cut blouse and a slinky skirt, called to Haines, "See something you like, handsome?" She hiked her skirt to mid-thigh and struck a pose.

I nudged Haines along, but he almost broke his neck twisting it for one more look. He grinned, hesitated, and it appeared he might walk over to the prostitutes.

"Listen to me for a minute," I said in my sternest voice. I put his bag on the pavement and grabbed his elbow.

He looked at me with surprise. "What are you—"

"If you want to make the team, keep your mind on *baseball*. When you're on the field, give it everything you got—hustle like you got a devil on your tail. When you're on the bench, watch the other players and listen to the coaches. And at night, stay in the hotel and get your rest. There's nothing on the streets that's going to do you any good."

A smirk tugged at his lips. "I believe I can take care of myself, but thanks for the advice, Mr. uh... I'm sorry, but I forgot your—"

"Mickey Rawlings," I reminded him. "I've been a major leaguer since you were in short pants and I've seen more players kill their careers by what they do *off* the field than from getting hurt *on* it."

He was taken aback. "You're a *player*?"

"Yeah. I'm also your competition. And if you want to take my job, you're gonna have to work your ass off, because I'm gonna be fighting to keep it."

He scratched the back of his neck. "I don't understand. If you think I might take your job, why are you giving me advice?"

"Because I want you to be at your best no matter what. If we both make the team, I want you to help us win. If I lose my job to you, I want it to be because you're a helluva ballplayer. And if I beat you, I want it to be because of what I can do on the field, not because you wore yourself out in a saloon or a whorehouse."

He appeared to mull that over for a moment, then nodded agreeably and began walking so quickly that it was a struggle for me to stay in the lead the rest of the way.

We turned onto Baronne Street and entered the Grunewald Hotel, the most elegant in New Orleans. One advantage of playing for the Yankees was that they always traveled first class, and these were the finest spring training accommodations I've ever enjoyed. The hotel's opulent lobby was decorated with Oriental rugs, dark wood paneling, and gilt-framed paintings. Massive crystal chandeliers hung from the high ceiling, casting a golden light that reflected brightly from the polished brass fixtures and decorative panels.

Even in this fashionable establishment, however, there was ready access to the same kinds of pleasures that were once found in Storyville. The Grunewald's basement was home to The Cave, which was modeled as a grotto with plaster rock formations on the walls and ceilings. It proudly claimed to be the first night club in the country and hadn't slowed its operation one bit with the coming of Prohibition. Booze flowed freely in The Cave and hostesses dressed as nymphs were available for company. Having such a place right in our hotel was another temptation for the players and another headache for manager Miller Huggins.

I spotted Huggins in his usual spot, a leather wingback chair near the elevator, from which he monitored the comings and goings of his ballplayers. The oversized chair made him appear even smaller than he was. Huggins, a former second baseman, was invariably referred to as "pint-sized" by sportswriters. Since I was about the same build as the manager, I didn't care for that description. To my mind, we were exactly the right size for infielders. Huggins was in his forties and still looked in shape to play. His gnomish face, however, was that of a much older man, with bags under his eyes and worry lines furrowing his brow. Managing a team like the Yankees could age anyone prematurely.

I ushered Haines across the marble floor. When Huggins looked up from his newspaper, I made a brief introduction.

Huggins eyed the newcomer up and down, giving no indication of approval or disapproval. "Rawlings here talk to you?" he asked.

Haines nodded uncertainly.

"Good," the manager said. "Learn everything you can from him. Rawlings has been around a while and he can teach you a lot—about playing ball and about being a ballplayer." He fixed Haines with a scowl. "And being a *team* player also applies to what you do *off* the field."

"Yes, sir," Haines said quickly. "He told me about that. I promise I won't be any trouble."

Huggins turned his tired eyes to me. "I wish you could convince your roomie to stay on the straight and narrow as easily as you seemed to have convinced this young man."

I shrugged. No one else had ever succeeded in correcting my roommate's behavior, either. Besides, I was being paid to play baseball, not nursemaid to an overgrown kid.

There was a sudden furor near the hotel entrance. Bellmen, guests, and lobby sitters rushed toward it as if pulled by a powerful magnet, and all eyes turned in that direction.

"There's my problem boy now," muttered Huggins.

Inside the door, basking in the attention, stood Babe

Ruth. His round face, with its flat nose, dark eyes, and wide mouth, was among the most famous in the world. A long black cigar was clamped in his grinning teeth, an oversized golf cap crowned his enormous head, and his large body was draped in a raccoon coat. He tottered slightly and his complexion was ruddy.

Clinging to the Babe's left arm was a shapely blonde in a gauzy white dress and a stained fox stole, a brunette with smeared lipstick had a hand on his right elbow, and a yawning redhead clutched at his collar. It would be obvious to anyone who saw them that these women were of the same profession as those who'd been standing outside *Creole Candy*.

Ruth paused to exchange greetings with the admirers who swarmed to greet him. He loved the adulation and they loved being in his almost mythic presence. All he had to do was walk into a room and it was a spectacle.

"That's *him*," Haines gasped. "That's the Babe!"

I certainly understood the rookie's awestruck reaction. Babe Ruth was big in every way. From his imposing physique to his towering home runs to his boyish charisma. Aided by newspapers that reported his every deed—and, until recently, omitted mention of his *mis*deeds—it was no wonder that Babe Ruth had become a national hero. He had also become my roommate, which gave me a unique perspective on the man.

After signing a few autographs, Ruth and his trio of dates made their way in our direction, heading to the elevator. None were walking steadily and it appeared the ladies were holding on to him partly to keep from falling.

As much as I admired Ruth, I was disappointed to see him like this. Last season had been a miserable one for him both on and off the field. He had begun 1922 with a six-week suspension and ended it with a pitiful World

Series performance. This spring he had promised to change his ways and give his best to baseball. He vowed to get his weight under two hundred pounds and swore that he would cut down on booze and women.

Desperate to try anything that might help the Babe keep his promises, Miller Huggins decided that I could be good influence on him and paired us together as roommates. Curtailing Ruth was like roping a tornado, however. The man was a force of nature and submitted only to his own impulses.

Now here he was, after a humiliating game in which he had contributed nothing to the Yankees' effort, out on a binge. That meant he'd be in even worse shape tomorrow and the downhill slide would continue.

When he got near us, Ruth bellowed, "See, Hug? I'm in by curfew!"

Huggins pulled out his pocket watch. Curfew was eleven o'clock and it was now nearly one. Different rules applied to the Babe, however, and he delighted in flaunting that fact to the manager.

Ruth suddenly guffawed. "I'm gonna be in *after* curfew, too." He gave the blonde a playful slap on her bottom. "I'm gonna be in *her*." Doing the same to the other women, he added, "And *her*, and *her*." Each one giggled in turn, then they all laughed together before turning toward the elevator. There was certainly nothing subtle about Babe Ruth.

He called back over his shoulder, "You might want to go out again, kid! I'm gonna be busy a while!" That was directed to me, I knew. So far, he had never called me anything but "kid" and his use of the room to entertain women was almost a nightly occurrence—except when he never returned to the hotel at all.

As they stepped into the elevator, Huggins said with

an exasperated sigh, "We *got* to find a new place for spring training."

It wouldn't help, I thought. Babe Ruth could probably find beer and women at the South Pole.

I had almost forgotten about Hinkey Haines until he elbowed me and whispered with astonishment, "He's got *three* of them."

"Yeah," I said. "He's cutting down this year."

While the manager took Haines to get checked in at the lobby desk, I looked around for a comfortable chair. I was starting to suspect that the real reason I'd been assigned as Ruth's roommate was not so much to be a good influence on him, but so that a starting player wouldn't have to lose sleep each night. Whether I played or not, I had the feeling that 1923 was going to be an exhausting season for me.

Chapter Two

As the train slowed, my heartbeat quickened. After four weeks of spring training in an unseasonably cold New Orleans, and a grueling exhibition tour on the way back to New York, we were finally pulling in to Pennsylvania Station.

Even though the Yankees provided topnotch accommodations, including this special train, I was tired of Pullman sleeping berths and hotel rooms, and especially tired of getting no sleep at all whenever my roommate had the urge for female companionship. I wanted a normal night at home—with one particular female.

The wheels were still rolling when a crowd that had gathered alongside the track sent up a roar. Their cheers almost drowned out the rumble of the rails and the shrieking of the brakes. Through tendrils of steam drifting back from the engine, I saw hundreds of fans, reporters, and family members who had turned out to welcome home their baseball teams. Most were undoubtedly on hand to greet the Yankees, but others had come over from Brooklyn to meet the National Leaguers with whom we had traveled.

Judging by the explosion of activity inside the train, I wasn't the only one eager to step foot in New York. Players from both teams jostled each other in the aisles, some plowing through as though trying to break up a double play at second base. While porters hustled to keep up with the demands for trunks and suitcases, there was a noisy crush for the exits, accompanied by the colorful kind of language that only baseball players and sailors could speak with effortless fluency.

By the time the train screeched to a complete stop, some of the exits were impassable. One was blocked by Babe Ruth, who stood on the top step of a luxury Pullman car and was going to be stuck there for some time. He was pressed by a large crowd of fans and reporters who peppered him with questions and made approving noises at his every utterance. A slightly smaller crowd prevented Miller Huggins from stepping down from another car until he had satisfied their every question about the Yankees' prospects for the season.

Roly-poly Brooklyn manager Wilbert "Uncle Robbie" Robinson, with Dazzy Vance and Zach Wheat standing behind him, was similarly besieged several cars away. His was a team of many names: I was among those who thought of them as the "Dodgers" which was shortened from "Trolley Dodgers," newspaper writers often referred to them by the club's preferred name "Superbas," while most fans called them the "Robins" in honor of the popular manager. I didn't much care for naming teams after managers, especially after seeing a recent headline that referred to the Yankees as the "Hugmen."

There was more shoving inside the train as players ran

into the blockages and then fought their way back to find other routes. Using my suitcase as a wedge, I pried a narrow gap between Bullet Joe Bush and Wally Pipp and slipped through the brief opening. After climbing over a small mountain of steamer trunks, I got to an open door and stepped outside. This was one time when the anonymity of my utility role was an advantage. No one was going to interview me or ask me for an autograph.

Before the soles of my brogues hit the platform, I was scanning the crowd for the only person I wanted to see. I heard her call "Mickey!" before I saw her. Then she came into view, working her way through the predominantly male crowd as forcefully as the players who were still pushing to leave the train. Margie made more rapid progress than the ballplayers, though. She had once been a movie star, appearing in her own series of action serials, and she was still lithe and athletic.

I don't think there's anything more beautiful than the sight of a loved one welcoming you home after a long separation. And when that loved one is Margie Turner, a homecoming could feel as exciting as hitting a grand slam. Or what I assume it would be like to hit a grand slam, anyway.

Margie's dark, heavy-lidded eyes resembled Mabel Normand's and they had such depth and sparkle that when she smiled it was like turning on a light. She was stylishly dressed for the brisk morning in a chocolate-colored velour coat with flare sleeves. Over her chestnut hair, she wore a cloche hat adorned with a bright silk florette.

She ran the last few steps to me with a beaming expression on her tawny face. I put down my suitcase and we embraced in a hug that told each other we'd been apart for much too long. I said, "I am so glad to see—"

Before I got out "you," Margie's lips were on mine in an ardent kiss. She always did have a way of getting right to the point.

I picked up my bag, she hooked her hand in my arm, and we headed to the station's concourse.

"How was the trip?" she asked.

"*Long.*" Traveling with the Brooklyn team we had taken a circuitous route home, stopping to play exhibition games in cities and towns from Muskogee, Oklahoma to Chattanooga, Tennessee. Two weeks, twelve games, and more than two thousand miles made the journey seem interminable. "I'll sure be glad to sleep in my own bed tonight," I added.

Margie smiled broadly. "I'm looking forward to that, too." Never coy or shy, she was once again right to the point. "But I suppose you must be tired," she teased.

"Not anymore." I instantly picked up my pace, almost dragging her along for a few steps. She laughed and I eased up—just a little.

"How are things at the studio?" I asked. Shortly after I left for spring training, Margie had landed a job with the D. W. Griffith movie studio in Mamaroneck.

"Slow," she answered. "Mr. Griffith is down South, so we don't have much to do. But the paycheck is regular, and I've met some nice people."

We emerged from the concourse into the building's spectacular main waiting room. It was famous as one of the largest indoor spaces in the world, a remarkable structure of steel, glass, and granite, with carved archways and fluted columns that supported a ceiling one hundred fifty feet high. I'd probably passed through Pennsylvania Station a hundred times during my career and I was always struck by its scale; it seemed to announce to arriving passengers that they were entering a city like no other in the world. Although I'd played in cities throughout most of the United States, New York was definitely in a league of its own. This was a city that had everything, and often had it bigger and better than anywhere else.

Margie said, "As a matter of fact, a couple of people from the studio came with me." Her words, along with our footsteps, echoed in the enormous chamber.

"Where are they?"

"Outside. I wanted to see you by myself first." She gave my arm a squeeze. "I'm sorry. I know you probably want to go right home, but I've told them all about you and they're really eager to meet you. I tried putting them off but—"

"I'd be happy to meet them," I said. It was refreshing, and rare, that somebody wanted me instead of Babe Ruth. "Are they actors?"

"One of them is an actress I knew in Hollywood— Natalie Brockman. She helped me get the job with Mr. Griffith. The other is her, uh… He's a director: Tom Van Dusen. They're waiting in his car."

We passed through the station's pink granite colonnade and walked down the steps to Seventh Avenue. Even the air was different in New York, carrying a unique mixture of smells: hot sausages and oysters from pushcarts, exhaust from the rapidly increasing number of motor vehicles, excrement from the dwindling number of horses, and occasional hints of the waterfront that surrounded the island. The broad avenue teemed with automobiles, street cars, and fast-moving pedestrians. Yes, I thought, New York was always big and bustling—and this year I was going to be part of it.

Margie said in a worried tone, "I'm not sure if you'll like them, but I had to… I mean… I think they want to…"

"It's okay," I assured her. "I don't mind at all." Maybe they'd even ask for an autograph.

"Margie!" called a tall slender man standing by a royal blue Franklin automobile with yellow spoked wheels. "Over here!" The car was double-parked, blocking a checker taxi, and despite the cold its canvas top was down.

"That's Tom," Margie said.

The first thing that I noticed about Van Dusen was that he looked every bit as "Hollywood" as his car. The director's outfit might have been copied from something he'd seen in *Photoplay Magazine*. He sported a double-breasted camelhair overcoat, with the belt knotted, and a paisley silk scarf worn as a giant ascot. A white, wide-brimmed fedora topped his head and highly polished two-tone wingtips were on his feet. He was probably in his late thirties, with a clean-shaven boyish face and nervous eyes.

We walked over and Margie made the introductions.

"I can't tell you how much I've been looking forward to meeting you," Van Dusen said, flashing an expanse of very white teeth. He pumped my hand like he expected me to spout water. "I am a *big* fan."

There was something phony about him, but that didn't prevent me from feeling flattered.

The taxi honked its horn angrily, but Van Dusen didn't appear to notice. "Allow me to introduce you to one of our studio's loveliest stars: Miss Natalie Brockman." He led me to the passenger's side of the car, where a waif-like woman in an ermine-trimmed coat was slouched in the front seat. She had bleached blonde hair cut in a bob, and a face that would have been pretty if it hadn't been fixed in an expression of determined boredom. Van Dusen added, "You may have seen her in *Way Down East* or *Orphans of the Storm*. Mr. Griffith uses her in all his big pictures."

I'd never heard of her, but pretended that I had. I told her how much I enjoyed her acting. She barely acknowledged me and whined to Van Dusen in a childlike voice, "I want lunch."

"Splendid idea!" he replied.

The taxi driver bellowed, "Hey buddy! Move yer damn car before I take a tire iron to yer head!"

Pointedly ignoring him, the director asked, "Perhaps you and Margie would join us? I know you're probably eager to go home, but we would be *so* grateful for your company."

Margie didn't object, so we were soon in the back of the gaudy Franklin, a cold wind blowing over us as Tom Van Dusen weaved his way through Manhattan traffic as recklessly as a Keystone Cop.

* * *

Natalie Brockman's idea of lunch was champagne. She had quickly tossed off her first glass, murmuring something about having missed breakfast, and was sipping her second before the rest of us had placed our food orders. Like most establishments in the city—or in most of the country, for that matter—this one ignored the strictures of Prohibition. Brockman was served her drinks as routinely as if they were sarsaparilla.

From the moment we entered the upscale café, on Thirty-third Street not far from the train station, Van Dusen spoke to the staff in a loud, imperious tone as if he was giving orders on one of his movie sets. The restaurant was busy, and almost every table was occupied, but that hadn't stopped Van Dusen from demanding instant service and ordering a waiter to set a special table exactly where he wanted. He gave another waiter his hat to hang for him, revealing sandy hair that was slicked back with pomade and so perfectly parted that it looked like it had been done by a surveyor. Snapping his fingers, he called the harried waiter back to take his coat as well. I wondered if the waiters would take turns spitting in Van Dusen's food before serving him.

The director soon proved to be nearly as overbearing in conversation, almost all of which was about himself. Brockman, with her peroxide hair and pale skin had almost faded from view; she sat quietly watching the bubbles in her champagne flute, completely mesmerized. Margie also spoke little during the meal, occasionally elaborating for my benefit on something Van Dusen had said.

I was quiet, partly from exhaustion and partly because I feared that speaking up would only prolong the ordeal. So I quietly picked at a greasy chicken leg, nodded every now and then, and hoped that no one would order dessert.

Van Dusen shifted the topic of his monologue to baseball and tried to convince me that he was an ardent fan. He assured me that he would have been excellent at the game himself except for the fact that he was of a more artistic nature and didn't actually engage in sports.

Throughout lunch, the arrogant director had issued an endless series of statements, pronouncements, and opinions but had never asked the rest of us any questions or sought our views. It came as a surprise when he asked me, "You have a few more exhibition games against Brooklyn, don't you?"

"Yes," I answered. "In fact, we have a game at Ebbets Field tomorrow." I downed the rest of my ginger ale and added, "I should probably rest up for it—it was a long trip home." I hoped he would take the hint.

"Of course, of course. You must be tired." He placed his coffee mug on the table and shoved his half-full plate to one side as if he no longer cared for anything as mundane as food and drink. "But I hope we can talk a little business first."

"Business," Brockman softly echoed as if it was a curse. I didn't remember seeing her in any movies but if her acting range was limited to the two expressions she'd shown today—bored and petulant—I doubted that she'd have much of a career. She lit a thin cigarette and inhaled deeply.

I glanced at Margie who was casually poking at a piece of baked haddock. She didn't seem in a hurry, so I nodded for Van Dusen to proceed.

"Very good!" he thundered. I doubted that he required a megaphone to give directions on a movie set. "As you know, I am a director at the D. W. Griffith Studio. But I am not a mere employee. I am an investor, with a significant share of the company." He leaned forward and dropped his voice so that only half the restaurant's customers could hear it. "May I speak frankly?"

That question always made me suspect that a lie was coming, but I said, "Please do."

"I'm not betraying any secrets here," he went on. "It's in all the trade magazines that our studio is struggling to stay afloat. Mr. Griffith is a genius as a movie maker, but as a businessman he's… Well, he has a tendency to lose whatever money he makes. Now he's in Louisiana preparing to film something called *The White Rose* and he's taking forever to scout locations. We didn't release a single movie last year and we'll be lucky to get the new one out this year." Van Dusen slapped his hand down on the table, causing the silverware to clatter. "If a studio doesn't make movies, it doesn't make money!"

I didn't know how to respond and couldn't see what this had to do with me. I gave a noncommittal nod.

Van Dusen quickly calmed and continued. "So I want to make some smaller movies. Nothing on a grand scale like Mr. Griffith's, just some short, simple pictures to keep the studio working and enough money coming in to pay expenses."

"Makes sense," I said honestly. I thought Griffith's movies were much too long; some of them ran two and a half hours, considerably longer than a baseball game. I preferred the twenty-minute two-reelers that used to be the standard program fare of nickelodeons, and I particularly enjoyed the weekly cliff-hanger action serials like those that Margie and Pearl White used to make.

"Well, here's my idea…" Van Dusen paused, prepared to gauge my reaction. "Adolph Zukor started Paramount Pictures as the 'Famous Players Film Company.' Zukor believed that famous actors and actresses, the biggest names from the stage, would draw people to the movies. And he was right. People are attracted to *stars*, not stories. So my thinking is: How about *baseball* stars? Everybody follows baseball—it's the American game." He paused again. "I want to get a baseball player to appear in a movie for me."

I finally understood where Van Dusen had been leading with all this: He wanted me to be in a movie. I looked at Margie and smiled. We had met on a movie set in 1914, when Casey Stengel and I were given small roles in *Florence at the Ballpark*. It was filmed at the Vitagraph Studios in Brooklyn, where Margie was making an episode of her *Dangers of the Dark Continent* serial. She introduced herself to me by hitting me in the face with a pie from the set of a slapstick comedy. My first view of her was through custard filled eyes, but our relationship improved considerably thereafter.

I tried to catch Margie's eye, certain she would know what I was thinking. But she gave only a hint of a smile in return and looked away. Something was troubling her.

Van Dusen said, "Margie tells us you're Babe Ruth's roommate. So... I was hoping you could ask him to meet with me. He'd be the *perfect* ballplayer to launch the new movie series."

Now I really did understand: Van Dusen was only interested in me because of my connection to the Babe. I remembered that Margie had been trying to tell me something just before we'd met Van Dusen, and I was sure this was it. I gave Margie a smile and a small nod to let her know that it was alright. She visibly relaxed.

I said to Van Dusen, "Ruth was at the train station. You could have met him there."

He shook his head. "I would have only been a face in the crowd. I need to talk to him one-on-one. Also I'm hoping you might use your influence to sell him on my idea. I assume you two must be pretty close."

"Sorry, but I barely know the man. I spend more nights with Ruth's suitcase than I do with him."

Van Dusen let loose a theatrical belly laugh. "Yes, he is rather renowned for his extracurricular activities. And that's why I believe this picture would be good for *him* as well as for us. With all the bad publicity he's been getting lately, a good clean motion picture could do a lot for his image."

It might take more than one movie, I thought. The Babe had been hit with a paternity suit in November, and in January even the discreet *New York Times* alluded to his sexual history by describing him as "a man of many infections." And, of course, there was no secret about his drinking. Another newspaper ran a headline just last month that announced "Ruth Training on Scotch."

A thoughtful expression briefly altered Van Dusen's pretty boy features. He added, "Of course I only mentioned Babe Ruth first because he would be the star. There would certainly be a part in the movie for you, too." No doubt Van Dusen assumed I would jump at the chance, but I didn't find the role of afterthought to be all that appealing.

Natalie Brockman roused herself. "I would love to meet Babe Ruth," she slurred. "From what I hear, he must be *quite* an athlete." She flicked a half inch of cigarette ash on to the floor and returned to contemplating her champagne.

I was pretty sure Brockman wanted more from Ruth than an autograph. I also suspected that the Babe would more agreeable to whatever she might propose than to anything Van Dusen had in mind.

For Margie's sake, I finally answered, "I promise I'll talk to him if I get a chance. But I don't see much of him when we're in New York. He stays at the Ansonia. We only room together on the road."

"Fair enough," Van Dusen said. "That's all I can ask."

Margie abruptly spoke up. "This was a lovely lunch, but if you'll excuse us I really need to get Mickey home."

I smiled at her. I was glad there was somebody in the world who was more interested in me than in my roommate.

Chapter Three

The temperature was barely fifty and wintry clouds scudded across the threatening gray sky. There was also an electricity in the air that had nothing to do with the weather. Wednesday, April 18, 1923, would be a day for the history books and it seemed that all of New York wanted to share in the occasion.

This was Opening Day for the most majestic ballpark ever built—no, not "ballpark," but *stadium*. Thousands of tons of steel and concrete had been put together in a structure so imposing that the usual names of "park," "field," or "grounds" were inadequate. The new home of New York's American League franchise, swathed in patriotic bunting, was being unveiled to the public as *Yankee Stadium*.

Almost two hours before the scheduled first pitch, Babe Ruth led us onto the park's fresh green turf. Even the Babe, who was larger than life himself, seemed staggered by the scale of this baseball palace. "Some ballyard!" he exclaimed. We all stopped for a moment to gaze around. The structure wasn't impressive only in size, but in design. The team's owners had spent wildly to make this a monument for the ages. The stadium looked as if it could last as long as the Roman Coliseum that some said it resembled. The structure featured splendid architectural embellishments, my favorite being the scalloped copper frieze on the grandstand roof.

This was the first ballpark in history to have three tiers of seating, and it easily had the largest capacity. Although tickets were expensive—from one dollar for the bleacher section to $3.50 for reserved—they all sold easily and a small army of ushers attired in tuxedos had been employed to escort patrons to their seats. As the stadium filled, we had received attendance updates in the locker room: fifty thousand, sixty thousand, seventy thousand. Then came reports on the number of fans that had to be turned away: ten thousand, fifteen thousand, twenty thousand. I had thought that the counts must have been exaggerated, but from what I could see now, there appeared to be a million people packed in the seats and standing in the aisles. It looked like a dark roiling sea of wool overcoats, felt derbies and cloth caps. A rumbling sound from thousands of throats filled the air and reverberated through the vast space.

To keep warm, all the Yankees wore long sweaters over our pin-striped white flannels. The sweaters were trimmed in navy and adorned with an interlocking "NY" that matched the one on our caps. The Babe stepped forward to a thunder of cheers, and the rest of us followed. I was near the end of the line but not last; behind me walked Hinkey Haines, who had made the roster as a utility outfielder.

Like the fans, most of us had hopeful eyes on Babe Ruth. Just as he was leading us onto the field, we were counting on him and his fifty-three ounce bat to lead us to the pennant. He was well aware of how much everyone was depending on him, and was eager for a good start. In the clubhouse, he had said wistfully, "I'd give a year off my life to hit one today."

I certainly didn't want to shorten his life span, but I hoped that he'd hit one, too. Last year, the Babe had missed all of April and most of May because of a six-week suspension. He was suspended four more times during the year, easily leading the league in that unfortunate statistic, and had ended the season by hitting a pitiful .118 in the World Series—less than half my lifetime batting average. Some sports writers suggested that Ruth was washed up. That made me wonder: If Babe Ruth could be over the hill at twenty-eight, what was I at thirty-one? And I had never even been *up* the hill!

At the moment, though, I felt no fears or worries, only excitement about what might be in store. Playing the first game of the season in this spectacular new stadium, with a crowd larger than many city populations, there was every reason for optimism. I was just a sucker for Opening Day and the promises of spring.

Of course, Opening Day in a new stadium required that the pregame ceremonies be interminably long. Every politician and dignitary wanted his moment in the spotlight and a photograph with Babe Ruth. We waited while public officials from the Bronx borough president to the superintendent of West Point had their images taken alongside the Babe. Every pose was documented by dozens of photographers. With each shot, smoke from the flash powder puffed into the air like naval broadsides.

The most awkward photographs of the day had to be those of Yankees owners Jacob Ruppert and Til Huston.

The two men had become such bitter enemies in recent years that Baseball Commissioner Kenesaw Mountain Landis had to stand between them as a buffer. The three men were a contrast of styles: Ruppert dignified and dapper, Huston a disheveled man of almost three hundred pounds, Landis a slightly built, white-maned federal judge who ruled organized baseball with an iron fist. All three of them waved to the crowd enthusiastically, and accepted the crowd's applause as if they had each personally put every stone in place.

When the smoke cleared from the photographs, John Philip Sousa himself led the Seventh Regiment National Guard Band around the park. Seventy-five instruments blasted out the old march king's compositions, but the park was so large that the music could barely be heard when the band was on the far side of the field. After one tour around the perimeter of the park, the band halted near home plate and struck up *The Stars and Stripes Forever.* In tight formation, the musicians marched to the flagpole in distant centerfield, with the players of both clubs following them in an orderly procession.

Boston manager Frank Chance was given the honor of raising the American flag while the band launched into a spirited rendition of *The Star Spangled Banner.* Miller Huggins followed by raising the Yankees' 1922 American League Championship pennant.

I looked over at our opponents and at the scarlet "Red Sox" across their jerseys. I had played for Boston myself in 1912 when Fenway Park was new. Now I had to face them as an enemy. Of course, going from the Red Sox to the Yankees wasn't unique to me. Most of the Yankees roster, including Ruth, Jumpin' Joe Dugan, shortstop Everett Scott, and virtually the entire pitching staff, had once worn a Red Sox uniform. I knew that changing clubs was part of baseball, and that today's teammate could be out to beat you as an opponent tomorrow, but the switch from Boston to bitter rival New York was almost like transferring from the American Expeditionary Force to the Kaiser's Imperial Guard during the Great War.

After the flag-raising, the players marched back to a spot near home plate, where Governor Al Smith prepared to throw the ceremonial first pitch. He astonished everyone who'd ever seen a politician throw a baseball by tossing a perfect strike to Wally Schang.

I was getting restless. The ceremonies were a requisite for the occasion, but they were all about the owners and the politicians. I was a *player*, and I was eager for the first real pitch of the actual game to start the new season.

Finally, the field was cleared of politicians and the umpires took their positions on the diamond. Instead of the usual two umps, the American League had assigned three to this game. The venerable Tom Connolly was given the honor of calling balls and strikes. He had officiated the first game in Yankee history in 1903, back when the team was known as the Highlanders and played in Hilltop Park on Washington Heights.

Because it was so difficult to hear in the vast stadium, two announcers were being used, one along each foul line. In resonant voices, they called out the starting lineups through hand-held megaphones. To no one's surprise, "Mickey Rawlings" was not among the names they announced.

I had held out some hope that I might get to fill in for shortstop Everett Scott, who had injured his ankle days earlier. But Scott had played in 986 consecutive games and was determined to reach one thousand. So I was relegated to the dugout bench.

Miller Huggins chose right-hander Bob Shawkey to pitch the opener for us. The tall veteran was the Yankees' workhorse, pitching almost 300 innings in 1922. Shawkey took the mound, his trademark red-sleeved undershirt sticking out of his uniform. It was ironic that he was the only Yankee with a splash of Red Sox color on him because he was the only starter in our rotation who had never pitched for Boston.

Behind the plate, Tom Connolly bellowed "Play ball!" and Boston lead-off man Chick Fewster stepped into the batter's box. Shawkey unleashed a fastball for the first pitch in the new park. It didn't even come close to the strike zone. He promptly buckled down, though, getting Fewster out on a grounder and retiring the rest of the side in order.

Then it was time for Yankee bats to make their stadium debut. Whitey Witt, Joe Dugan, and Babe Ruth were the first three to face Howard Ehmke, who relied on slow, tricky pitches delivered with a hesitation move. Witt and Dugan were quick outs for the Boston hurler. Ruth, spurred on by the cheering crowd, fared somewhat better, lifting a high fly ball to left, but it was easily caught to end the inning.

In the top of the second, Boston's George Burns singled to right for the first hit in the new park. The first Yankee hit was by our second baseman Aaron Ward, and Bob Shawkey scored the first run.

In the bottom of the third inning, with two runners on and two outs, it was the Babe's turn again. As the crowd roared louder with each pitch, Ehmke cautiously worked Ruth to a two-two count. Then the wily pitcher served up a side-armed offering so slow that it didn't look like it had enough stuff on it to reach home plate. Thanks to the Babe, it never did.

Ruth shuffled forward in the batter's box and unleashed his massive bat. The crack of wood on horsehide was louder than anything Sousa's entire band had achieved. As the sound echoed through the park, the ball soared toward the frieze in right field... Home run!

The big guy went into a happy trot around the bases while the screaming, joyous crowd littered the new field with shredded programs, half-eaten hot dogs, and more than a few hats. Fans danced in the aisles and jumped on the seats. Dozens of photographers who had been kneeling along the foul lines triggered their cameras to document the event. All of us on the bench bolted from the dugout, cheering as we swarmed the Babe.

The game couldn't continue until smoke from the photographers' flash powder had cleared and groundskeepers had swept the field clean of debris. When Connolly again called "Play ball!" what followed was anticlimactic.

Relying on nothing fancier than a hard fastball and a sharp curve, Shawkey completely dominated the Red Sox batters. By the fifth inning, with the Yankees up 4-0 and the skies growing dark and ominous, much of the crowd began to leave.

I was as thrilled as anyone in the park by the Babe's home run and our solid lead, but I could never be completely happy about a game unless I was in it. I was a *player*, not a spectator, and I needed to get a bat in my hands and my cleats on the field. I hoped that Everett Scott might be pulled from shortstop after he had been in long enough to keep his consecutive game streak alive. But he stayed in for the duration, and my posterior remained on the dugout bench.

* * *

Three days later, as the series finale against the Red

Sox went into the ninth inning, my butt was in the exact same spot. I had initially chosen to sit near Miller Huggins so that he couldn't miss noticing me; whenever we needed a pinch runner or a defensive replacement, I wanted to be the first player he saw. It soon became my regular location and proved to be an instructive one. I listened in on his discussions with the coaches and studied his strategies. As much as I learned, however, my restlessness only grew.

The dugouts in Yankee Stadium were better than any other in baseball, with cushioned benches and convenient hooks for caps, gloves, and equipment bags. I had no complaint with the facility, but a strong aversion to being confined to it. I didn't want to be comfortable and I didn't want a regular spot on the soft green bench. I wanted to play ball!

Even Hinkey Haines had already gotten into a game. When we needed a pinch runner in the ninth inning of game three, Hug looked right past me and sent in Haines. Ten years ago, I would have been the one chosen. I didn't begrudge the kid his first appearance in a big league game, but I fretted that the years might have slowed my steps a little. If so, my value to the team was diminished. But, after some thought, I considered the situation as Huggins must have done: Haines was faster than me and he ended up scoring the tying run. It had been the right choice.

As for the fans, the enthusiasm of opening day had sputtered out quickly. For the stadium's second game most of the seats were empty. And, although the Babe hit some powerful drives, not another one left the confines of the spacious park.

My chance to play in the series ended when spitballer Carl Mays got the final out in a 7-6 victory to complete a four-game sweep of the Red Sox. The win was greeted by a smattering of cheers from the sparsely populated grandstand.

As we trudged to the clubhouse, I saw Miller Huggins intercepted by a brawny man in an ill-fitting gray suit and a ridiculously small polka dot bowtie. He had the freckled face and unruly ginger hair of a twelve-year-old, but his demeanor and size would discourage anyone from teasing him about it. They spoke briefly in voices too quiet for me to hear.

When I tried to pass by them, Huggins grabbed the sleeve of my jersey and pulled me up short. "They want you in the office," he said softly. A sad scowl dragged at Huggins features, but since that was a common expression for him, I didn't read much into it. The circumstance alone was enough to tell me what was happening. I knew that when a utility player who hasn't made a single appearance all year is called into the front office, it isn't because he's earned a bonus.

The big man spoke up in a high, pinched voice, "Colonel Ruppert wants to see you right away." An odd whistling issued from his bent nose as he said the words. He hunched his broad shoulders as if his suit was binding him and I had the feeling he'd have been more comfortable in boxing trunks.

"This is Andrew Vey," said Huggins. "He'll show you the way."

I didn't see why firing me should be such an urgent matter. "Can't I change first?"

While Vey pondered the question, Huggins answered, "Of course." To Vey, he said, "You don't want him scratching up the nice new floors with his spikes, do you?"

"Suppose not," muttered Vey, and the three of us

proceeded to the locker room. Vey hovered directly behind my shoulder as if he thought I might try to flee.

I followed Huggins into the Yankee clubhouse expecting it to be for the last time. The manager went directly to his small private office without a glance back at me. I was disappointed not to get a "good-bye" from him.

Near the clubhouse entrance was the Babe's maroon locker, with "Ruth" stamped on a metal tag at the top. Next to the locker was a telephone that had been installed for his personal use, and on the floor was a wastebasket into which he threw most of his mail unopened. With a postgame cigar in his mouth, Babe was loudly regaling a crowd of newspapermen with colorful details of a nighttime escapade that he knew would never see print. Edging my way around the Babe's enraptured audience, I wondered if I was being let go because I had failed in my assignment to keep him reined in.

At the far end of the clubhouse was a locker with "Rawlings" written on it in chalk. The starters got metal name plates; utility players and rookies got chalk.

With the silent Andrew Vey standing so close that I felt like he had me under arrest, I changed quickly from my perfectly clean Yankee pinstripes into a suit and tie. The uniform belonged to the team, but the spikes, along with my mitt and an old homemade bat, were mine and I wasn't sure if I should take them. I decided against lugging the equipment with me. I left my gear in the locker and closed the door quietly, figuring I could come back later. Maybe, I thought hopefully, I'll be going to a ball club that will actually want me to put the equipment to use.

Some of the other players were already in the showers, sending wisps of steam to the ceiling. Most sat around in various stages of undress, chatting, smoking, and chewing tobacco. I tried not to catch anyone's eye as I followed Vey out.

Vey led the way upstairs through hallways that smelled of fresh paint and plaster. The playing field had been finished by opening day, but much of the stadium's interior was still under construction. My escort didn't say a word, but continued to hitch his shoulders like he had ants in his suit. I was content to forego conversation since I was busy wondering where Margie and I would be headed next, and trying to figure out how we would get by financially if I wasn't quickly picked up by another team.

We arrived at a pebbled glass door with "Edward G. Barrow" painted on it in gold lettering. Vey rapped on the glass. At the gruff command to "Come in!" he opened the door for me to pass through. I did so, and Vey followed me to take a position like a sentry just inside. Three other men were in the room and I wondered how many they thought it took to fire a mere utility player.

The spacious office was still unfinished and painters' drop cloths covered parts of the floor. It was furnished, however, and appeared fully operational as the team's headquarters.

Ed Barrow, a hulking man with hedgehogs for eyebrows, sat at a massive mahogany desk with several empty bookcases towering behind him. Barrow was the Yankees' business manager and the only man in the room whom I'd met before. That was a few months ago, in the team's Times Square office, when I had signed my contract to play for New York.

I had never met Jacob Ruppert in person, but the club's primary owner was easy to recognize. As usual, he was impeccably dressed and groomed. The wealthy Ruppert, whose fortune had been made in beer, was known to employ an extensive staff of servants including a full-time valet. He was in his mid-fifties with thin graying hair and a trim mustache that was almost pure white. Ruppert paced agitatedly in front of a credenza. His aristocratic face was flushed, as if he had over-imbibed in the Knickerbocker beer his brewery used to produce. He was muttering to himself in a German accent.

Leaning nonchalantly against a file cabinet was a lean, dark-haired man I didn't recognize. He wore a rumpled khaki suit and a world-weary expression. A long-stemmed briar pipe was between his lips, but no smoke came from the bowl, and an old fedora was atop the file cabinet. He held a notepad in one hand and a pencil stub in the other. Probably a reporter, I thought, although I couldn't see that my dismissal from the team was all that newsworthy.

"Thank you for coming, Mr. Rawlings," Barrow began courteously. "I'm sorry to have to get you up here so quickly, but we've run into a bit of difficulty and it needs immediate attention."

Ruppert squawked, " 'Difficulty' you call it? It's a *disaster* is what it is! He's out to ruin me!"

How the hell was I going to ruin Ruppert? I wondered. Was my three thousand dollar a year salary going to bankrupt him?

Barrow let the team president rant for a while before calmly replying, "It isn't a disaster yet, Colonel, and we are going to do everything we can to prevent it from becoming one." Ruppert had once been given the largely ceremonial rank of "Colonel" in the National Guard and he enjoyed being addressed by that title. Barrow looked up at me with sharp dark eyes under his massive brows. "And you, Mr. Rawlings, seem to be in a unique position to help us with that task."

"I don't understand," I said honestly. I didn't recall ever being so thoroughly flummoxed.

Ruppert continued to mumble about impending disaster. From what I could catch of his ramblings, everyone from New York Giants manager John McGraw to Yankees co-owner Til Huston was out to ruin him.

The man at the file cabinet spoke around the stem of his pipe. "What do you know of a man named Spats Pollard?" He kept his thin face at a downward angle and looked at me the way people with spectacles peer over the top of them.

There was something familiar about the Pollard name, but I couldn't place it. "I don't think I know him at all."

Barrow cleared his throat loudly. "Permit me to make the introductions." He jerked his head toward the man in khaki. "This is Detective Luntz of the New York City Police Department." Looking directly at me, Barrow said, "You were teammates with Spats Pollard on the Cubs."

That would have been 1918. "Oh, yes." Now I remembered the name, but I barely remembered Pollard. That had been a chaotic, war-shortened season, with new players continually coming up to replace those who went into the service.

"Did you know him well?" Barrow asked.

"No. He was a dead-armed pitcher who would have had trouble making a minor league team if it wasn't for the war. He could put the ball over the plate, but it usually came right back at him. I think he was only on the club for a couple of months and didn't pitch in more than a handful of games."

The detective spoke again. "How well did you know him *off* the field?"

"I never had anything to do with him."

"Any particular reason?"

I tried to recall what I knew of Pollard. "I didn't like him all that much," I answered. "He thought he was the best pitcher since Cy Young and he blamed everybody else when he didn't win. And I heard that he always had some racket going—crooked card games, selling stolen watches. But I never had any dealings with him myself, so I can't say for sure. Why?"

Barrow and the detective exchanged looks. The business manager straightened a sheaf of papers on his desk before answering. "Mr. Pollard was found in the wall of a concession stand this morning." He adjusted the papers again. "More precisely, his body was found. With three bullets in it."

Geez. Not a murder.

Ruppert stopped his pacing and cried, "It's to ruin me, I tell you! What will happen to my beautiful new stadium when people learn it has bodies buried in it?"

Luntz said quietly, "Only one body." He smiled wryly. "So far."

There was no indication that Ruppert heard him. The owner walked up to me and said solemnly, "Rawlings, you do what I ask of you. Find out who is behind this terrible thing." He made a slight bow. "You do this for me, and I promise you will have a friend in Jacob Ruppert."

Before I could answer, Ruppert strode to the door. Andrew Vey jumped to open it for him and the president was gone.

I looked back and forth from Barrow to Luntz in growing confusion. I was still trying to absorb the truly important news that apparently I was *not* being released, and couldn't fathom what Ruppert had been talking about. I hoped that one of the men would enlighten me.

Ed Barrow spoke up. "Colonel Ruppert has gotten right to the point: We would like you to investigate this matter."

"Why me?" I gestured at Luntz. "You got a detective right here. What can I do that he can't?"

Barrow answered, "For one thing, you knew Pollard personally—"

"Barely. Until you reminded me, I didn't even remember his name."

"Also, it is no secret that you've done this sort of thing before." A small smile creased Barrow's bulldog face. "And you have had some rather impressive successes."

That didn't mean I wanted to get involved in "this sort of thing" again. "I'm sorry, Mr. Barrow. But all I want to do is play baseball. And I really don't know any more about Spats Pollard than what I already told you." Actually, if Barrow knew how little I was following things so far, he would probably realize that I wasn't suited to investigating anything more than stolen bases.

Barrow tried to look understanding. "We have no intention of interfering with your playing. I was happy to sign you to a contract and I consider you a valuable member of the team." The words were soothing but the tone was totally lacking in conviction. He went on, "Of course, Detective Luntz will lead the official investigation. We simply hope that, as a player, you might have access to avenues of information that he doesn't."

Luntz spoke up again. "You're correct about Pollard being a petty crook, but he was trying to break into the bigtime. With Prohibition, he decided to get into the bootlegging business."

Then it's a job for the Prohibition Bureau, not Mickey Rawlings, I thought. "I don't know anything about bootlegging," I said.

Barrow countered, "You know one of Pollard's customers."

Luntz answered my blank stare. "Pollard had a list of names in his jacket—names of customers, it appears."

Barrow said, "One of them is your roommate." He spread his hands. "As I said, you are in a unique position to look into this for us."

Oh no. I knew that having Babe Ruth for roommate was going to be trouble for me.

"Here's what we would like you to do." Barrow leaned forward and his eyebrows drew together in one thick furry line. "You talk to Ruth, maybe some others, and see what you can find out about his connection to Pollard. Whatever you find out, you report to Mr. Vey— he's my personal assistant and talking to him is the same as talking to me." He paused. "But do *not* talk about this to anyone else." Luntz tapped the stem of his pipe on his teeth and Barrow added, "Of course, you may speak with Detective Luntz as well. The important thing is that this entire situation—"

"You mean Pollard's murder?" I interrupted. Calling it a "situation" wasn't going to change the fact that the former pitcher had been shot and killed.

"Presumed murder," Barrow acknowledged. "But whatever it's called, it *must* be kept quiet. Mr. Ruppert has put a lot of money into this ballpark and we can't risk bad publicity." He shook his head. "A body turning up in the new park, Babe Ruth being involved with gangsters... Those kinds of things can be devastating to us." Barrow paused again. "Of course, you can only do this for us if you're on the team, so you can think of it as job security."

There it was, an unspoken threat: If you *don't* do it, you're likely to find yourself *off* the team.

"I'd like to think about it," I said. "I wouldn't even know where to start."

"Start with Pollard," suggested Luntz. "I always try to learn about the victim first, and work back from there."

"Haven't you done that yourself?"

"I tried to." He took the pipe from his mouth and looked down at the bowl. "The problem is Pollard disappeared two years ago. How he ends up in a wall that didn't exist until a month ago beats the hell out of me."

Chapter Four

"A little to the left," Margie said.

I moved the painting to the left, putting it exactly where it had been before she'd instructed me to move it to the right.

"Perfect!" she decreed.

I marked the spot, hammered a nail into the wall, and hung the picture in place. It was a still-life of a blue vase filled with brightly colored flowers that looked the same to me as every other painting of that sort. Margie had found it, along with a few framed prints of similar themes, at a second-hand shop on Tremont Avenue.

This was the first chance I'd had to help her set up our new home in the Bronx. I didn't know anything about decorating, but it turned out to be easy: I put things wherever Margie wanted them and agreed with whatever she suggested. I felt badly enough that we'd had to relocate again, and I was happy to let her set up the flat however she liked.

We had been unexpectedly uprooted in February. I'd had a solid season with an outstanding St. Louis Browns team last year—coming within one game of winning the American League pennant—and I had expected to remain with them for 1923. Then I was traded to the Yankees for "a player to be named later" and Margie and I had to make an abrupt move to New York. I had been traded for that "player to be named later" so often, that I sometimes wondered if I had ever ended up being traded for myself.

Together, we'd found this second-floor furnished apartment on East 170th Street, not far from Claremont Park and within walking distance to the stadium. The one-bedroom walkup was small but clean. Its kitchen was modern and we had our own bathroom supplied with hot running water. We had barely signed the lease when I had to leave for spring training in New Orleans, leaving Margie to take care of the new place alone.

As usual, she took care of things quite well. Margie got the furniture moved in, painted the bedroom, and found herself a job at Griffith's movie studio. All that was left for me to do now was move a few things around—and I suspected that she'd only left me this task so that I could feel I was making some kind of contribution to our new home.

"I think the cabinet might look better on the other side of the door," Margie murmured, with her forefinger pressed against her chin.

I stifled a groan. With all our moves over the years, we'd learned to limit ourselves to the bare minimum of furniture. There were two luxuries we always took with us, though: my floor-model Victrola and a china cabinet of Margie's that she kept as a family heirloom. Moving that massive walnut piece would require first removing every piece of china to avoid breakage and then a great deal of muscle strain on my part.

"Well, let's leave it there for now," she decided, much to my relief. "I want to get the prints up first." Standing away from the wall, and eying the possibilities like an artist stepping back from his easel to study a partially finished painting, she said, "How about putting the one with the daffodils to the left of the window?"

I grabbed a framed print of a flower-filled basket. The blossoms in the picture nearly matched the color of Margie's gingham frock.

"Those are lilacs," she said.

I put the wrong print back on the floor and picked up another. At Margie's nod, I lifted it to the wall and slid it around until I hit the spot she wanted.

I had to tell Margie about my meeting with Jacob Ruppert and Ed Barrow, but I wasn't eager to raise the subject. She had readily gone along with us suddenly moving halfway across the country, but I doubted that she would be as agreeable to me getting involved in another murder investigation. When I opened my mouth to broach the subject, my tongue balked. The words that came out instead were, "How are things at the studio?"

"Confusing," she answered. "With Mr. Griffith away, no one seems to know what to do. I was hired to help design stunts and double for the actresses in action scenes. It would be like making my old serials again. But for some reason, Tom Van Dusen has me organizing clothes in the wardrobe department."

"It safer than doing stunts," I said. Margie's career as a leading actress had come to an abrupt end when she fell off a camel while filming one of her exotic action pictures. The injury required hip surgery and she was left with a slight limp that was exaggerated on screen. I thought it just added an appealing little hitch to her walk.

"It's not about safety," Margie snorted. "Tom simply

likes to play the boss while Mr. Griffith is away. He *loves* giving orders."

"He did seem awfully full of himself," I said. "I know he's a friend of yours, but—"

"Oh, Tom's a complete ass—and we're *not* friends. I was friends with Natalie in the old days, and she's his…" Margie stepped back and studied the print. "You know, you were right," she said. "The lilacs would look better there."

I swapped prints again. I hadn't liked Natalie Brockman much more than I did Tom Van Dusen, but who was I to judge Margie's friends? After all, I'd certainly had a few odd—and sometimes unsavory— companions during my baseball career. "How did you and Natalie get to know each other?" The mounting wire on the frame was frayed at one end, so I unwound it and tried to make it more secure.

Margie sat down on the sofa and tucked her legs beneath her. "When I first went to Hollywood, a few of us girls rented a bungalow together. Natalie was one of them. She was *so* much fun—always playing pranks and cracking jokes. She once crashed a stuffy party at Mary Pickford's house by pretending to be a countess from Transylvania!" Margie laughed. "We were like kids. Nobody took the movies all that seriously back then, so we had fun at work and even more fun after work. And it was all pretty innocent—not like what you read about."

"I can't imagine Natalie being fun," I said, recalling Brockman's bored expression and whiny voice.

"Oh she was." Margie's smile faltered. "Then she started to enjoy the parties a little too much, and they weren't as innocent any more. Eventually she'd show up at the studio too tired to work. One of the older actors gave her a 'pick-me-up' and she got hooked on them.

You remember what happened to Wally Reid?" Only three months ago, Wallace Reid, the All-American movie star, had died in a sanitarium from morphine addiction at the age of thirty-one.

"She was an addict?" I asked, putting the final twist on a loose strand of wire.

"Natalie would try whatever drug anybody gave her, and if she liked it she'd take a *lot* of it. She got hooked on dope and it almost killed her. Eventually she kicked the habit, but she's never been the same. Now she goes from day to day and doesn't seem to care about very much at all. Instead of making movies, she attaches herself to the men who make movies. They keep her in bit parts and nice clothes. And champagne—she won't take anything stronger than champagne."

I hung the repaired picture. "She seems so different from you," I said. "Why do you still want to be friends with her?"

Margie appeared thoughtful. "Because I remember who she really was—who she really *is*. Maybe someday *that* Natalie will come out again. And she's always been nice to me. She went out of her way to get me the job with Mr. Griffith."

"Through Van Dusen?"

"No, she persuaded Mr. Griffith herself." Margie smiled. "I think at one time he was quite smitten with Natalie. Mr. Griffith often develops attachments to his actresses."

"And now she's with Van Dusen."

"Yes, but I don't think either of them takes it very seriously. Oh! Did you ask Babe Ruth about meeting him?"

"Uh, no. He's been surrounded by reporters and fans all the time. I hardly ever get a chance to talk to him."

Actually, I had never intended to tell him about Tom Van Dusen's movie idea.

"Could you?" Margie swung her legs off the sofa and sat upright. "Van Dusen may be a louse, but he is a capable director. He'd probably make a good picture."

I promised her that I would talk to the Babe and suggested we take a break. Margie got a bag of ginger snaps from the cupboard while I cranked a couple handfuls of beans through the coffee grinder. Soon we were sitting at our small dining table by the front window, with a pot of fresh coffee and a plate of not-so-fresh cookies.

Looking down at the street, I saw a dozen shabbily dressed boys playing a noisy baseball game on the patchy asphalt. They had to avoid potholes as they ran, none of them had a glove, the only bat had a taped handle, and even from this distance I could see that the muddy brown ball was no longer round. But they were having so much fun that I almost wished I could go out and join them.

Margie fingered the dingy green curtain that adorned the window. "I'm thinking of changing this. White would look cleaner. Maybe lace."

"Sounds good," I said, absently dunking a cookie in my coffee as I continued to watch the game outside. The kids made some good contact with the ball but there was never the satisfying "crack" of a bat. The only sound it made was a feeble "squoosh." I decided I would try to bring a couple of baseballs home from the stadium for them. And maybe a bat that wasn't broken.

Margie spoke up again. "Maybe I'll make the curtains myself out of some of your old underwear."

"That sounds good, too," I answered, before her words registered.

When I looked at her, I expected to see the

mischievous smile that I knew so well, but her face expressed only concern. "What's bothering you?" she asked softly.

I took a breath before answering. "They found a body in Yankee Stadium. Some crook who used to be a ballplayer. He was murdered."

Margie simply stared at me, her big bright eyes gradually growing wider.

"And they want me to investigate," I added.

"Who's 'they'?" she asked.

"Jacob Ruppert and Ed Barrow. Ruppert owns the team and Barrow runs it, so I really don't have much choice."

"But why *you*?"

I had asked myself that question a number of times. After all, if a New York City police detective couldn't figure it out, how could a utility infielder be expected to solve the crime? Yet, for whatever reason, Ruppert and Barrow had decided that bringing me into the case was the best course of action. Sometimes I wondered how baseball owners ever made their fortunes, because they never seemed to be very smart.

I gave Margie a complete account of the meeting in Barrow's office, and concluded, "They seem to figure that since I was once teammates with Pollard, and because he might have had a connection to my new roommate, I might be able to get information that others can't. Barrow also knows that I've been involved with some murder investigations in the past."

"Yes, too many of them!" Margie shook her head hard enough to make her lustrous brown hair flutter about her shoulders. "After what happened in St. Louis, you're going to get involved in something like this *again*?"

"I don't want to, but—"

"Then why do it?" Her voice rose. "You were almost killed last year! Can't you just play baseball and forget about crime?"

I wished that I could, but that didn't seem to be what the Yankees had planned for me. "Mr. Barrow made it clear to me: If I want to stay on the team, I have to find out what happened to Spats Pollard."

"And if you do this for them, they'll keep you?" Margie sounded skeptical.

"No promise of that," I admitted. "But I figure it'll give me some time. Eventually the Yankees will need me to fill in for one of the other players. And when I get that chance, I'm gonna play so hard they'll want to keep me no matter what."

"But—" Margie gave up on words and again simply shook her head. I knew she was worried.

"I don't see how I'm going to have any real trouble," I said, trying to reassure her. "All I'm going to do is ask a few questions, report to Mr. Barrow, and that's it. Besides, the police are looking into it, too, and if they find out what happened my job is done."

She didn't appear convinced. "Promise me you'll think about it."

"I will."

There was a shout of joy from the street below and I watched a boy in patched knickers legging out a hit that had bounded off a parked Model T. That's what I wished I could do: simply play baseball.

* * *

I kept my promise to Margie: I thought about it. And I was still considering exactly what to do when I left early for Yankee Stadium that afternoon. I didn't know where it would lead, or how far I would go, but I decided to start by seeing where Spats Pollard had been entombed.

As I approached the ballpark, soft breezes stirred dust clouds from the roads and parking lots surrounding it. They had been recently cleared and not yet paved. Much of the area around Yankee Stadium had a similarly barren appearance. The West Bronx was sparsely populated and so rural that New York Giants manager John McGraw derisively referred to the neighborhood as "Goatville."

With no land for a new ballpark available in crowded Manhattan, the Yankees had found an old lumberyard in the Bronx owned by the William Waldorf Astor estate. After purchasing the site, Jacob Ruppert's partner Til Huston, an experienced civil engineer, personally supervised the construction. In less than a year, baseball's most imposing edifice was unveiled. And, only a few days after opening, it was becoming known by the name sportswriter Fred Lieb had given it: The House That Ruth Built.

Although enough construction had been completed to begin the season, as I neared the entrance I saw that some work was still being done. Construction trucks were parked haphazardly in the players' lot and various craftsmen scurried about carrying pipes, paint buckets, and electrical cable.

Inside the stadium, I passed dozens of men in overalls who were applying the finishing touches of paint and plaster. The clang of metal pipes reverberated throughout the corridors as plumbers did their work, and I had to step carefully because of electrical wires lying in loose coils on the walkways.

Since I had telephoned ahead, I was let right in when I reached Ed Barrow's office. The paint job in his office must have been completed because two burly workmen, grunting heavily, were moving furniture in place against the walls. Big Andrew Vey, who stood near Barrow's desk, probably could have done the moving himself with no strain at all, I thought.

Barrow peered up at me from under his bushy dark eyebrows. "Ah, Rawlings. I'm glad you've decided to help us out with this Pollard matter. I promise you I won't forget it, and neither will Colonel Ruppert." The business manager sounded genuinely pleased, but not at all surprised, that I was complying with his wishes. He made a slight gesture toward his assistant. "Mr. Vey will show you where the body was found." Barrow's gaze went down to the paperwork on his desk and I knew the conversation was over.

Vey held the door open for me as we left the office. He was again wearing a tiny bow-tie, this one solid orange. It was a poor color choice with his ginger hair and ruddy, freckled face. "This way," he said in a reedy voice as he joined me in the hallway.

We walked some distance without Vey speaking another word. He didn't fidget in his suit jacket as he had the last time I'd seen him, but now and then he dug a finger into his stiff shirt collar as if it was too tight. I noticed that his freckled hand was the size of a small ham, the knuckles were lumpy, and his fingers misshapen.

Since Vey was supposed to be my primary contact with the front office, I decided to get some conversation going. "You work for Mr. Barrow long?" I asked.

"A while." The words seemed to whistle from his broken nose.

"What exactly do you do for him?"

"I'm his assistant." Vey tugged at his collar again.

Geez, talking to this guy was like talking to a catcher's mitt. "What do you assist him *with*?"

"Whatever he needs."

"Such as?"

Vey shot me a look and his broad face twitched in something like a smile. "I'm thinkin' that if you keep after this Pollard thing the way you're keepin' after me, you'll have it figured out in no time."

"I'm not so sure," I replied honestly. "Detective—" I had to search my memory for the officer's name. "Detective Luntz said that Spats Pollard has been missing for two years. This place was a vacant lot back then—so how does he end up in a wall that's just been built?"

"Yeah, that's a puzzler." Vey rubbed the palm of his hand over his unruly red hair causing it to spike up like a porcupine. "But Pollard ain't in the wall no more. What do you expect you're going to see?"

"I don't know yet. But what Luntz suggested about starting with the body makes sense. I know what Pollard was doing five years ago: pitching for the Cubs. And we know where he was a few days ago: buried in a wall. But nobody seems to know much about where he was between those times. I figure I'll try to fill in that gap until we know what led to him being killed." Five years was an awfully long period of time, though, and I was doubtful that I could fill it all in.

On the left field side of the stadium's mezzanine level, we reached a built-in refreshment stand. This was another innovation by the Yankees' management. At most ballparks, fans could only get food and drink from vendors who hawked their goods in the grandstand. Yankee Stadium provided a restaurant near the main entrance and half a dozen refreshment stands conveniently spaced around the concourse.

"This is the place," Vey squeaked.

The stand's varnished wood counter was piled with trays of hot dog rolls and hamburger buns. They smelled freshly baked and sent a craving through my stomach.

Along the wall behind the counter were a grill, a refrigerator, and a sink, all of them sparkling new and white enameled. Menu prices were written in chalk on a small blackboard above the grill. A door set in the side wall was open, revealing a storage area packed with wooden crates of green glass bottles. The stand was of simple, utilitarian construction; its only decorative feature was a brass chandelier with three frosted white globes painted to look like baseballs.

Leaning against the refrigerator was a short round man who looked like a sixty-year-old Fatty Arbuckle. He was bald, with only a thin horseshoe of gray hair remaining above his ears. Dressed in sagging white cotton pants, with a shirt and apron of the same color and a black bowtie, he looked like a butcher or a baker. The man was supervising two younger ones, similarly dressed but with their ties removed and their shirts unbuttoned, who were moving cases of soda pop and near beer into the storage room.

"Mr. Zegarra!" Vey called. When he got his attention, Vey said, "This is Mickey Rawlings. He's going to be looking into that, uh, matter for us. Mr. Barrow would appreciate it if you would give him your full cooperation."

"Of course," Zegarra replied in a strong Brooklyn accent. "Be happy to." He waved me to come around the counter. " 'Rawlings,' huh? Name sounds familiar." Through deep-set eyes he studied my face as if trying to recognize me.

"It should," said Vey. "Rawlings joined the club this year. Plays a helluva second base. Good hitter, too."

I gave Vey a nod of appreciation. Since I hadn't played for the Yankees at all so far, it was the kindest assessment I'd gotten this season.

He nodded in return. "I'll be in the office if you need

me for anything." With that, he dug a finger behind his shirt collar and walked away.

"Well, well," said Zegarra. "I never met a big-league ballplayer before." He shook my hand enthusiastically and exposed his stained teeth in a broad smile. "I'm Joe Zegarra. Call me 'Joe.' " His jowls quivered when he spoke.

"Thanks, Joe. I won't take much of your time."

In a lowered voice, he asked, "But why are yuh lookin' here? I thought Mr. Barrow didn't want no publicity."

"He doesn't. I guess he figures it's better if *I* poke around instead of the police or the newspapers. It'll be quieter this way."

"Huh." Zegarra jammed his hands in his trouser pockets. "But why *you?* I mean... you're a *ballplayer.*"

I stifled a chuckle. The "why me" question was a recurring one. "I knew the dead guy years ago. We were teammates."

"Oh, damn. Sorry about that." Zegarra's fleshy face drooped mournfully. "Was yuh close friends?"

"No. Played ball together is all."

One of the young men set a crate of near beer down heavily, causing the bottles to rattle. Zegarra yelled at him, "Watch what you're doing, dammit! Anythin' yuh break is comin' outta yer pay!" He said to me, "Nephews. Take my advice: If you ever get the chance to hire relatives, don't."

I wanted to get to the purpose of my visit. "Where was Pollard found?"

"I'll show yuh." He yelled at his nephews, "Get outta there, the botha yuz!" When they stepped out of the storage room, he led me inside. "Right there," Zegarra said, pointing at the back wall.

There wasn't anything unusual to see. I stepped nearer

to the wall and inspected it closely, even running my hand over the surface.

"They got in quick and patched things up," Zegarra said. "Soon as they got the body out, they had plasterers sealin' the wall again."

"If he was inside a wall, how was he discovered?"

"It was the damnedest thing." Zegarra leaned lightly against a tall stack of crates. "Yuh know they're still doin' a lotta work on the joint, especially the plumbin'. There's all those restrooms—*sixteen*, I hear—and water fountains, and of course we all need water for cookin', so there's a whole mess of pipes runnin' through the building. I guess they got some of them hooked up wrong and had to redo some fittings. So they broke into the wall to get at the pipes... and there was your friend. With a couple bullet holes in him."

"You saw the body?"

"Hell yeah." Zegarra gave a shudder, causing his flesh to ripple. "And I don't never want to see nuthin' like that again."

"Were the bullet holes fresh, or did he look like he was dead for a while?" I had wondered if Pollard had been killed recently or if he'd been dead for the past two years and his body moved here.

Zegarra took out a handkerchief the size of a pillow case and swiped it across his bulbous nose. "Well, I wouldn't say nothin' about him was 'fresh.' Smelled to high heaven, he did. The blood was dry, though, if that's what yuh mean."

"How did you happen to be here when he was found?"

"I hardly been anyplace *else*. I was workin' day and night to get everything set up and runnin'. Most of my savings is in this little business."

"Doesn't Mr. Ruppert own it?"

"Nah. He got the main restaurant downstairs, but he leases out the stands. We each pay a monthly rent and Ruppert takes a percentage of the sales. This ain't gonna make me rich, but if attendance keeps up and the fans stay hungry and thirsty, I figure I'll at least turn a profit."

A couple of scruffy delivery men brought some more cases of near beer and stacked them on the floor next to the counter. Each green bottle bore a red label that read *Fervo*. Before Prohibition, fans could enjoy Jacob Ruppert's Knickerbocker or Ruppert brands. Now the closest they could get was a "cereal beverage" with less than half a percent alcohol. It couldn't even be marketed as "near beer" since the word "beer" wasn't allowed to be used. To me, the substitute brew didn't deserve the name anyway—whoever first called it "near beer" must have been a terrible judge of distance.

"You selling much of that stuff?" I asked.

Zegarra laughed and his belly shook. "What else are people gonna do at a ball game 'cept drink beer? Of course, it ain't *exactly* beer—but it comes awful close." I suspected that "awful" was probably the apt description. He walked me a few steps on a tour of the refreshment stand. "Look at what I got here: sausages, burgers, soda pop and beer. That's it. Let the vendors sell the nickel stuff—peanuts and crackerjack and candy. To me, that crap ain't worth the space."

I looked it over and agreed he had a pretty good setup. "You said you've been here day and night. You ever see Pollard around here before?"

"Never seen him before in my life."

"Anything else you can tell me about him?"

"Yeah. I almost lost my lunch when they pulled him outta that wall."

"Who *did* pull him out? Who else was here?"

"Oh, well, let's see..." His brows went down, causing the fringe of hair around his scalp to bob up. "There was the workmen who broke into the wall... then a stadium cop... Mr. Vey and Mr. Barrow showed up... then a few more cops, and later a detective." Zegarra paused, and seemed to give up the search of his memory. "I tell yuh, there was so many people through here I don't know who they all was. Eventually a coroner took Pollard away, and they got the wall sealed up again."

I nodded toward the young men working in the storage room. "Were they here? Or any delivery men?"

He snorted. "Them lazy bastards? Nah. They don't put in the hours I do."

"Has anybody else talked to you about Pollard?"

"Just you. And the police and Mr. Vey when they found the body. I told them the same thing I'm telling you: I didn't know nuthin' about the man. He was just a body in the wall."

"Alright. Thanks, Mr. Zegarra. I appreciate you talking to me."

"Call me 'Joe,' " he reminded me. "Just do me one favor, will yuh?"

"If I can."

"I was told to keep quiet about this, and except for talkin' to you I have. I know Mr. Barrow wants you nosin' around a little, but could yuh keep it quiet, too?"

"I'll try."

"Yuh know how people are," he went on. "They hear a dead guy was found in my place, it could spook 'em. Hell, they'll probably even start rumors about what's in my sausages. Speakin'a which—" He yelled to one of his helpers, "Hey, Carlo! Remember to clean the damn grill!"

I thanked Zegarra again, wished him well with his

business, and left for the clubhouse.

* * *

Like everything else in Yankee Stadium, the locker room was better than any other in baseball. The lockers actually locked, each player had his own chair, there was an adequate supply of clean towels, and the showers had plenty of hot water. I'd played in some old ballparks where I had to hang my clothes on a nail in the wall and wash up in a trickle of liquid rust. Being a Yankee was definitely the big time. And I wanted to stay.

A few other players were already in the clubhouse. Bob Shawkey, who would be going against Washington Senators' ace Walter Johnson, was getting a rubdown from the trainer. Shawkey was a veteran of the Great War as well as a veteran pitcher; because of his naval service aboard the battleship *Arkansas,* he'd been tagged with the nickname "Bob the Gob." Hinkey Haines was early, too, talking to centerfielder Whitey Witt about how to play balls hit off the fence. The main job of a rookie is to learn, and I was glad to see Haines putting in the time and effort.

With a passing nod at Haines and Witt, I walked to Miller Huggins' small office. He was alone, seated behind a plain oak desk, scowling down at a lineup card. Through four games we were undefeated on the season, but he looked as mournful as if we'd lost ten in a row.

I knocked on the open door. "Got a minute, Hug?"

The manager looked up. "Sure. Come on in." He slid the card aside and leaned back in his chair.

After less than a week of use, his office already smelled faintly like the rest of the clubhouse, a mixture of sweat, leather, tobacco juice, and liniment. A canvas satchel of baseballs and a jumble of bats were in one corner, and a coat rack with several uniforms and sweaters hanging from it was in another. There was also a small bookcase with works by famous authors—actual literature. Most managers read nothing more challenging than the *Sporting News* or the daily newspapers, but Huggins was something of a bookworm.

"Mr. Barrow and Col. Ruppert talked to me," I began, "and I'm not sure what to do. I figure I work for *you*, so I want to ask you about it."

"Yeah, they told me what's going on." Huggins waved me into the room's only other seat, a spindle back arm chair next to the bookcase. "I'm sorry they're getting you involved. Ruppert has it in his head, though, that he's under some kind of attack and he wants to know who's behind it."

"*He's* under attack? Spats Pollard is the one who got killed."

The manager smiled wryly. "That's not the way Col. Ruppert sees it. As far as he's concerned, Pollard was merely a means by which to give the new stadium a bad name."

I took a breath. "So what's my job here? Am playing baseball for you, or detective for the front office?"

Huggins pondered that before answering. "Well, just like anybody else in organized baseball, you have *two* jobs—and they're both important. One job is on the field, playing the best you can and helping the team to win. Then, as in any profession, you also have the responsibility of keeping your bosses happy. Maintaining a career in baseball has a lot to do with who you know and who your friends are." He didn't point out—and didn't need to—that it was especially important to get along with the boss when one didn't exactly have the athletic skills of Babe Ruth.

I remembered Jacob Ruppert's offer to be a friend.

"So I need to do what they ask."

"That would be the wise choice," he said. "We are all called upon to do a little more than should be required of us sometimes. Especially for the man who signs the paychecks." A rare smile slowly took over his face. "Let me talk straight with you." At my nod to continue, he leaned forward. "You're thirty-one. You've been a utility player for your entire career—a good one, but still utility. Now you're worried you only have a few years left and you don't know what you're going to do afterward. Am I right?"

I was taken aback that he had such an accurate read on me. All I could do was nod again.

"Mickey, you're me ten years ago. And I got you pegged to be a manager yourself someday." He paused. "When I needed a pinch runner the other day, and I put in Hinkey Haines, did you think that was the right move?"

I hesitated briefly. "It was the right move for the *team*, I suppose."

"You're not sure?"

"If I was in your job, I'd have put in Haines because he's a helluva runner. But I can't say it was right for *me* because I'm still a ballplayer, not a manager, and I want to be in on every play. When I'm in the field, I want the ball hit to *me*. When we're facing a tough pitcher, *I* want to be the one going to bat. I know other fellows might be better than me, and if I ever do become a manager I'll put in whoever's most likely to help us win. But I can't give up on being a player yet. I can't!"

"Believe me. I understand." Huggins smiled. "There are times when I'm itching to get in a game again myself."

There was a rap at the door. Charley O'Leary, a former shortstop who'd been coaching for Huggins ever since his retirement as a player, stuck his large head inside. "We got a problem, Hug." The rubber-faced O'Leary performed in a comic vaudeville act during the off season, but there was no humor in his expression now.

"What is it?"

O'Leary hesitated and gave me a glance. Huggins nodded that it was okay to speak in front of me. "Babe had himself quite a night last night," the coach said. "Might not show up—and if he does, probably won't be in any shape to play."

I said softly, "He'll be here. And he'll play."

Huggins gave me a quizzical look.

"This is the kind of game he lives for," I explained. "A Sunday game against Walter Johnson is sure to be a full house—and Babe does like an audience."

"You're probably right," Huggins said after a moment's thought. To O'Leary, he added, "Just in case, tell Haines he might be starting today. Even if Ruth does show up, I might let the kid start for him. Maybe it'll teach that big sonofabitch a lesson."

When O'Leary left us alone again, Huggins resumed our earlier conversation. "As I was saying: I know what it's like to want to play. And when I can use you, you'll get in the game. But I won't put you in unless the situation calls for it. You are only going to play when I feel you're the best man at the time to help us win." He leaned back. "When you're a manager, you'll understand, and I know you'll do the same."

I already understood, but I didn't necessarily like it.

"Meanwhile," Huggins went on, "there are some other ways you can help the team."

"How?" I asked, wondering what else the team could possibly want of me. I was already playing nursemaid to

Babe Ruth on the road and looking into a dead ballplayer for Jacob Ruppert.

"Teach the other players," he suggested. "Especially the young kids like Haines. Coach them some."

"Sure, I could do that."

"And maybe help *me* out a little, too. I might ask your advice from time to time. You know, I've noticed you on the bench: You listen when I'm talking strategy, and you always have your head in the game. Most of the other fellows are yapping about their dates and their dinner plans for after the game, but you're always focused on what's happening on the field. That's part of what makes a good manager."

"I'll help however I can," I said. It was refreshing to be asked to do something that involved baseball.

"Good." Huggins studied me for a long moment. "Let me ask your opinion on something right now: What do you think of Scott's chances against Johnson?"

"Lousy," I answered promptly. "But hardly anybody has much of a chance against Johnson." Walter Johnson's fastball bordered on invisibility, and you can't hit what you can't see. Relying on that fastball and extraordinary control, the Senators' pitcher had dominated the American League for more than a decade.

"True," Huggins said with a faint smile. "But any particular reason you think Scott might have trouble today?"

"His bad ankle. It's hurting him and he has to take an extra split second to step off it when he's hitting. He's playing hurt and doing the best he can, but with Johnson pitching he can't afford that split second—the ball will be past him before he can get his bat around." Everett Scott, although an outstanding shortstop, was not a particularly strong hitter and that slight delay could be fatal for him against Johnson.

The manager smiled more fully. "You noticed that little hitch in his swing, huh? So have I, and I believe your evaluation is correct." He looked down at the lineup card. "Can *you* hit Johnson?"

"I have before." I chose not to mention that it was only once and just a single—although it had felt like a grand slam at the time. I stared at the lineup card on the desk, trying not to let my eagerness show. Was he going to put my name on it? Would I finally get into a game as a Yankee?

"Scott's starting," Huggins abruptly said. "He's got that streak on the line, and he deserves a chance."

I swallowed hard and tried to shrug off the bad news.

Huggins dismissed me with jerk of his head toward the door. As I left, I made an effort to keep my disappointment from showing. I walked out the door with my back straight and my shoulders high. My steps suddenly became lighter when Huggins called after me, "Get some extra batting practice today!"

* * *

My flannels were still perfectly clean through the first three innings. I sat near Huggins, my scarred old baseball mitt clasped between my hands. I was so antsy about getting into the game that I kept squeezing and kneading it like a lump of raw dough.

Just as he had for so many years in so many other games, Walter Johnson completely dominated the Yankee batters. The tall right-hander, with arms that dangled nearly to his knees, had an easy motion and a side-armed delivery that flung blurry white bullets across home plate. The "Big Train," as Johnson was called, was on track today. With a clear sky above, a temperature of seventy degrees, and a near-capacity crowd murmuring at his every pitch, he retired batter after batter in order. Meanwhile, he had been staked to an early lead when Senators left-fielder Goose Goslin knocked in a pair of runs with a triple.

Babe Ruth did make it to the park shortly before game time, and Huggins elected not to give Hinkey Haines his spot. It was again the right decision for the team; against Johnson, we needed Ruth's bat in the lineup. But Haines couldn't have fared any worse than the Babe did in his first at bat. Ruth clumsily struck out on three straight pitches and stormed back to the dugout spewing profanities in every direction.

With the Yankees failing to put any runners on base, it wasn't until the bottom of the third that Everett Scott, batting in the eighth spot, came to the plate. I watched closely as the shortstop dug in, certain that Huggins had his eye on him too. Scott went into his normal stance—a mistake, I thought. With his delayed step, he should have moved back in the box to give himself a little more time.

Scott took Johnson's first pitch for a strike, then a fastball low for a one-one count. When he swung at the next pitch, the delay in his step as he strode forward was noticeable. Scott's bat wasn't half way around when the ball popped into the catcher's mitt. The final pitch was almost an exact repeat of the previous, and Scott was out on strikes. There was certainly no shame in being struck out by the tall man from Kansas—Johnson had struck out about three thousand batters during his illustrious career—but Scott's effort was completely futile.

I glanced at Huggins. Although the manager gave no indication, I was sure that I would be going into the game when it came time for Scott to bat again. It turned out I was mistaken. After Bob Shawkey grounded out to end the inning, Huggins barked at me, "Rawlings! See if you can use that mitt for something more than a squeeze toy. You're going in at short."

Scott had already taken a couple of steps out of the dugout when he heard that he was pulled from the game. The usually mild-mannered shortstop hurled his glove at the bench in anger. "Rest that ankle of yours," Huggins said to him calmly. "You'll be back in tomorrow."

I trotted out to my position, enjoying the feel of my cleats digging into the well-tended ground of the new ballpark. As I did, I was aware that too many thoughts were running through my head. I almost wished that Huggins hadn't gotten me started thinking like a manager—it was tough enough to play baseball without having to think so much!

Instead of simply appreciating the fact that I was about to make my first appearance as a New York Yankee, I was considering Huggins' rationale for putting me in at this point in the game. I had assumed that I wouldn't take over for Scott until his next at bat, but I realized that Huggins' judgment was sound. Although Scott was the best fielding shortstop in all of baseball, the position required so much range that it put a great deal of stress on the feet and legs. One tough play and his strained ankle could be injured far worse. By putting me in now, Scott got some time to let it heal, his consecutive game streak was still on track to hit a thousand, and I could get my feet wet in the game before having to face Johnson's fastball.

While we threw the ball around in infield warm-ups, I became aware that Yankee Stadium was most impressive from the vantage point of the playing field. I was surrounded by sixty thousand fans in three tiers of stands, the biggest crowd I'd ever played before. And while my eyes were diverted to a quick scan of that enormous crowd, they were all treated to the sight of me dropping an easy toss from Wally Pipp. Furious at myself, I picked up the baseball and threw it back to him hard. I could feel my face turning red. What a way to make my Yankees debut: an error on a warm-up throw. I'd probably just given Huggins a heart palpitation and Scott a good laugh.

From that moment, I kept my eyes and mind on the field of play. *Forget everything else*, I told myself, *just play the game*. By the time Bob Shawkey threw the first pitch to start the fourth inning, I was fairly relaxed. The only jitters were in my feet, but that was an asset; I was ready to move in any direction that the ball might be hit.

The Senators' first two batters went down on an easy fly ball to Babe Ruth and a hard liner up the third base line that Joe Dugan snagged with a low dive. Then came my first fielding opportunity: Roger Peckinpaugh hit a slow chopper directly at me. It was a catch that any of the street kids who played near my apartment could make, but I felt good about playing it cleanly and throwing Peckinpaugh out to end the inning. I trotted off the field happy that I had done my job well.

In the fifth inning, with the Senators up 3-1, two outs and nobody on, I got my first chance to hit. I picked my bat off the ground and gripped the handle tightly. As I approached the plate, I looked directly at Walter Johnson as if to show that I had no fear of him. His expression was stolid, and I was pretty sure he had no fear of me, either.

As soon as I scratched my cleats into the hard-packed dirt of the batter's box, I had the calming sense of being in a familiar place. I'd played in a hundred ballparks over the years, but one small rectangle of earth was always the same: the batter's box. I tapped my bat on the outer edge of the plate and took my stance. The Louisville Slugger in my hands, the red clay under my spikes… it felt so natural and so comfortable, all the worries of the past weeks were gone. This was exactly where I belonged.

My strategy for hitting Johnson was simple: I would reduce the strike zone as much as possible and then swing at what remained. If the gentlemanly pitcher had any weakness it was that he didn't want to injure anyone. One of his fastballs to the head could kill a batter instantly. My new teammate Carl Mays had killed Indians' shortstop Ray Chapman with a pitch a couple of years ago and Mays didn't throw nearly as hard as Johnson.

I dug in at the back of the box to give me more time, but close to the plate, trusting that his kind nature would keep him from throwing inside. I also crouched a little more than usual to cut down the height of the strike zone.

From behind the plate, catcher Muddy Ruel chuckled, "He ain't even thrown the damn ball yet, and yer already duckin'."

I kept my eyes riveted on Johnson as he went into his wind-up. I looked for his release point when he threw. There would be no time to react if I waited to pick up the ball after it was in flight, so I watched his hand with the idea that I could tell where the ball would be heading. Of course, everyone had a system for hitting Walter Johnson; the problem was that none of them worked any better than the systems used by gamblers to bet horses. Still, I felt I had more control of the situation by going in with a plan.

With his side-armed delivery and long right arm, Johnson's first pitch seemed to come at me from the direction of third base. It was all I could do not to hit the ground in panic.

"Strike one!" bellowed umpire Billy Evans.

I'd barely seen the ball as it blurred past me. It popped into Ruel's mitt with the sound of a rifle report.

"Sounded outside to me," I quipped, trying to hide my nervousness.

"What are you, a comedian?" the umpire growled.

"He sure as hell ain't a ballplayer," said Ruel. He tossed the ball back to Johnson and added, "That was just his changeup. The next one's gonna be a fastball."

From that, I guessed curve and was right. Low and outside—judging by where Ruel caught the ball—for ball one.

I correctly figured a fastball would come next and swung hard. It grazed the handle for a foul tip that went all the way to the backstop. At least I got a little wood on it.

"Hey, how about that?" Ruel piped up. "The ball actually hit your bat. You gonna stick it out there again and hope Johnson puts it on the sweet spot?"

"Keep talking and I'm gonna stick it in your ear," I replied.

"It's your own ear you better worry about."

I shuffled back from the plate an inch or two. Ruel wanted me to think the next one would be coming in tight. Fine, I'll play along. But I was sure he'd set up for a knee-high pitch on the outside corner.

Johnson whipped his right arm around again and I lunged, trying to poke the ball into right field. It cued off the end of the barrel, sending a tremble through the wood. It wasn't a solid hit, but thanks to Johnson's speed I didn't need to get much on it. The ball went out on a looping arc over the first baseman's head.

I ran hard out of the batter's box while Sam Rice bolted in from right field, Joe Judge scurried backwards from first base, and Bucky Harris raced over from second. None of them had a chance as the ball dropped two feet inside the foul line. It had heavy spin on it from going off the end of the bat, and instead of taking a true bounce the ball squibbed into foul territory. A few strides from first base, my brain and feet together made a spontaneous decision to go for two. I touched the first base bag with the side of my foot and propelled myself toward second. Charley O'Leary, coaching first base, tried in vain to stop me. My legs suddenly felt eighteen again as I sprinted the final feet and did a hook slide under Peckinpaugh's tag. Safe!

As Peckinpaugh tossed the ball to Johnson on the mound, I popped up and dusted myself off. I was aware of three things: I had just hit a double off Walter Johnson, there were more people cheering me than I'd ever heard before, and Johnson had an expression on his face that indicated I wouldn't be getting any more hits off him any time soon.

Unfortunately, the last proved to be true in this game. I grounded out and popped out in my two remaining at bats, and Johnson beat us 4 - 3 to put the Yankees in the loss column for the first time this year. Still, I felt like my season had finally begun. I only wished that Margie had been there to see the game.

After a shower and change, and a lot of good-natured kidding from my teammates about my hitting prowess, I stepped out the players' entrance to find that she *was* there. And standing next to her was Karl Landfors.

Chapter Five

Post-game traffic outside the stadium was so snarled that the three of us elected to walk to our apartment. We made a few attempts at conversation along the way, but noisy crowds and the harsh, incessant rumble of automobiles made it difficult to sustain them.

Once we were in the quiet of our parlor, Margie said to me, "I hope you don't mind us showing up like that. When Karl wrote that he'd be coming to New York, I thought it would be fun to surprise you." She and Landfors both looked well-satisfied at having sprung him on me.

"It was a nice surprise," I replied. I always enjoyed seeing my old friend, even though he really wasn't much to look at. Landfors had a pale, angular face with a sharp nose. Resting upon that nose was a pair of thick steel-rimmed spectacles. His bony frame was clothed in an off-the-rack black suit that would have been considered drab by an undertaker. "But how did you get to the clubhouse door? The stadium cops don't let anybody past the gate."

Landfors removed his black low crown derby, revealing that his translucent hair had thinned almost to the point of invisibility. "The same way you get to do anything else in New York," he sniffed. "You pay a cop to look the other way."

Margie walked to the kitchen, saying over her shoulder, "I picked up some dinner. Hope everybody's hungry!"

I assured her that I was. Landfors, who seldom concerned himself with food, muttered, "At least the cop only demanded two bits. Worth it, I suppose."

Our small dining table was furnished with only two seats, so I dragged over the parlor's one Morris chair for Landfors. Glancing out the window, I noticed the boys playing in the street again with their taped bat and misshapen ball and reminded myself to get them something better.

As I went to help Margie in the kitchen, I called back, "What brings you to New York, Karl?" I hadn't seen him since St. Louis.

"A story," he answered tersely. Brushing back his coat, he sat down primly on the front edge of the Morris chair. Landfors was a writer of the muckraking type. He'd written for a number of newspapers and magazines, always trying to expose some kind of social injustice and usually disappointed when his stories failed to generate the public outrage he'd expected. There probably wasn't a progressive cause or radical organization that he hadn't championed at one time or another. He'd also been a great ally to me in some of the tough situations I'd faced over the years.

"What kind of story?" I asked. Margie handed me a blue ceramic platter that held a cold glazed ham and a small wheel of cheddar cheese. I placed it in the middle of the table. Plates, forks, spoons, and glasses were handed to me next, and I arranged them in the appropriate spots.

Landfors hesitated. "It's the Dot King murder."

Margie came in with French bread and a plate of pickles and olives. "That's something different for you, isn't it?" she said.

I was about to make the same comment. The death of a Ziegfeld chorus girl, dubbed "The Broadway Butterfly," had been in all the newspapers for weeks. The stories were full of lurid details about her many suitors and her fast lifestyle, but there was nothing political that I recalled.

Margie surveyed the dinner spread. "I'm forgetting something… Oh!" She briskly walked back to the kitchen, her long skirt swishing.

"I *want* something different," said Landfors. "I'm tired of causes. I've been working on them for years and it's gotten me nothing. Worse than that, nobody seems to care anyway. If all the public wants is salacious stories about chorus girls, fine, I'll give it to them. I'll bet any of the Hearst newspapers would be happy to have me write for them. In fact, I think I have an angle on the case that could prove *very* interesting."

I suspected that if Landfors was soured on radical causes it was because something had gone wrong between him and a certain lady friend who shared his politics. I didn't ask, though; I figured he would tell me about it in his own time.

"Here we are!" announced Margie, holding aloft a bottle of red wine in each hand. "And it's the real thing."

Landfors blinked eagerly behind his thick lenses. I preferred beer, but he was the guest and was partial to wine.

"Where'd you get it?" I asked.

"Mr. Tomasetti, the grocer on the corner. Very nice man. I've been shopping at his store for a few weeks. The first time I went in, he recognized me from my old movies. Today I told him it was a special occasion and he got these bottles for us from his back room. From Italy, before the war."

I poured a generous amount for each of us and Margie proposed a toast, "To good friends." After we clinked glasses and sipped the dry red wine, we began tearing off pieces of bread and cutting slices of ham and cheese. I hadn't realized before how hungry I was.

Shifting his gaze back and forth to indicate the question was intended for both of us, Landfors asked, "How do you like being back in New York?"

While I chewed a mouthful of ham, Margie said, "It's almost like last time: Mickey's involved with another murder."

Landfors blinked rapidly. "What murder?"

Margie again answered. "Some ballplayer was found dead in the new stadium." She ripped apart a piece of bread. "And I don't see why that should be Mickey's problem."

"You can't seem to stay away from crime, can you?" Landfors said with a tight smile. "Tell me about it." He eased back in the chair, causing it to suddenly recline. The pickle he'd been directing at his mouth struck his right nostril instead.

I managed to stifle a laugh and helped him move the backrest of the chair upright. After refilling the wine glasses, I gave him a quick account of Spats Pollard turning up in the Yankee Stadium wall. "But I'm only doing this to keep my job," I insisted. "I'll make enough of an effort to keep the front office happy, and then I'll let it drop." From the expressions on their faces, neither Landfors nor Margie appeared to believe me.

Margie raised her glass and neatly changed the subject. "Another toast," she said. "To Mickey, who got more hits than Babe Ruth today."

"Thank you." I lifted my glass. Trying to sound more modest than I felt, I added, "But it was just a cheap hit and it was only one."

"A double off Walter Johnson is more than most players get," she said. "I cheered like crazy when you slid into second."

I nodded my thanks again and drank half the glass. She was right: Today's game was something to celebrate.

"Ah, baseball," said Landfors. "The only profession in which a man can fail seventy percent of the time and be considered a great success."

I stared at him for a long moment and decided not to respond. I finally asked, "Do you have a place to stay?"

"Yes, with a writer friend in Greenwich Village."

I was glad to hear that. Because as much as I liked Karl Landfors, he sometimes made it difficult for me to remember why.

* * *

The Forty-fourth Precinct was headquartered in a three-story yellow brick box of a building on Sedgwick Avenue in the West Bronx. The traditional green lamps that designated a New York City police station were on either side of the front door.

On Monday morning, I went through that door and checked in with a surprisingly jovial desk sergeant. He told me how to find my way inside and let me pass through into a dreary office space with peeling beige walls and soot-stained ceilings. The stationhouse was furnished with a mismatched jumble of battered desks, chairs, storage shelves, and cabinets.

In a windowless corner of the second floor, I found Detective Jim Luntz seated at one of the better desks, looking much the same as when I had seen him in Ed Barrow's office. He even wore the same rumpled khaki suit which had acquired a scorch mark on the lapel. His old fedora was atop a pile of file folders on his desk and a half-full mug of black coffee rested on a smaller stack of papers. The pipe clamped in Luntz's teeth was burning a blend of tobacco so noxious that I thought he might use it to coerce confessions from suspects.

The detective peered up at me with a weary expression on his drawn face. At closer proximity to him than I'd been in Barrow's office, I noticed a touch of gray in his dark hair. "I got a message you'd be stopping by," he said. "You learn anything about Pollard?"

"Not yet," I admitted. "I need more to go on, and I was hoping I could get it from you."

He flicked a finger in the direction of a Windsor chair that was missing half its spindles. I pulled it closer to his desk and sat down. Luntz leaned back and drew so hard on his pipe that his cheeks pulled in. "So how can I help?" he asked, expelling a cloud of smoke along with the words.

"I have a five year gap that I don't know how to close," I began. "I did what you suggested: I started with the body. I went to the place where Pollard was found, but I don't think I really learned anything. And I only remember a little about him from 'eighteen when we were on the Cubs. I got a couple more ideas I might look into, but first I wanted to see what you know about him."

Luntz nodded and pulled a slim sheaf of papers from one of the accordion portfolios under his hat. "This is all I got. Anything in particular you want to know?"

I had a number of questions, but started with the simplest. "You said Pollard was missing for two years. He hadn't been dead all that time, though, had he? The fellow at the refreshment stand said the bullet holes looked fresh."

"Here's the coroner's report." Luntz briefly reviewed an official-looking form. "The cause of death was three very big bullets—.45s probably, but they passed right through him so we don't have the slugs. And he wasn't dead for more than a few days before he was found."

"So he was alive during those two years he was supposedly missing. Any idea *where* he was?"

Luntz shook his head. "Wherever he could find something to steal, probably. Gangsters don't work regular jobs."

"That's another thing I've been wondering about," I said. "In Barrow's office, and now again, you called Pollard a 'gangster,' not a 'crook' or a 'bootlegger.' Was he with a particular gang? Do you think he could have been killed in a gang war or something?" There were almost daily newspaper stories about deadly shootouts between the city's various gangs.

A hint of a smile crossed Luntz's face. "You're asking questions like a cop. Usually *I* do the interrogating."

"Hope you don't mind," I said. "I've been involved in a couple of murder investigations before, and I figured those were sensible questions to ask."

"They are," he chuckled. "I'm just not used to other people asking them." After a long draw on his pipe, the detective answered, "Pollard mostly operated in Manhattan, so the information I have is from detectives there. He was a two-bit criminal who worked on the fringes of several organizations, but never at a high level. Like most petty crooks, he was hoping to make a big score someday so that one of the major gangs would take notice and take him in." He tapped the pipe stem against his lower teeth. "As to who killed him, of course the logical guess is another gangster, but I have no idea who or why." The detective rarely looked at me when he spoke, generally keeping his gaze on his paper-strewn desk or on the bowl of his pipe.

"Your investigation hasn't turned up anything?"

Luntz hesitated. His cheeks began to work like a bellows until clouds of smoke rose to the stained ceiling. I could barely breathe from the overpowering stench of the tobacco. With the pipe clamped firmly in his teeth, he finally mumbled, "I've had a lot of other work to do."

I was puzzled. There were higher priorities than murder?

The detective sat upright and slowly withdrew the pipe from his mouth. In answer to my unspoken question, he said, "I'll be honest with you: I love the Bronx. I grew up in Highbridge and I got family in just about every part of the borough. So when I joined the force this is where I asked to be assigned. There's more action and faster promotions in Manhattan or Brooklyn, but this is my home and these are the people I want to serve. The Bronx is a nice borough and I want to keep it that way— quiet and peaceful, where decent people can walk the streets safely." He paused. "So if some gangster gets himself killed, I figure what the hell, that's one less hoodlum out there hurting civilians and one less arrest I'll have to make later."

I had no doubt that dead criminals were seldom mourned by law enforcement, but I was surprised that a police officer would so freely admit that he was happy to have murders lighten his work load. "So you don't investigate at all?" I asked.

He put the pipe back in his mouth and appeared disappointed to find that it had gone out. "Oh, I look into everything that happens in my precinct. But if it turns out to be gangsters killing gangsters, it drops way down on my list of priorities." Luntz struck a match and held it to the bowl. Sucking wetly on the bit, he went on, "I wouldn't be doing much of anything about this Spats Pollard thing if it wasn't for Jacob Ruppert pressing us. He's convinced that there's some kind of plot against him and he's got the influence to make the department do whatever he wants."

"You think there's anything to his notion that somebody's really out to hurt him?"

"Nah. I don't even understand what he was talking about—didn't make any sense to me at all." Luntz drew hard to get the pipe burning again. "As far as Huston being behind it, everybody knows those two men don't get along. But you don't kill somebody to annoy your business partner."

I agreed with him there. The Yankees' co-owners had been feuding for years, but Til Huston had been the driving force to get the stadium built on time. No matter how much he disliked Jacob Ruppert, he wouldn't do anything to damage the reputation of the ballpark that was largely his creation.

Luntz abruptly gave me a sharp look. "Maybe *you* could answer a question for *me*."

"Sure."

"When we were in Ed Barrow's office, what was Ruppert saying about John McGraw?" he asked. "Did you make any sense of it?"

"Well, there's even worse feelings between Ruppert and McGraw than there are between Ruppert and Huston." That was no secret; the Little Napoleon's New

York Giants had been the premier team in baseball until Babe Ruth and the Yankees overshadowed the city's National Leaguers. "McGraw is jealous of the Yankees' success," I explained. "That's why he kicked them out of the Polo Grounds and they had to build their own park."

"Huh." Luntz drew slowly on the pipe. "Then McGraw probably wouldn't mind giving Ruppert a great big problem in the new park."

"Probably not. But he wouldn't kill anybody."

"Maybe Pollard wasn't murdered at the park. Maybe he was moved there—dumped. Does McGraw know the kind of people who might need to dispose of a body?"

I considered that idea for a moment. John McGraw certainly did know such people. The Giants manager was on friendly terms with a number of underworld figures. He was even business partners with a few, owning a couple of pool halls and making regular bets at the racetrack. "He might know them," I answered, "but he wouldn't be involved with something like that."

"What makes you so sure?"

"I played for him. McGraw would love nothing better than to humiliate the Yankees—but he wants to do it on the field. He did it in last year's World Series and he made Babe Ruth look like a bush-leaguer to boot." To make it even sweeter for McGraw, it was the first World Series to be broadcast on radio. "He's happy as he can be right now, and he'll be gloating all year. No reason for him to do anything else."

"All right." Luntz appeared thoughtful. "I suppose that makes some kind of sense—and I don't intend to go asking McGraw if he had anything to do with it." He poked the stem of his pipe in my direction. "How about you? You going to do anything more with this Spats Pollard thing?"

"Yeah. Some of Pollard's other teammates from 1918 are still playing. If the schedules work out so that our teams are ever in the same city at the same time, I'll talk to them and ask if they remember anything about Pollard, or if any of them saw him again after that season."

Luntz nodded approvingly. "I don't see how that can hurt. Anything else?"

"Yes. I'm going to talk to Babe Ruth. You said he's on Pollard's customer list so I'm hoping he can tell me something about him, too." That was a fairly faint hope, however, because Ruth was notoriously forgetful about people. This brought me to my next question for Luntz. "Can I see the other names on the list?"

For a few seconds, his only response was a scowl. When he spoke it was only one word: "Why?"

"It might help to know how old the list is, and if it was really Pollard's or somebody else's. If I talk to some of people on it, I should be able to pin that down."

Luntz puffed away for a while. "No," he finally said. "I don't believe I can allow that. There are some important names on that list. I don't think it would be a good idea to bother them with a fishing expedition."

"But I—"

"Sorry. The answer's 'no.' " He leaned back, took the pipe from his mouth, and gave me a quizzical stare. "Why are you doing all this anyway?"

"You heard Ed Barrow. I'm doing this because he wants me to. And doing what he wants means I get to keep playing baseball."

"You must really love the game, then."

"More than anything."

Luntz slowly smiled. "Very well. Come see me again if I can help." When I stood, he added, "Like I said, I don't mind hoodlums killing other hoodlums. But I don't like civilians getting hurt. So be careful."

Troy Soos

Chapter Six

No matter how many times I glanced over at the front row box—and it was often—I couldn't believe what I saw: There was the President of the United States of America, less than twenty feet from where I stood. Warren G. Harding, the man who had promised the country "a return to normalcy," was in a seat of honor next to the Washington Senators' dugout. The presidential box was draped with patriotic bunting and a banner displaying the Great Seal of the United States hung from railing. I'd never seen a president in person before, and had assumed that the occupant of such an august office would have a more imposing appearance. Harding, who bore a resemblance to Ed Barrow, looked dignified in a black fedora and a Chesterfield coat, but weak and haggard.

I was situated in the first-base coach's box, where my primary responsibility was to remind Yankees runners not to get picked off. Coaching first base generally wasn't considered an important assignment—it was usually filled by any player or coach who wasn't otherwise engaged—

but Miller Huggins had given me the task because he liked my aggressive base running in Sunday's game. I'd had another good performance yesterday, too, coming in after Everett Scott had played the first three innings. I picked up two more singles in a losing effort against the Senators' Cy Warmoth. Having gotten some rest, Scott today felt that his ankle was up to full strength and Huggins had agreed to let him play the entire game. At least my coaching assignment meant that I wouldn't have to spend the game on the bench, but my position in the coach's box required that my backside face the president. I worried a little that I was violating some kind of protocol.

Ever since William Howard Taft initiated the practice in 1910, it had been an annual tradition for U. S. presidents to throw out the ceremonial first pitch for the Washington Senators at their home opener. They rarely appeared at other games, and today marked the first ever presidential visit to a New York ballpark. The current president was known to be a genuine baseball fan as well as a personal friend of Walter Johnson. With no advance notice, Harding had simply shown up at the stadium to cheer for his team. Even if he hadn't been president, it would have been easy for him to get a seat. Only about one in ten was occupied, and I was sure Jacob Ruppert wished he could have advertised the president's appearance in order to boost ticket sales.

In addition to Harding and his small entourage, the sparse crowd included Margie, Tom Van Dusen, and Natalie Brockman. I had arranged for them to meet Babe Ruth after the game so that Van Dusen could talk to him about making a movie. I wasn't looking forward to spending time with Margie's coworkers again, but I was happy to set up the meeting as a favor to her.

After the initial fanfare of the presidential visit settled down, Sad Sam Jones took the mound to face the Washington lineup. Jones, another pitcher acquired from the Red Sox, got his nickname because he wore his cap so low over his eyes that some thought it made him look mournful. It also made opposing batters wonder nervously if he could adequately see them. As a result, they were hesitant to dig in, eager to bail out, and susceptible to his masterful curveball. Relying largely on that curve, Jones set the Senators down in order in the first.

During our half of the inning, with the Yankee bats equally ineffective, I had nothing to do but steal glances at the president. Harding had Walter Johnson's young son balanced on his lap, and the chief executive looked like any other man out at a ball game.

Jones continued his domination of the Senators. Then, with the game scoreless, the bottom of our batting order went on a hitting spree. Second baseman Aaron Ward singled as did Everett Scott, and Jones drove in Ward for the first run of the game. With two on and two outs, Ruth came up and knocked in both runners with a line drive to right. I cheered them all on from behind first base, but none of them required any coaching.

When Wally Pipp grounded out to end the inning, I trotted to the dugout to take my place on the bench near Miller Huggins. Before I could step inside, I noticed Andrew Vey standing at the railing trying to get my attention. Even with the thin crowd, it was difficult to hear his high, weak voice calling my name. I thought if he didn't wear his little bow ties so tight, he'd probably be able to produce more sound.

When I stepped to the rail, Vey said, "Mr. Barrow would like to see you." He pulled at one of his shirt cuffs, which must have been the wardrobe problem he was struggling with today.

"Be happy to," I said, although I wasn't happy at all. "As soon as the game is over."

"Well—"

I cut him off. "Mr. Barrow used to be a manager. I'm sure he knows not to bother a player during a game."

"Actually—" He tugged hard at his other cuff.

"And in the future, I'd appreciate if you didn't, either."

Vey's face always had a slightly startled appearance, as if he'd just been slapped and didn't know why, but now his eyes widened even more and his freckles seemed to burn. "I'm sure after the game will be acceptable," he said.

I stepped into dugout and gave one more glance at Vey. As he turned around to leave, I noticed he was trying hard not to grin.

We held the 3-0 lead into the bottom of the fifth inning. Then Babe Ruth stepped into the batter's box and with one swing of his bat gave the fans a far greater thrill than seeing the president. He connected with a high fastball and sent it on a towering flight to right field. As soon as he made contact there was no question that it was going over the fence—the only question was whether it would leave the borders of the Bronx.

The crowd was instantly on its feet and Ruth went into his home run trot as they cheered wildly. When he got to first base, I jokingly coached him, "Turn left, Babe!" He roared with laughter and continued his triumphant circuit of the base paths. When he got to home plate, he pounced on it with both feet, then theatrically doffed his cap and bowed to the president.

The crowd roared again, and Harding grinned with delight. The Babe went into the dugout and soon came out holding a bright red poppy. He brought it to Harding's box and pinned it to the president's overcoat. The game was stopped while photographers documented the meeting of America's two most famous men.

Ruth's home run held up as the final tally of the game and Sad Sam Jones earned the Yankees' first shutout of the season. Going into the clubhouse, everybody on the team was in high spirits. Except me. I had to see Ed Barrow.

*   *   *

Work on the business manager's spacious office had been completed. The walls and trim were freshly painted, the furniture was carefully placed in position, and expensive area rugs covered most of the floor. Barrow had also decorated the walls with plaques, photographs, testimonials, and awards that documented highlights of his colorful career.

The most unusual piece in the collection was a sepia photograph of a young bare-chested Ed Barrow in tight pants. His fists were raised in a boxing pose, and facing him in the picture was a similarly clad, and magnificently mustachioed, John L. Sullivan. Barrow made sure that everyone knew he had once boxed the former heavyweight champion of the world; although Barrow had never played professional baseball, his abilities in the ring earned him the respect of players who might have otherwise dismissed him as a mere administrator. In the photo, Barrow's face exhibited the bulldog determination that stood him well in every confrontation from boxing matches to contract negotiations.

The rest of the keepsakes were from his varied baseball career, starting as a concessionaire with Harry M. Stevens, then as owner of some small minor league teams such as the Class A Paterson Silk Weavers, and later as president of the Eastern League. There was a photograph of him with a young Honus Wagner, whom Barrow had discovered in 1896 and signed to his first professional contract. Of more recent vintage was a large engraved plaque honoring the World's Champion 1918 Boston Red Sox whom Barrow had led as field manager—I had the feeling that this office was the only spot in Yankee Stadium where a Red Sox championship would ever be commemorated. After leaving the Red Sox at the end of the 1920 season, Barrow had come to the Yankees. He promptly helped build the team that earned the two American League championship trophies that rested on a shelf behind his desk.

I had time to examine Barrow's mementos because he was engaged in a telephone conversation and had yet to acknowledge my presence. Andrew Vey stood dutifully by his boss's side while Barrow issued an uninterrupted stream of orders into the mouthpiece. From what I could gather, he was interested in acquiring a couple of pitchers from the South Atlantic League. He ended the phone call with, "Get me scouting reports on both of them—and they better be *thorough*!"

When he hung up, Barrow fixed me with a stern expression. Without any preliminaries he said, "We might have a problem."

A bigger problem than a murdered man buried in the stadium? I wondered. "What is it?" I asked.

"The newspapers are getting curious. Rumors have been making the rounds about dead bodies in the ballpark." Barrow knitted his beetle brows. "Have you said anything to anyone?"

"I've talked to a few people," I readily admitted. "I have to, if I'm supposed to find out what happened to Spats Pollard."

"Of course you do," he snapped. "But I expect you to be discreet."

"I'm only asking questions, and I'm only talking to people who might have information." As soon as I spoke, it occurred to me that I did tell Karl Landfors about Pollard's murder. But I was sure Landfors wouldn't try to turn it into a news story. Well, I was *almost* sure.

"Very well." Barrow peaked his fingers and rested his chin on the crest. "So far, Mr. Vey has been able to dissuade the papers from publishing anything. However we don't know how long they can be kept at bay."

I shot a look at Vey's impassive freckled face. I was curious exactly *how* he had managed that dissuasion; reporters didn't give up easily when they got wind of a juicy crime story.

Barrow went on, "Also, Colonel Ruppert is becoming quite anxious over the state of the club's finances. Do you know what today's attendance was?"

I gave my most precise estimate: "Lousy."

Vey uttered a soft chuckle and looked down at the shirt cuff that he was absently fingering.

Barrow scowled. "Barely *eight thousand*. Not nearly enough to pay the bills."

I had no reply to that statement. My concern was hitting, catching, running, and throwing. Monitoring gate receipts and balancing the accounting ledgers was somebody else's job.

"I remind you," Barrow continued, "that among those bills is your salary. Now, tell me what you've found out so far."

Okay, so maybe to some extent the team's financial condition *was* my concern. I quickly gave Barrow a summary of my talk with Joe Zegarra at the concession stand and my meeting with Detective Luntz.

Barrow briefly considered my report. "It sounds to me like you have a lot more work to do—and you have to do it fast." He leaned back in his leather-padded desk chair. "You see, if this does hit the newspapers, we need to know how to handle it. Was Pollard's death some random crime? Was it a conspiracy by Colonel Ruppert's enemies?" He spread his hands. "We have to be prepared so that we can minimize the damage to our public image." Sitting upright again, he added, "Frankly, the police don't seem to be making as much progress as we had hoped, so we are relying on you."

It's tough to make progress when you're not doing anything at all, I thought. Luntz had made it clear that the murder of a small-time hood like Spats Pollard was not going to be a priority for him. It occurred to me that the Yankees didn't care about his death, either, except for the fact that it might bring the club bad publicity. Nobody seemed interested in actually having Pollard's killer brought to justice.

"What are you planning to do next?" Barrow asked.

We were leaving for Boston after one more game, so there wasn't much more I could do in New York. "I'm having dinner with the Babe tonight," I said. "His name was on Pollard's customer list, so I'd like to find out how well they knew each other. I'm also planning to talk to some more players to see if they remember Pollard. He wasn't in the majors long, but maybe somebody knew him in the minors."

"Sounds like a sensible course of action." Barrow nodded approvingly. "Remember: Be discreet—and keep me informed."

"I'll do that," I said. "But not during games."

Barrow's huge eyebrows twitched upward.

"I've already told Mr. Vey, and I'm asking you: Don't come to me with this business during a game. I'll help you all I can before and after, but on the field my only job is baseball."

"Well... Yes, of course. My apologies." Barrow gave his assistant a meaningful look. "It won't happen again."

Vey responded with a hint of a smile and a small nod of acquiescence.

* * *

I was never a heavy drinker, but I'd certainly been in my share of saloons over the years, from richly appointed bars in upscale hotels to squalid blind pigs hidden away in dark alleys. The essentials were all the same: an almost exclusively male clientele, a long bar equipped with a brass foot rail, and a few tables for those too lazy or too drunk to stand. The available beverages were generally limited to beer, whiskey, gin, or rum, sometimes accompanied by a heavily salted lunch spread of pickled eggs, stringy beef, or boiled ham. As far as I knew, such establishments were standard in every town and city in the country, and probably had been since before the nation was founded. Now, however, it seemed they were becoming obsolete.

Of course, putting saloons out of business was the goal of the Prohibitionists, but the Eighteenth Amendment inadvertently resulted in an expansion of drinking to new venues and new customers. Night clubs and speakeasies were taking the place of traditional bars, especially in the cities. Instead of a simple watering hole for men to talk sports and politics over their drinks, these new places provided diverse entertainments and catered to both men and women. There was a thrill and romance to indulging in illicit activity, and little risk since the law was seldom enforced, so it had become fashionable for couples and groups to go "night clubbing" together. New clubs were opening almost every night and vying with each other to offer the most enticing attractions. In New York City, there were thousands from which to choose.

Our choice for this evening—more precisely Tom Van Dusen's choice—was Katie Day's on Forty-ninth Street. One of Manhattan's newest hot spots, it featured an Irish theme that was overdone to the point of caricature. Almost everything in the club was colored in hues of green, from the streamers that festooned the ceiling to the seat cushions on the chairs. Pennants displaying the names and coats of arms of various Irish counties hung on the walls. Behind the stage was a large mural of a rainbow leading to a pot of gold. Half a dozen dwarves, dressed as leprechauns, cavorted about while a red-haired fiddler played a lively jig.

The club buzzed with a hundred conversations and the fiddler had to play hard to be heard above the din. Tables were packed so closely together that we could barely squeeze between them. One of the leprechauns, with a realistic white beard, slowly ushered us to a prime spot that cost Van Dusen a ten-dollar tip, and we sat down at a small round table with a bowl of shamrocks as a centerpiece.

Van Dusen wore a belted tweed suit with knickers and argyle socks; his outfit looked like something that the Griffith studio's wardrobe department might have assembled for the role of an English squire. Natalie Brockman was in a low-cut fringed black dress that contrasted sharply with her pale skin and platinum blonde hair. She had a thoroughly bored expression on her face, for which I couldn't fault her. We were all weary of Van Dusen's grousing by now. After the game, the four of us had met for dinner at a small German restaurant. Throughout the meal, Van Dusen did nothing but complain about failing to get his picture taken with President Harding. Van Dusen had made a fool of himself at Yankee Stadium, first pleading and then ranting, trying to convince anyone who would listen that the president would certainly want to meet such a famous movie director as himself. No one in Harding's entourage had heard of Tom Van Dusen, however, and his request for a joint photograph was unceremoniously declined.

We'd been seated in Katie Day's only a few minutes, waiting for Babe Ruth to arrive, when Van Dusen began renewing his complaints. "I don't know what kind of fools Harding surrounds himself with," he griped. "They don't even recognize one of the country's most important motion picture artists!" He fixed his boyish face in a pout that would make a two-year-old proud.

Brockman, who had dined on a single potato pancake and several glasses of Reisling, said in a tired voice, "Tom, if you say one more word about it, I'm putting my cigarette out on your nose." She took a deep drag, making the tip glow bright, and held out the ivory holder as if she was prepared to carry through on her threat. I'd finally found something that I liked about Natalie Brockman and couldn't help but smile.

Van Dusen sullenly ran a hand over his pomaded hair. He began to mutter something but stopped abruptly when Brockman feigned a jab with the cigarette.

Margie, dressed simply but looking beautiful in a white shirtwaist and blue silk skirt, had managed to maintain good spirits all evening but now seemed uneasy at the growing tension. She made a show of looking about the room. "This is quite a place," she said in an effort to change the conversation. "I've never been here before."

Van Dusen made a dismissive gesture. "It's nothing special. Just another place to serve liquor and bring in the suckers."

Brockman said coolly, "You picked this joint, so I guess that makes you a sucker, too."

He shot her a brief but lethal look and addressed himself to Margie and me as if the actress was no longer present. "This is where the fashionable people are going at the moment," he said, "but it won't last. When people get tired of seeing shamrocks and midgets in funny costumes, they'll move on to someplace else. Everything loses its novelty, and something new always comes along." Van Dusen began to inspect his manicured nails. "Katie realizes that, and she's got a great system for making money fast before the place goes bust."

"You know her?" I asked. The way he spoke her name sounded as if he did.

"I know *everybody* worth knowing," he replied with his usual arrogance. "And I've known Katie for years. She used to be a showgirl—tried the movies but never caught on."

I chose not to point out to the director that if he really knew everyone worth knowing, he wouldn't need me to introduce him to Babe Ruth. The more Van Dusen talked, the more I wished Ruth would hurry so that I could sooner be free of Van Dusen's company.

A petite young lady in a green peasant dress with a white lace collar and loosely-tied bodice came to take our drink orders. The ladies opted for champagne while Van Dusen ordered a Manhattan and I asked for a beer. I had the feeling that if the evening turned out to be a long one I would need quite a few of them to make it tolerable.

Van Dusen gazed around. "Yes, it's quite a racket

Katie has here." He went on to explain in a confidential tone, "You see, it's all a matter of maximizing income and minimizing expenses." That didn't sound like a particularly innovative business strategy to me, but I didn't know anything about running a speakeasy. "Notice," he said, like a pompous professor, "there's no dance floor. Why waste floor space on dancing when you can fill it with more tables? And, if nobody's dancing, you don't need to pay a band—that damned fiddler certainly can't cost her much. With a three-dollar cover charge, every customer she can pack in is that much more profit. And with the drink prices—a dollar a beer, four dollars for real drinks—Katie makes a small fortune every night."

Margie spoke up. "There's no entertainment at all? People come here just to sit and drink?"

"Sounds pretty good, if you ask me," said Brockman. With a hopeful glance over each bony shoulder, she added, "I wish the drinks would come soon. I'm *thirsty*."

Ignoring her, Van Dusen answered Margie, "Katie Day herself is all the entertainment this place needs. You'll see when she comes out.

"*And* I'm hungry," whined Brockman.

Van Dusen snapped at her, "You should have eaten something at the restaurant." To Margie and me, he added, "All they serve here is drinks—who needs the expense of cooks and a kitchen when the real money is all in booze, anyway?" He lowered his voice and continued, "As far as that goes, by the way, it's not kept on the premises—it's stored next door under another name. When you place your order, the waitress goes to the back room, relays the order through a hole the wall, and picks it up from the same place. It takes a little longer, but if there's a raid on the club, everyone simply downs the drink they have at the moment and presto!—the place is dry as the Sahara desert. Hey, there's Katie now!"

A tall, attractive woman, with flaming red hair that owed more to chemistry than to nature, strode to a small stage. She was about thirty years old, full-figured, and walked seductively in a satin dress that clung to her every curve. After mounting the platform, Katie Day paused and looked around the room while the fiddler put aside his instrument. Her lips were brightly painted in a Cupid's bow and she had them tightly pursed. All eyes were soon turned toward her and conversations ceased. For a long minute, she let the silence continue and the expectations build.

A bright smile slowly spread on her heavily rouged and powdered face. In a brassy Bronx voice she said, "I'm just going to let you all look at me for a while." There were some good-natured laughs and chuckles. "That is why you're here, isn't it?—to drink in the sight of me?" She did a slow turn, accompanied by an exaggerated wiggle of her hips, and struck a pose like a model in a rotogravure. There was more laughter. She grinned broadly and winked. "Of course, if there's anything *else* you'd like to drink, I'm sure we can provide whatever your heart—or your liver—desires."

At that moment, our own drinks arrived. The champagne was served in plain white coffee mugs, Van Dusen's Manhattan was in a dainty tea cup, and I was handed a pale green bottle with an orange *Moxie* label. I gave it an uncertain look.

Van Dusen said to me, "It's what's inside that counts."

"Unlike the movies," put in Brockman. She took a long drag of her cigarette and expelled smoke from the corner of her mouth in the director's direction.

"Skoal!" Van Dusen toasted, and we each eagerly took

our first sips. The beer in the Moxie bottle was an excellent lager, and I downed a good part of it before setting the bottle on the table.

Meanwhile, Katie Day had been exchanging banter with customers, most of which consisted of her making wisecracks at their expense—and they seemed to love it. She now directed her attention to a balding, florid-faced man in a red-and-black plaid suit. "You there, wearing the checkerboard," she called to him. "Where are you from?"

He glanced around to be sure that he was the one being addressed. "Nebraska!" he answered proudly.

"You don't say! Well, how do you like visiting the United States? This must be quite a change from North Dakota."

"Nebraska!" he repeated. "Omaha, Nebraska."

She leaned over, put her hands on her knees, and slowly shook her head. "It doesn't really matter, does it?"

The crowd laughed. Making fun of out-of-towners was standard comedic fare in New York. The man from Omaha smiled blandly; he didn't seem to mind being insulted as long as he was part of the show.

Day continued, "What do you do out there in North Dakota?"

Not bothering to correct her again, he answered, "I'm in ladies' clothing."

"Well, I'm sorry to disappoint you, dearie, but you're not getting in *this* lady's clothing!"

The club erupted in laughter, but it soon dwindled away as attention was diverted toward a commotion near the entrance. I was pretty sure I knew the cause, and Katie Day confirmed it when she announced, "Ladies and gentlemen, here he is, the man with the biggest bat in baseball: Babe Ruth!"

Cheers and applause greeted his appearance. Ruth stood for a moment, his habitual black cigar sticking out of his beaming broad face. His clothes were perfectly tailored, his thick hair impeccably groomed, and a diamond stickpin was centered in his silk tie. After a wave and a bow to acknowledge the crowd's reception, he followed one of the leprechauns to our table, where an extra chair was promptly pulled up for him.

The four of us already at the table were aware that attention was on us now, too, and we all sat a little straighter and tried to look cheerful. I could sense nearby eyes gawking with envy that the Babe was joining our party. I also noticed that Natalie Brockman's eyes had a particular gleam in them.

Ruth paused to wag his cigar and bow once more before sitting down.

From the stage, Day said loudly, "You see, ladies and gentlemen, *everybody* comes to see Katie!" She then stepped off the platform and came to our table, where she exchanged some banter with Ruth and personally took his drink order—scotch with beer on the side.

When she left, I introduced Ruth to Margie and her coworkers. Tom Van Dusen immediately leaned forward and began speaking to Ruth as if the rest of us weren't there. He expanded on my introduction, enumerating his many accomplishments as a movie director. Van Dusen made it sound as if he had practically invented motion pictures.

I got right to the point, explaining to the Babe, "Mr. Van Dusen would like you to be in one of his movies."

Van Dusen gave me a sharp look for interrupting his autobiographical monologue. Returning his attention to Ruth, he said, "Let me tell you, Babe—mind if I call you 'Babe'?"

Ruth gave him his trademark grin. "Call me anything you like, as long as it isn't late to dinner."

Brockman laughed as if it was the funniest thing she'd ever heard.

The director continued, "Babe, I'll tell you straight out: You are the biggest star in America, a hero to every man, woman, and child." He paused as if expecting Ruth to be surprised at this news. When Ruth's only reaction was a nod of agreement, Van Dusen added, "Believe me, I know stars. I've worked with Pickford, Fairbanks, Valentino…"

Ruth's drinks were placed before him. He promptly downed half the scotch. "I don't know them people," he said. "I don't go to the movies much." I was sure he was pulling the director's leg.

"You don't have to go to them to be *in* one," Van Dusen replied. "And you don't have to worry about acting, either. I tell you, Babe, you can be a bigger movie star than any actor—all you have to do is be yourself, and I'll take care of the rest."

"Nah, I already tried that. A couple years ago a fellow talked me into making a picture for him." Ruth frowned. "I forget the name of it… Something about home."

"*Headin' Home*," I put in. I had seen the movie when it came out, believing that a picture about baseball was sure to be worth watching. Ruth was indeed fun to see, but the story was pure hokum.

"Yeah, that sounds right." One more swallow emptied the Babe's glass. "Anyway, that fellow gave me a check for twenty-five thousand dollars! Can you believe it? That was the biggest single check anybody ever gave me. I carried it around for months just to look at." He belched and patted his stomach. "Turns out it was just a piece of paper—soon as I tried to cash it, the damned thing bounced."

Van Dusen pulled himself upright and said haughtily, "I represent the D. W. Griffith Studio. I can assure you that *our* checks are good." When we'd first met, Van Dusen had admitted that the studio's finances were not all that strong. Now, trying to sway the Babe, he went on to speak at length about the film company's solid profitability and enormous prestige.

Without any of us ordering them, fresh drinks arrived for everyone. To give the waitress access to our table, Brockman scooched her chair closer to the Babe's. When the waitress left, she didn't bother to move it back.

Van Dusen and Ruth continued to chat as if the rest of us were invisible. Eventually, the director changed tactics. He reminded the Babe that his image was recently tarnished because of his poor World Series performance and the newspaper reports on his drinking and marital problems. Making a wholesome motion picture, Van Dusen assured him, would not only restore the shine to his image but practically put a halo over his head.

I looked at Margie, who had managed to sustain a cheerful smile through an evening that had provided little to enjoy. I wished that she and I could simply spend the rest of the night together alone; I gave her a small smile and the glimmer in her eyes told me that she'd caught it.

With his arm now draped around back of the actress's chair, Ruth turned to me. "What do you think, kid? Should I make a movie for Von Doodlebug here?"

Van Dusen visibly bristled at the mangling of his name, but I knew the Babe meant no offense. He didn't remember anyone's name, including his roommate's— he'd probably still be calling me "kid" long after we both retired.

"I don't know," I replied, causing Van Dusen to shoot

me a startled, angry look that I chose to ignore. No doubt he'd been expecting my unequivocal endorsement. Addressing the Babe, I went on, "As far as your public image, you don't need to make a movie to fix that. If you keep playing baseball the way you have been lately, nobody will remember the mistakes you made off the field." He had gone three-for-three in today's game, bringing his season average above .400.

"Well, I promised I was gonna turn over a new leaf this year, and I'm trying my damnedest." Ruth winked at Brockman. "I got a feeling this is gonna be my best season ever."

I looked again at Margie and reminded myself that I was really here for her, not for Van Dusen or Ruth. I continued my answer to the Babe's question. "So I'd say you don't *need* to make a movie. But on the other hand, why not? Margie tells me Van Dusen is a top-notch director, and he's sure to make a better picture than *Headin' Home.* I'll bet kids would love to see you in a good movie. Hell, I see you every day in person, and I'd still go to see you in picture."

Ruth chuckled. "Ah, what the hell. Maybe it'll be fun." To Van Dusen, he said, "What's the offer? Gimme the details."

The two of them began to discuss dollar figures and distribution rights. If Tom Van Dusen had assumed the Babe to be a novice in such matters, he was mistaken. Ruth addressed the business matters knowledgeably and capably. In addition to negotiating a landmark contract with the Yankees, the Babe had all sorts of endorsement deals and public appearance agreements. He was even a published author, thanks to his ghostwriter Christy Walsh.

While Van Dusen and Ruth were engrossed in the

details of a potential moving picture deal, I excused myself to use the men's room. I wished that Margie and I could have excused ourselves from the place entirely, but I knew we would have to linger a while longer.

I was alone in the clean spacious restroom, washing my hands, when a gruff voice near the door said, "Hey, ain't you Mickey Rawlings? With the Yankees?"

"Yes." I was flattered to be recognized. Being spotted in a men's room wasn't quite the same as Babe Ruth walking into the club and being cheered by the entire crowd, but I was happy for every small notice.

"I been hopin' to meetcha."

I turned to look at the man, whom I guessed to be in his late twenties. He had dark, brooding eyes and wavy black hair that was kept in place by a liberal application of scented grease. He'd probably be considered handsome except for a small vertical scar below his left eye that resembled a jagged teardrop. His compact frame was clothed in a loose double-breasted suit with an oversized silk tie that was sloppily knotted.

"Glad to meet you," I said, drying my hands on a towel. "What's your name?"

He didn't seem to hear me. "I saw you sittin' with the Babe. And a couple real pretty ladies." His drew his teeth back in what might have been intended as a smile. But he resembled a wolf baring its teeth. I had the sense something was wrong about this guy.

"Yeah, well, it was nice to meet you," I said, trying to remain polite. I took a step toward the door, hoping to leave the room without further conversation.

"You stay right there," he growled, pulling his jacket open enough for me to see the handle of a pistol that was tucked in the waistband of his trousers. I'd seen the exact same model during my stint in the army: an M1911 Colt

.45 automatic. While he held the jacket open with one hand, he moved the other to within inches of the gun. I didn't take another step.

"What do you want?" I asked, assuming it was a stickup. If so, this fellow had badly overestimated a utility player's salary.

Keeping the jacket drawn back, and the pistol in easy reach, he said, "I hear you got an interest in Spats Pollard. You need to forget about him. Pollard is dead and ain't nothin' gonna change that. You gotta think about people who are still alive—and about keepin' 'em that way. You don't gotta know my name, or nothin' else about me, except that I know who you are and I know who your friends are." He bared his teeth again, seeming quite pleased with himself. "And I can find any one of you, any time, just as easy as I did tonight." He let the jacket fall back over the gun. "Forget about Pollard and everybody else stays healthy."

He backed out of the restroom, not breaking eye contact with me until he was through the door. I was frozen where I stood, astonished at the encounter, and unable to make sense of had happened.

I didn't snap out of it until the businessman from Omaha burst into the restroom, tottering under the influence of Katie Day's bootleg liquor. "Must think you're something awful special," he grumbled at me, "trying to make this your own private bathroom."

"Huh?"

"Those goons you had outside wouldn't let me in." He lurched toward a stall and was soon noisily sick.

By the time I walked out to rejoin Margie and the others, the man with the gun was gone from view. But I suspected that he still had me in his sight.

Chapter Seven

After the team had returned from our long, arduous exhibition tour from New Orleans to New York during spring training, I had hoped that I wouldn't have to ride the rails again for some time. Now, embarking on our first road trip of the season, I was looking forward to getting away from New York and spending a few hours on the *Mayflower Express*.

Soon after we pulled out of Pennsylvania Station most of the players headed to the dining car, where they could eat and drink their fill on the Yankees' tab. I went alone to the club car, which smelled of old leather and stale cigar smoke, carrying a two-day-old copy of the *New York Tribune*. I had no interest in actually reading the newspaper; I only wanted to hold it in front of me to discourage anyone from trying to strike up a conversation. I had some thinking to do, and didn't want interruptions.

At the far end of the car, Waite Hoyt and Herb Pennock were beginning a game of pinochle. "Long Bob" Meusel, one of the team's night owls, had barely made the train and was already fast asleep in a capacious arm chair.

I chose a seat well removed from the others and unfolded the newspaper. It opened to a half-page advertisement for *Safety Last*, the new Harold Lloyd movie playing at the Rialto. I allowed myself to imagine Margie and me having a normal night out together: a quiet dinner for two at a nice restaurant, a first-run movie at one of the city's motion picture palaces, and then maybe a dance hall where Margie could once again try to teach me to move my feet in rhythm.

Such thoughts only served to emphasize the stark difference between the kind of evening I would *like* to have and the one we actually did have at Katie Day's. I knew that life would return to normal only if I could find a way to solve the problem of Spats Pollard's murder.

My daydream of a romantic evening with Margie soon receded to the back of my mind, and I began working my way through a tangle of questions. Some were relatively simple to answer, such as whether or not Karl Landfors was responsible for the recent press inquiries into Pollard's death. I was pretty sure the answer was "no," but I needed to be certain. I'd been unsuccessful trying to contact him before leaving town, so Margie promised that she would find Landfors and tell him that the Pollard murder had to be kept quiet. If Ed Barrow found out that I'd spoken to a writer about the murder, I would probably be sent down to a low minor league club somewhere.

Other questions were more difficult: Who was the man that threatened me in Katie Day's night club? How did he know I was investigating Pollard's death? What was his interest in the case? How seriously should I take him?

It was odd, but during the actual encounter, I had felt no fear. In France, during the Great War, I had faced machine guns, cannons, tanks, and chemical gas, so I certainly wasn't going to panic at the sight of a single pistol. I was taken by surprise, though, and it took a few minutes before I could absorb what had happened and compose myself. When I'd returned to our table, Tom Van Dusen was telling the Babe about a jazz club on Lenox Avenue and he tried to convince us all to move the party there. I loved jazz, but didn't want to go that night and never wanted to go anywhere again with Van Dusen. When Margie and I begged off, the three of them went on to Harlem without us. I said nothing about the gunman until Margie and I were home. She asked many of the same questions that I was now still trying to resolve in my own mind.

Although I didn't know the man's identity, I had no doubt about his occupation. He practically wore the uniform of a gangster, as readily identifiable as a fireman's leather helmet and rubber slicker. But why did he warn me off the case? As Detective Luntz had said, it was most likely that Spats Pollard had been knocked off by another gangster—was the fellow who'd confronted me in the men's room that man? Or was he an associate of Pollard's who feared I might jeopardize some of their criminal enterprises by looking into his murder? Come to think of it, how many "associates" might be involved? At least a couple of them had been posted at the restroom door to keep anyone from walking in while I was being threatened.

I had never seen the gunman before, but he seemed to know a lot about me. How had he learned that I was investigating Pollard's murder? The death of the former pitcher hadn't garnered a single line in the newspapers.

And how did he know I would be at Katie Day's night club—was I being followed?

That led to an embarrassing question: How could I have been so careless? It was an easy one to answer, but it was no excuse. Since my only reason for probing the Pollard murder was to placate Yankees management, I had made only a token effort and had looked at it as an inconvenience more than anything else. I had lost sight of the fact that Spats Pollard had been *murdered*, and murder is not a thing done lightly. Nor does a murderer necessarily stop with one victim. Whether or not the gunman in the night club was Pollard's killer, I knew I should take him seriously. Merely flashing a gun didn't mean he would use it, but I could not take the threat casually—especially since he'd extended it to my "friends," and that included Margie. Now I *had* to look into Pollard's murder, not merely to satisfy Ed Barrow or Jacob Ruppert, but to find out how the gangster who'd confronted me was connected to the crime—and how I could remove him as a threat.

I was compiling mental lists of everyone I'd spoken with about Pollard, and everyone who might have known that I'd be at Katie Day's last night, when the newspaper I was holding suddenly rattled from a sharp slap. I lowered it to see Miller Huggins' dour face. "Give your eyes a break from reading," he said gruffly. "You're going need them for hitting."

"I will?"

"Ward's come down with a damned flu. You'll be starting at second base." He turned on his heels and walked across the club car to speak with Waite Hoyt about what to expect from the Red Sox hitters.

I hadn't felt so happy all season. Without any concern for Aaron Ward's health, all I could think of was that this would be my first time in the starting lineup as a New York Yankee.

* * *

Unlike the cold, threatening skies that hovered over the first game at Yankee Stadium, Boston's Opening Day weather was ideal for baseball. The sun was high, the sky clear blue, the grass a vibrant green, and the temperature unseasonably warm. It felt like mid-summer instead of April twenty-sixth.

As I looked around the park, I had the sense that I'd come home. I had played for the Red Sox in 1912, the first year of Fenway Park's existence. Although I was now a Yankee, I still had a fondness for Boston, and especially for this field. Yankee Stadium was newer, grander, and three times the size, but cozy Fenway Park was exactly what a ballpark should be.

The roles of the two teams were reversed from a week ago, with New York the visitors and the Red Sox hosting their first home game of 1923. The obligatory Opening Day rituals that preceded the game had a distinctly Boston flavor. The full house of twenty thousand fans was first treated to an impressive drill exhibition by a squad of marines from the Charlestown Navy Yard. The marines then led the teams to the flagpole, where the Stars and Stripes was raised as a brass band played with less precision but more life than Sousa's. Finally, Boston's fabulously corrupt mayor James M. Curley took the mound to throw out the ceremonial first pitch. Massachusetts governor Channing Cox donned a catcher's mitt and bent down behind the plate to receive the throw. In an entertaining twist, Red Sox manager Frank Chance stepped into the batter's box to face Curley's offering. To the delight of the crowd, Chance took a Ruthian swing at the pitch. He had enough political savvy, however, to miss it by a wide margin—otherwise, he might have found a sheaf of parking tickets on the windshield of his car after the game.

With the ceremonies over, Boston's Howard Ehmke took his warm-up tosses and prepared to face the top of our batting order. The rivalry between the Red Sox and the Yankees was as intense as that between the National League's Dodgers and Giants, but the Fenway fans had been respectful when the Yankees were introduced and even gave us polite applause. Their behavior reverted to usual, however, once the game began. In their turn, Whitey Witt, Joe Dugan, and Babe Ruth were greeted by boos and catcalls as they approached the batter's box. These noises were followed by hoots of glee as each one made an easy out.

Perhaps it was the familiarity of this ballpark, or maybe it was the relief of being able to focus on something other than murder and murderous threats, but I felt loose and comfortable as I trotted out to second base for the bottom half of the first. I was relaxed, with no more jitters than if I was playing a sandlot game against a bunch of kids.

I had no fielding chance with the first batter since Waite Hoyt struck out Boston's Nemo Leibold on a sequence of well-placed fastballs. Veteran Shano Collins was next for the Red Sox, and he strode to the plate wagging his bat like the tail of a happy dog.

On a two-one count, Collins smacked a hard chopper up the middle that looked sure to go through for a hit. I dove and snagged the ball behind the second base bag. The air whooshed out of me as I landed hard on my stomach. I twisted in the dirt, rolled, and made a side-armed throw to nail Collins by half a step. Hoyt cheered my play with a "Way to go!" but it had felt as effortless to me as going around-the-horn during warm-ups.

When I came to bat, I discovered that hitting was unfathomably easy for me today too. In the top of the second, I connected solidly with one of Ehmke's slow curves for a line single over the shortstop's head. Batting again in the fifth, I noticed Norm McMillan playing deep at third base and dropped a bunt down the line that I easily beat out for my second hit of the day.

I was two-for-three going into the top of the ninth, but our team was down 4–2 on the scoreboard. With one out, Everett Scott, still nursing a tender ankle, hobbled his way to the plate and hit a slow grounder that squeezed its way between first and second for a single. Huggins immediately pulled the slow-moving Scott from the game and put Hinkey Haines in to pinch run for him. It was the sensible move, but I was a bit annoyed because Scott's injury was worthless for me today. I was already in the lineup, and I preferred that other players save their injuries for games when I could go in to replace them.

Following Scott in the batting order, I approached the batter's box with an unusual confidence. The partisan crowd loudly called for Ehmke to finish the job of sending the Yankees to defeat. I fought to block the sound of the fans until it was little more than a dull hum in my ears. I concentrated completely on what I would have to do at the plate.

Since we were down two runs, my job was simply to get on base and let the following hitters drive Haines and me in. *Just a single*, I told myself. Ehmke won't want to put the tying run on base with a walk, so I should be getting decent pitches to hit. I'd noticed that his fastball no longer had the pop that it did in the early innings, and I was sure I could get around on anything he put across the plate.

As I dug in, I quickly noted where the infielders were positioned, looking for a hole. Boston's first baseman George Burns was playing close to the bag to keep Haines from getting much of a lead. That left a gap on the right side of the infield. All I had to do was punch the ball through that hole and we'd have two runners on base. With Haines' speed, he might even make it all the way to third.

Ehmke's first pitch was a curve that broke wide and low. Catcher Val Picinich had to stab the dirt to prevent a passed ball. I guessed the next pitch would be a fastball and that Ehmke might ease up a little to make sure he put it in the strike zone. As a right-handed hitter, I readied myself for an inside-out swing to hit the ball the opposite way and shoot it through that hole between first and second.

The wily right-hander's next offering was indeed a slow fastball, chest high, in the middle of the plate. It looked so fat and inviting, that my brain went momentarily blank and impulse took command of my actions. On pure reflex, I hitched my bat a little higher, drove myself forward with my back leg, and unleashed a hard swing. *Contact!* I had never gotten such solid wood on a ball, and was thrilled to see it rising toward the left field fence. I took off running for first, and not until I rounded the bag did I realize there was no need for speed. I had just hit a two-run homer to tie the game.

The angry cries of the disapproving crowd suddenly registered in my ears like a small explosion. Not until I rounded second base did I realize that I was still running as hard as if I was legging out a triple. I slowed to a trot, stumbling slightly as I adjusted speeds, and let myself savor the moment and enjoy the sweet sound of jeers from the stands. I was being lustily booed for hitting a home run in Fenway Park. Now I was truly a New York Yankee.

When I got to the dugout, my teammates greeted me with congratulations and slaps on the back. They also gave me some good-natured ribbing about my unexpected display of power. "I didn't know your bat had a homer in it," said Joe Dugan.

As I approached the bench, however, I saw there was nothing good-natured in Miller Huggins' expression. "What the hell was that?" he growled at me. I knew that Giants manager John McGraw had once fined a player for hitting a home run when he was supposed to have laid down a bunt, and I wondered if was in for a similar punishment.

"Sorry, Hug," I said. "But that ball came up to the plate just *begging* for me to let loose on it."

He snorted. "The next time a baseball talks to you, you tell it to shut the hell up. You should have been swinging for a single."

"Yeah, I know." I tried to look contrite, but I was feeling too elated about the home run to achieve a convincing expression of regret.

Huggins' angry façade dropped, too, and he cracked a rare smile. "What the hell," he said. "Enjoy it. I know they don't come often." He was certainly right about that; I'd only had a few home runs in my career and most of them were inside-the-park.

I got to enjoy my game-tying homer for all of about fifteen minutes. In the bottom of the ninth, the Red Sox scored a fifth run off Bullet Joe Bush on a George Burns single and the game was over.

It was a disheartening loss and the locker room was quiet afterward. No matter what an individual player achieves during a game, there is no celebrating when the team loses. Today's loss was even harder to take than most because our ninth inning rally to tie had gotten our hopes up for a win.

The clubhouse wasn't completely silent, of course. There were words of commiseration for Waite Hoyt because of his strong pitching effort. And there were some more comments, mostly kidding, about my hitting prowess. On his way to the showers, Bob Meusel said loudly, "This got to be the damnedest game *I* ever saw— Rawlings hits our only homer and the Sultan of Swat gets our only stolen base."

After taking my own shower, I dressed in one of my better suits, a gray herring-bone that Margie had picked out for me. I was considering where I might want to have dinner when the Sultan himself sauntered over to me.

The Babe was dressed in a tailored suit that made mine look like something rejected by the Salvation Army. The usual long black cigar was clamped in his teeth. He puffed a few times before speaking. "Come on, slugger," he said with his famous grin. "I'll give you a ride."

* * *

I was soon seated next to Ruth in a pristine 1922 Packard Twin Six Special Runabout. The car's maroon body gleamed like polished china and its black leather interior could have been used to upholster the chairs in a British gentlemen's club. Like the numerous other automobiles the Babe owned, its doors were monogramed with "G. H. R."—George Herman Ruth— in gold lettering. Although Ruth had traveled to Boston on the team train, I wasn't surprised that he had a car available to him here; he had played for the Red Sox until 1920 and still lived nearby in the off season.

The car's canvas top was lowered so that we were

open to view, and fans thronged around yelling praises to the Babe. I tried not to show it, but I thoroughly relished the envious looks I got from the crowd. Judging by the look of pleasure on Ruth's face, though, it didn't compare to how much *he* enjoyed people looking at him.

Half a dozen Boston police officers, including two on horseback, eventually cleared a way for us to get through the congestion on Lansdowne Street and we were on our way. I assumed our destination was the Copley Plaza. When I caught on that we were heading out of the city, I shouted over the noise of the powerful engine and the rushing wind, "Aren't we going to the hotel?"

Ruth answered around the massive cigar, "Nah, Huggins cramps my style, kid. I'm staying away from him." He took his eyes off the road to glance at me. "But since he wants you to babysit me, I figure I'll take you along." He grinned, tugged his driving cap tighter on his big head, and stomped down on the accelerator.

A pang of concern shot through me as he sped up. Babe Ruth was a notoriously reckless driver. He liked to do everything in an extravagant manner, and that included the way he operated his automobiles. Ruth bought the fastest and most luxurious cars—from a Stutz Bearcat to a custom-built Pierce Arrow—and ran them at their upper limits. It was a good thing for him that he could afford any automobile he wanted, because he had crashed some of the finest cars ever produced.

I wasn't familiar with the roads outside of Boston, but I could tell that we were heading west. The countryside was becoming increasingly rural and the sparse traffic allowed the Babe to drive at greater speed.

"Where are we going?" I yelled to him.

"Home Plate!" he answered.

There wasn't much chance for conversation in the

noisy car, but I didn't need him to elaborate. "Home Plate" was what Ruth had named his eighty-acre farm in Sudbury, about twenty miles west of Boston. It had been featured in numerous newspaper stories this past winter. After his disastrous World Series performance, Ruth had promised to spend the off season getting in shape and living a clean healthy lifestyle on his rustic homestead. Compliant photographers took pictures of him decked out in a plaid winter coat and a fur cap with ear flaps as he chopped wood, shoveled snow, and fed chickens. One particularly amusing image showed him perched on a rail fence with a piece of hay in his mouth, looking like an oversized Tom Sawyer. The Babe was also frequently photographed during these months as a devoted family man, with his wife Helen and their adopted baby Dorothy.

Not often reported—at least not in print—was the farm's primary function: The remote location provided Ruth and his pals a place to hunt, fish, and have a good time away from the view of reporters and team officials. I'd heard there were frequent parties fueled by large quantities of bootleg booze, and that these sometimes got out of hand. In one famous escapade, Ruth decided to demonstrate his great strength by hurling a piano into the nearby pond.

Our drive to Sudbury was delayed by a patrolman who stopped us near Waltham. The young officer was at first irate about the reckless speed we'd been traveling. When he recognized Ruth, however, he apologized for holding us up. The Babe obligingly gave the officer an autograph, and the grateful young man stepped out into the road to stop an approaching car so that we could pull right out. During the exchange with Ruth, the officer had given me some quizzical looks as if wondering who would be important enough to have Babe Ruth as his chauffeur.

It was almost dusk when we arrived at Home Plate. The house, an expansive two-story colonial on Dutton Road, was not what I would ever describe as a "farm." If it had been located on Fifth Avenue, it would qualify as a "mansion." The interior was spacious, but the furnishings fairly simple and mostly masculine. It didn't appear that Helen Ruth had much say in the décor. I'd heard that she often lived apart from the Babe and was sometimes brought in only when a family photograph was needed to bolster his image.

Ruth led me into a high-ceilinged den with a flagstone fireplace that spanned almost an entire wall. The mounted head of an eight-point buck was above the mantle and various animal pelts served as rugs. Several wood-and-leather easy chairs and sofas were positioned around the enormous white hide of a polar bear; the beast's head was still attached and its jaws gaped open in a sad silent roar.

Except for the faint sound of chickens and pigs in the barnyard, the house was quiet. "Is Helen home?" I asked.

Ruth's prominent lips twisted in distaste. "If she was, we wouldn't be here. She cramps my style worse than Huggins. Helen stayed in New York this trip. But never mind about her—it's dinner time!" His expression brightened considerably. "You must have worked up an appetite running out that homer," he joked. "How about steaks?"

"Sounds good." I suddenly felt myself ravenous.

"Lemme go find the cook."

Left alone in the den, I wandered about the room, looking over the mix of sporting equipment, awards, and mementos. A set of golf clubs was in one corner, a few bats in another, and several expensively engraved shotguns rested on a walnut rack next to the window. Much of the wall space was filled by framed photographs of the Babe posing with celebrities, athletes, and politicians. Among the faces I recognized were Jack Dempsey, Governor Al Smith, Buster Keaton, President Harding, and Jackie Coogan in costume as "The Kid."

The fireplace mantle was crowded with plaques, medals, and trophies. Most of them were for his baseball accomplishments, but there were several for bowling, shooting, and golf. He even had a loving cup for taking first place in a farting contest sponsored by a Yale fraternity.

When I got to the baseball equipment, I picked up a well-used hickory bat and hefted it a couple of times. It weighed about fifty ounces compared to my usual thirty-two, and I couldn't fathom how anyone could successfully hit with such a massive piece of lumber. So I decided to give it a try. I slid my hands down to the knob and took a couple of ponderous swings. The bat was so heavy that I could barely keep it horizontal as I cut through the air. Taking care not to hit any lamps or trophies, I swung as hard as I could and nearly fell over from the way the bat pulled me off balance.

An outburst of laughter from the doorway told me that Ruth had returned—and that he'd witnessed my poor attempts to imitate him. Still chuckling, he said, "You planning to be a slugger now, kid? You get a homer today and figure you can keep beltin' 'em out?" He had changed to a soft-collar shirt and carried a schooner of dark beer in each hand.

I fought to keep from blushing. "Nah, I was just wondering how you swing this damn thing so easily." I moved to put it back in the corner. "Hope you don't mind."

Ruth put the beers down on a side table and took the bat from me. "I'll show you how I do it." He rolled up his sleeves and took a few cuts, swishing it through the air as effortlessly as if it was a piece of straw. "See, it's easy," he said. "You just have to be as strong as me." He grinned. "But there *ain't* anybody as strong as me."

"It's more than strength," I said. "You have to see the ball right, time the swing, step into the pitch…"

"Yeah, you do have to put it all together." Ruth let loose another swing that would have decapitated anyone standing in the way. "I always had the natural ability, but somebody had to teach me to really play ball."

"Who?"

"Brother Matthias, at the St. Mary's Industrial School for Boys in Baltimore." Ruth added in sincere tone, "He is the greatest man I know."

The Babe motioned toward a couple of easy chairs. We sat, drank our beers, and he told me about growing up in Baltimore. By the age of seven, he'd already gotten into enough trouble that his parents placed him in the Catholic reform school. There, Brother Matthias, a Canadian monk and the school's Prefect of Discipline, had become a father figure to him and taught him the finer points of baseball. Recognizing Ruth's natural athletic ability, and wanting to give him a healthy outlet for his energy, Matthias spent hours and hours teaching him to hit, field, and pitch. Since there wasn't much equipment available, the left-handed Ruth made do with an old right-handed catcher's mitt that he had to wear jammed on the wrong hand.

When the call came that dinner was ready, Ruth led us into an airy dining room painted in pale green with white trim. The table, chairs, and china cabinet were rustic pine. Decorative plates adorned one of the walls and

French doors provided a spectacular view of the sunset.

A short fussy woman in a pristine dress and spotless apron asked if there was anything else we wanted. "If we need more," Ruth answered, "I'll give a yell. Thank you, Mrs. Mullaly."

I added my thanks but barely noticed her as she left. I was staring in wonder at the heaping platters of food on the table. There was one plate piled high with thick steaks and another of pork chops. Surrounding these were bowls of baked beans, sauerkraut, mashed potatoes and sliced tomatoes. A fragrant loaf of brown bread was on a wooden serving board and there was a basket of golden dinner rolls. Smaller dishes of mustard, gravy, butter, and various sauces were conveniently placed. A dozen bottles of beer were chilling in an ice-filled bucket. It looked like there was enough to feed the entire starting lineup!

"Is anybody else coming?" I asked. The table could seat eight, but only two places were set. I had thought there might be others joining us, and that I would get to witness one of Babe Ruth's infamous parties first hand.

"Nope." Ruth sat down and pointed for me to do the same. Without any further word or ceremony, he enthusiastically forked a couple of steaks onto his plate. He then speared some pork chops and put them around the steaks as if they were a garnish. Before I had a chance to get a single morsel of food on my plate, he was already tearing into his first steak like a starving man.

I selected a well-done pork chop, along with some beans and mashed potatoes. After a couple of bites and a long swallow of beer, I looked up at the Babe. "Why me?" I asked.

His mouth full of the better part of a steer, Ruth mumbled, "Why you what?" Juice dripped from his lips.

"I don't want you to think I'm ungrateful, but why did you bring *me* here? Why not your regular pals on the club?"

"I *like* you, kid." A grin broke over his big round face. "I know Huggins wants you to play nursemaid to me and keep me out of trouble, but you never act like you're better than me and you never give me no problems." He pointed at me with his fork. "And most important, you never get on me about needing to change my ways. I get enough of that crap from the newspapers and the do-gooder civic clubs and Jacob Ruppert and that little runt Huggins."

"Why should I tell you that you need to straighten out?" I said. "You're a big boy—you know it yourself."

He put down his fork so hard that it splattered drops of gravy on the tablecloth. "Oh, so you don't say it but you *think* it!" Ruth's voice rose. "You think I need to be a good boy and drink my milk and be in by curfew and do whatever Miller Huggins tells me?"

I hadn't meant to make Ruth angry, nor did I want to be an ungracious guest. "What I think," I answered calmly, "is that you're probably the best athlete who ever lived. And you know better than anyone what your body is capable of doing and what kind of shape you have to be in to perform at your best." I paused. "And your best is something other people can only dream about. So if you piss your talent away, you shatter a lot of dreams."

The Babe stared at me for a long moment with an impassive expression. I couldn't tell how he was going to react. He finally snorted, "You gonna give me the speech about how I'm disappointing all the runny-nosed little kids who look up to me?"

I cut into the pork chop. "To hell with the little kids," I replied. "You'd be disappointing *me*. I want to play in a

World Series more than anything, and if you're not at your best there's no chance of us getting there."

Ruth continued to stare at me for a moment, then chortled, "At least you're honest about it." He speared another chunk of beef. "Don't you worry, kid. We're going to the World Series—and this year, we're gonna *win*." I hoped he was right, because I probably wouldn't have many more chances to get into a Fall Classic. The 1923 Yankees were the team that could take me there, and Babe Ruth was the key.

We talked for a while about our upcoming games, and whether Cleveland or Detroit would be our main competition for the pennant. As we spoke, I noticed that Ruth's beer consumption was light and his eating had slowed. He eyed the full steak and two pork chops that remained on his plate with a pronounced lack of enthusiasm. Sighing heavily, he raised his knife and fork and began to saw off a piece of meat.

I said, "It's just the two of us here, Babe, and you don't have to impress me."

He looked at me with surprise. Setting the utensils back down, he chuckled. "It seems like I always got to be putting on a show for somebody." Leaning back, he folded his hands over his full belly. "Everybody expects me to do things big—and they're never satisfied. If I hit fifty home runs, they want me to hit sixty. If I hit one into the second deck, they want me to knock the next one clear out of the park." He belched softly. "Somebody sees me eat five hot dogs, the next person expects me to eat ten." He began to look sorry for himself at having to bear the burden of so many expectations.

I couldn't help but tease him. "And if you take two girls to your hotel room one night, then you have to take three the next?" I shook my head in mock sympathy.

"Must be rough on you."

He guffawed. "That's purely for fun, and there's no limit on *that*. More than one time I've gone into a whorehouse and didn't leave until I sampled every girl in the place!"

I smiled, but hoped he wouldn't recount the details. Glancing at the door, I noticed the night was pitch black. "It's been a great dinner," I said, "and I really appreciate you inviting me. But shouldn't we be getting back for curfew?"

Ruth waved a hand dismissively, his big diamond ring flashing brightly. "The hell with curfew. We're staying here tonight. I already told the housekeeper to get a room ready for you."

Since I had no way to get back to Boston without the Babe driving me, I had to accept his hospitality. I hoped that Miller Huggins wouldn't be too angry at this violation of team rules.

We went back to the den, where several logs were already burning in the fireplace. The Babe offered me one of his black cigars, which I declined. He lit his and puffed contentedly. Soon, in the comfort of two easy chairs, amid the fragrant smell of woodsmoke and tobacco, we were drinking beer and talking baseball. We discussed hitting techniques, swapped stories about Ty Cobb and John McGraw, and talked about the experiences we'd each had playing for the Red Sox.

After another draught of the excellent porter, I held the glass in front of me and eyed the rich dark color. "This is good stuff," I said. "Where'd you get it?"

"Some fellows in Boston keep me supplied with suds and liquor." The Babe took a long swallow from his own glass. "And it's all top-notch, none of that bathtub brew."

"How about in New York?"

Ruth laughed. "They never even heard of Prohibition in New York! If I want something, there's a dozen fellows ready to get it for me."

"Was Spats Pollard one of those fellows?"

"Spud *who?*" he asked with a frown.

"*Spats*," I repeated. "Spats Pollard. I hear he did a fair amount of bootlegging, and claimed you were one of his customers."

"Name doesn't ring a bell, but I'm not real good with names."

"Pollard used to play ball. He pitched for the Cubs in 'eighteen." I hoped that might prod the Babe's memory.

He appeared to consider it, but shook his head. "I remember that series, though," he added with a smile. "I won two games, including a shutout in the opener." That was back when he was primarily a pitcher and had led the Red Sox to three pennants in four years.

For a while longer, we talked about that series, but the Babe appeared to be getting sleepy. After letting out an enormous belch, he got to his feet and said, "Well, I'm gonna call it a night, kid. I'll have Mrs. Mullaly show you to your room."

"Thanks, Babe," I said. "By the way, I know you're not much for names, but mine is 'Mickey.'"

He hesitated. "You got it... *kid.*" With a big grin, he turned and walked away. I couldn't help but smile, too. The Babe was just a lovable character, no matter what he said or did.

When I got into bed, I finally realized what this evening had been about. Ruth was doing exactly what the Yankees—and the newspapers and the fans—wanted him to do. He was trying to behave and keep himself in shape for baseball.

Ruth didn't come out to the farm tonight because Miller Huggins "cramped his style," as he'd claimed. He wanted to put himself out of reach of the city's temptations. And he didn't bring his regular buddies along with him because he didn't want a party. So he had himself a quiet night with only a utility infielder named Mickey Rawlings for company.

Babe Ruth would probably forget about my visit by morning. I would remember it forever.

Chapter Eight

Knowing how innocuous our evening had actually been, I was unprepared for Miller Huggins' heated reaction when we arrived at the Copley Plaza hotel the next morning. I had the impression that with every hour that we were late, his anger had doubled. Since we'd missed curfew by a full twelve hours, the Yankees' manager was furious.

The drive from Sudbury back to Boston took considerably longer than the trip out. It drizzled on and off all morning, leaving slick roads and poor visibility, and the Babe navigated his Packard with some caution. It wasn't until after eleven Friday morning that the two of us walked into the hotel.

The dazzling lobby of the Copley Plaza looked like it could be the ballroom of some European castle, with coffered ceilings, marble floors, crystal chandeliers, and gilded woodwork. Ruth fit in perfectly with the elegant surrounding; he was attired in a fresh cashmere suit with a diamond stickpin in his tie. I was in the same clothes I'd worn out to Home Plate and felt a bit grubby.

We hadn't made it more than ten feet into the lobby when I spotted Miller Huggins in a chair that a French king might have used as a throne. He noticed us a second later, and bolted from it like he was jumping off the dugout bench to argue an umpire's bad call. I knew Huggins hadn't waited in that chair all night for us—after a certain hour, he generally assigned the lobby-sitting job to a coach like Charley O'Leary—but he looked as tired and grumpy as if he had.

"Where the hell you two been?" he screamed from halfway across the lobby. Dozens of heads turned to look at the angry manager.

Ruth answered at twice the volume that Huggins had achieved. "None of your damn business, you little squirt! I'm here by game time, and that's all that counts!" I hoped Huggins knew that my belligerent roommate wasn't answering for me.

The two men met in the middle of a blue Persian rug that probably cost more than most houses. The argument grew loud and heated. Trying to intimidate the little manager with his size, Ruth stepped so close to Huggins that their chests were almost in contact. Huggins had to crane his neck up to see the Babe's face. Here, in one of Boston's most elegant buildings, amid its genteel clientele, the two men exchanged words as if they were on a sandlot, using language that turned the air as blue as the rug on which they stood.

Huggins finally squawked, "That's it! Fifty dollar fine for breaking curfew! If you think you're too good to follow the rules, it's gonna cost you."

The Babe pulled a thick roll from his pocket and peeled off a hundred dollar bill. "Here you go," he said, shoving the bill into Huggins' vest pocket. "I might not be in tonight, either." With that, he stormed off to the elevator.

The apoplectic manager grumbled a few indistinct words and turned his attention to me. "You're just as late as he is, so it's the same for you—fifty bucks!"

I didn't make Babe Ruth's salary and I didn't carry a roll of money like he did. I began to explain, "I don't have—"

Huggins briefly hesitated; he might have realized that the penalty was a bit stiff for me. "You don't need to pay me now," he said. "Mr. Barrow will take it out of your next paycheck."

I nodded. What the hell, I did miss curfew, so if there's a price for that I had to pay it. But I hated to have to tell Margie that I was losing almost a week's salary.

Huggins asked in a somewhat calmer tone, "What kind of trouble did that big ox get you into last night?"

I wished I could have told him the truth about what a tame evening it had actually been. The manager might then have known that he and the Babe were actually seeing eye-to-eye on some things. But I think they simply enjoyed feuding with each other. Besides, whether good or bad, you don't tell your manager what other players have been doing. I answered, "We just stayed out a little too late, Hug. Sorry."

He eyed me up and down, obviously dissatisfied with my answer. "Well, you must be tired after your big night. I'll let you rest on the bench today."

I didn't mind the fine as much as I did being benched—especially after my performance yesterday. My only hope was that the game would require me to go in. I had confidence that Miller Huggins would make the right moves to win. If the situation called for it, I might still get to play.

* * *

It turned out that I didn't miss a thing because no one got to play. The light rains that had followed the Babe and me all morning during our drive to Boston had settled over the city and turned into a cold deluge. The game was called off by mid-afternoon, and I decided it was ideal weather to do some reading.

Across the corner of Copley Square, an infield toss from our hotel, was the magnificent Boston Public Library. It was a solid building of granite and sandstone topped by a red tile roof with copper cresting. The interior was lavish, with murals, statues, vaulted ceilings, and heavy green velvet drapery. There was also an open air courtyard, which was deserted on this rainy day.

Inside the library, I made some inquiries and was directed to the reference section. I'd had no luck learning about Spats Pollard by asking questions, so I hoped that a review of the printed records would be more productive.

I was assisted by a stooped, impeccably dressed old gentleman who wore pince-nez and smelled of peppermint. Since reference books couldn't be taken from the room, I had to use them under his supervision. He asked why I was conducting my research, and I told him I was a ballplayer looking for some former teammates. The librarian appeared skeptical that a baseball player would know how to read, but he patiently brought me every volume I requested, handling each one as if it was the Gutenberg Bible.

Soon I had five years' worth of baseball record books piled around me on the reading table. They included the annual *Who's Who in Baseball*, published by *Baseball Magazine*, along with the *Spalding* and *Reach* guides.

I pored through the books, turning the pages carefully, and scrutinizing every item that might prove useful. I made notes on stationery that I'd brought from the

Copley Plaza, meticulously recording the name of every teammate of Spats Pollard that I could find.

The record books carried information on all of organized baseball, major league and minor, so the process was a lengthy one. After compiling the names of Pollard's past teammates, I checked to see which of them were still playing. Pollard's career hadn't amounted to much, so this yielded a much shorter list.

Finally, I reviewed this year's team schedules to see when I would be in the same city as one of these players. That whittled the list down to a single ballplayer. According to the National League schedule, I could meet him in Brooklyn in one week.

Chapter Nine

The Yankees' train pulled into Pennsylvania Station again on the first Friday in May, after a brief two-city road trip. We had dropped two of the three games against the Red Sox, but came back to take three out of four against the Senators in Washington. Our record was now ten wins and six losses on the young season. That put us in second place, half a game behind Detroit. Bunched within a game of us were Cleveland and Philadelphia.

As for me, I got into three more games during the road trip, picking up two singles and scoring as a pinch runner. I was now batting over .300 for the season, more than fifty points higher than I usually managed to achieve. Miller Huggins' anger at me had faded after a day. In addition to giving me a few more chances to play, he continued to use me as a base coach and occasionally asked my opinions on strategy.

Tomorrow, we would open a home stand against the Athletics at Yankee Stadium. After the busy road trip and with a difficult schedule coming up, Huggins had told all of us to take it easy today and rest up. So how did I choose to spend my day off? I took Margie to a baseball game.

* * *

Ebbets Field was an intimate ballpark that had opened ten years ago in the Flatbush section of Brooklyn. The site had once been a desolate plot of land known as "Pigtown" because of all the local hog farms, but no trace of those humble origins remained.

Surrounded by a maze of trolley lines, the modern double-decked park featured a grandiose entrance on Sullivan Place and a spectacular marble rotunda. Dodgers' owner Charlie Ebbets had built a jewel of a ballpark that would probably last a century. Unfortunately for Brooklyn fans, he seldom could assemble a team of the same caliber. Although the team had won two pennants during the park's existence, it usually finished in the bottom half of the league standings. They were currently dead last, and attendance was so light that I had no trouble getting us good seats.

Margie and I were comfortably ensconced in a fourth row box midway between home plate and first base when Brooklyn's Leon Cadore loped out to the pitcher's mound to face the top of the Phillies batter order. Margie was playing hooky from the Griffith studio for the day, and had dressed for the occasion in a pastel yellow frock with a white middy collar. I wore seersucker, and both of us would have a challenge keeping our clothes clean since we'd provisioned ourselves with hot dogs, peanuts, and sodas from passing vendors. It was a beautiful afternoon for a ballgame and a rare treat for me to be able to sit back and enjoy it as a fan.

Being at Ebbets Field again also brought back memories. I pointed to a section not far from us and said to Margie, "That's where your friends from Vitagraph sat:

Florence Hampton, Arthur V. Carlyle, and that funny director…"

"Elmer Garvin," she said with a wistful smile. "Oh, that seems so long ago."

"It was. You know, sometimes everything from before the war seems like a hundred years ago."

Margie playfully poked my chest. "You've held up remarkably well for a man of a hundred and twenty!"

"And you," I replied, "look as pretty as the first time I saw you."

She turned her head and gave me a kiss, causing her bonnet to collide with my straw boater. "It was that same day," she said.

Oblivious to the unfolding baseball game, we reminisced about everything that had happened that memorable day in 1914—making a moving picture with Casey Stengel and Florence Hampton, meeting Margie at the Vitagraph Studio here in Brooklyn, and joining the movie crew for a party that night. Neither of us mentioned the tragedy that followed.

Margie took a sip of soda and suddenly giggled. "I was just thinking about all that champagne we drank—and you had never had it before."

"You said champagne and oysters make the best meal in the world."

"They still do!"

"I learned my lesson," I said. "Champagne can make people do funny things."

"You mean like your dancing?" she teased.

"My dancing is more dangerous than funny," I replied. Margie had tried to teach me to dance at that party, and it was a talent that I still was unable to learn.

From several rows behind us, a leather-lunged Brooklyn partisan bellowed at umpire Bill Klem, "Hey

Catfish! Why dontcha open yer damn eyes? Yuh been robbin' us all day, yuh bum yuh!" One thing about Ebbets Field was that the crowd, no matter how small, always took a vocal interest in the game.

I soon turned my attention to the game, too, as the Phillies and Dodgers exchanged leads in a well-played contest. It looked like Philadelphia had the contest clinched when Cy Williams hit a three-run homer onto Bedford Avenue in the eighth, but Brooklyn came back to give Cadore a 7-6 win. I was happy to see him get the victory; three years earlier he and the Boston Braves' Joe Oeschger had locked horns in a twenty-six inning marathon that was called a tie because of darkness. I couldn't imagine pitching almost three full games and coming away with no decision.

The reason I had come to Flatbush today wasn't to watch the ballgame, though, nor to reminisce with Margie. I wanted to talk to the Dodgers' backup catcher Tim Concannon. When the game ended, Margie offered to wait for me in the rotunda while I met with him.

I had an easy time reaching Brooklyn's clubhouse door and getting a message to Concannon. Since the Yankees and Dodgers had traveled together on the exhibition tour in spring training, the players and officials of both clubs knew each other pretty well. I'd spoken with the catcher a few times during that trip. We were both part of that smaller fraternity of major league ballplayers, the ones who spend most games warming the bench while waiting for a chance to play.

He recognized me the moment he came out. "Rawlings," he said. "What brings you across the river?"

"I came to see you."

Concannon was about my age, with a catcher's thick powerful build. He was dressed in a plain brown suit and wore a pork pie hat. His eyes were intelligent—catchers are often among the brightest players on a team—and the expression on his ruggedly handsome face was placid. Concannon struck a match on the sole of his shoe and lit up a cigarette. "What about?" he asked.

"I had a teammate on the Cubs," I said. "A pitcher named Spats Pollard."

The placid expression was instantly replaced by one of revulsion. "Sonofabitch," he muttered.

"I guess you knew him," I said. "You were both with the Chattanooga Lookouts in 'nineteen."

"Don't remind me." He pulled a shred of tobacco from his tongue and flicked it away. "I didn't much like playing in the Southern Association—too damn hot for me—and I *sure* didn't like being on the same team as that bastard Pollard."

"Could you tell me about him?"

"I got a date, but I guess I can talk until my trolley comes." I agreed and we began walking toward the streetcar tracks on McKeever Place, where some fans were still waiting for cars to take them home.

"As a pitcher," Concannon began, "Pollard wasn't much. The only decent pitcher we had on that club was Wiley Marshall—he hasn't made it to the majors yet, as far as I know. Anyway, with a lousy staff and some players still in the service, our manager Sammy Strang really had to juggle to keep a starting rotation together. Somehow Pollard got himself a spot in it. He thought of himself as an ace, but he didn't have much of an arm. He'd barely make it as a batting practice pitcher in the big leagues."

"That's the way I remember him," I said. "The only reason he made the Cubs was because of the war, and he didn't last long anyway." We stopped talking long enough to weave our way past a couple of slow-moving automobiles. When we were safely on the other side of the street, I asked, "What else can you tell me about Pollard? Why didn't you like him?"

"He was a complete turd of a human being—didn't have an honest bone in his body."

"What did he do?"

Concannon took the cigarette from his lips and spat. "Stole, cheated, did anything he could to make a quick buck for himself." He eyed an approaching trolley. "This might be… nah, it ain't mine. Anyway, Pollard probably took money from every guy on the team, including me. He got a lot of it in card games, until we found he was using marked cards." Concannon smiled for the first time since I'd mentioned the former pitcher's name. "Pollard got a good thrashing from us for that—it cost him a couple of teeth. Then later he had a scheme for selling moonshine that he was gonna get from some hillbilly in Georgia. He got some of the boys to invest in a cargo that turned out to be nothing but vinegar—we figured Pollard kept the money and sold the real liquor himself. That earned him another beating, but he still didn't learn his lesson."

"What else did he do?"

"The *last* thing he did was steal Strang's pocket watch. Can you beat that for stupid?" The catcher shook his head. "He steals the manager's watch, gets caught with it, and tries to claim it's his own—even though it had Sammy's name engraved right on it. He didn't get a beating, but Strang cut him loose right in the middle of a road trip. We were on our way to Little Rock, and he put Pollard off the train in Forrest City. As far as I know, the thieving sonofabitch is still in Arkansas—and as far as I'm concerned, he can damned well stay there." He tossed his cigarette on the ground. "This one's mine," he said, as a street car squealed to a stop.

"Thanks for the talk." I saw no reason to tell him that Spats Pollard was no longer in Forrest City.

From the steps of the trolley, Concannon yelled to me, "Hey, we're going to Coney. Maybe my date has a friend for you, if you want to come."

I waved him off. "Got my own, thanks!"

I hurried to the rotunda to meet Margie. That evening, after dinner at a restaurant near Times Square, she again tried to teach me to dance.

*   *   *

Only a half dozen of us were in the Yankees' clubhouse, early arrivals before the series opener against the visiting Athletics. Most of us had removed some of our street clothes but none of us were in uniforms yet. I was sitting in front of my locker, untying my shoes, when Andrew Vey came in. At the sight of Ed Barrow's big ruddy-faced assistant, I assumed I was going to be called in to the business manager's office again.

As usual, Vey wore a thin bow tie that appeared to be choking him. He dug a finger into his collar and cleared his throat to get our attention. Like every other sound that he emitted, it was high and pinched. He announced, "I have your paychecks." Several players jumped up to collect them.

Vey pulled a handful of envelopes from his jacket pocket and began to make the rounds, starting with Hinkey Haines. He brought mine last. As he handed it to me, he said, "I'm afraid there's been an adjustment to yours." Vey appeared genuinely sorry.

"Yeah, I know," I said. "Had a late night in Boston and missed curfew."

Waite Hoyt and Sad Sam Jones arrived in the

clubhouse and Vey went to give them their checks. As he did, I tore my envelope open and peeked inside. As expected, it was fifty dollars light.

Vey came back to me. "Mr. Barrow would like a report," he said.

I was happy that at least this time he wasn't bothering me during a game. "When?" I asked.

"How about if we step outside now?" Vey suggested.

"Mr. Barrow is *here*?" I couldn't picture him venturing outside of his office.

"No, he's out of town for a meeting—that's why I'm handing out payroll. He asked that you give me the report, and I'll pass it on to him."

I agreed and followed him into the empty runway in my stocking feet.

"What have you found out?" he asked, his broad freckled face expectant.

"Not much," I said. "But I think there's one thing Mr. Barrow *doesn't* have to worry about: The Babe didn't have much—if anything—to do with Spats Pollard."

"You sure?"

"Not a hundred percent. But I spoke with him and I'm convinced he doesn't remember Pollard at all. Maybe he got some liquor from the man, but no more than he gets from a hundred other sources." I was convinced that even if Ruth had merely forgotten Pollard's name, he would have remembered him as a former pitcher if he'd had any dealings with him.

Vey nodded approvingly. "That's good. Anything else?"

"Found out a little more about Pollard. I get the feeling his death wouldn't be mourned by anybody who knew him." I asked Vey a question, "Are you still hearing from the newspapers about it?"

"Not lately."

"Then can I drop this whole investigating business?"

"That's up to Mr. Barrow, and Mr. Barrow told me to keep you on it." As he spoke, Vey's broken nose whistled along with the words.

"*Why?*"

"We had another problem." Vey ran a palm over his unruly bricktop. "At another concession stand."

"A body?"

"No, this one was alive—but barely. Beaten worse than anything I seen in the ring."

"What happened?"

"It's the fellow who leases the stand. A stadium cop found him behind the counter. Broken bones, face bloodied pretty bad. But he wouldn't talk, wouldn't say who did it. I convinced him that it happened *outside* the park, not inside, in case he does decide to report it—so we don't get bad publicity."

"Another concession stand," I said. "That can't be coincidence."

"That's what Mr. Barrow figures—and it's why he still wants you nosing around."

I sighed, agreed to continue, and turned to go back into the clubhouse to get ready for the game.

"One more thing," Vey said.

I faced him again, wondering what more the Yankees could possibly want me to do. Vey pulled another envelope from his pocket. "Mr. Huggins told Mr. Barrow that you've assumed some coaching duties for him and suggested that you be given a bonus." He handed it to me with a small smile. When I looked at the check later, I saw that it was for fifty dollars.

Troy Soos

Chapter Ten

This was my second stint playing for a New York baseball team, and I had visited the city many times while I was on the roster of other clubs, but I had rarely ventured into Greenwich Village. The south Manhattan neighborhood was one of the city's oldest, and didn't quite seem to fit in with the parts that were built later. Its streets were narrow and meandered in all sorts of directions, unlike the grid plan that was followed in most of the city. The buildings were primarily residential, of quaint construction, and wedged closely together.

The people who lived in the Village had a distinctive character, too. Newspapers often referred to the inhabitants as "bohemians" because of their unorthodox lifestyles. The neighborhood was home to a thriving community of writers, artists, actors, and musicians, many of them exploring new and unusual ways of expressing themselves.

Monday evening, I walked along Grove Street in the Village, looking for an address that Margie had written down for me. The windows of the homes I passed were dappled in amber by the setting sun, making them appear as if they were illuminated by candles. When I found the number I was seeking, on a tree-lined block near Seventh Avenue, it appeared so old and rundown that it very well might have lacked electric lights. The narrow, four-story red brick building, with white lintels and black ironwork, was sandwiched between two structures of similar construction. They were all built in a style that might have dated from the American Revolution, and struck me as something that I might expect to see in Savannah or Charleston instead of modern New York.

Cradling a bottle of Mr. Tomasetti's best Chianti in one arm, I climbed a footworn staircase to the third floor. With one more check of the address to be sure I had the correct apartment number, I knocked on *3-C* and soon heard a clattering and banging from within. It almost sounded as if the place was being ransacked. The sound grew louder as someone inside approached the door.

With a squeak of the knob and a creak of the hinges, Karl Landfors pulled open the door and greeted me with something that resembled a smile. He was dressed in his customary stark black suit with a tie of the same color. Squinting through his spectacles, he poked his pale, bony head into the hallway, looked left and right, and asked, "Where's Margie?"

"She had to work late at the studio," I said. "They're doing some big Civil War picture and Margie's working out some of the stunts." I held up the bottle. "I hope I'm still welcome without her."

"Of course, of course." Landfors stepped aside to let me in, and followed behind. "The place is in a bit of a disarray, I'm afraid."

The condition of the small apartment was worse than "a bit of a disarray." The place looked like the aftermath of an explosion in a second-hand furniture shop. The mismatched chairs, sofas, and tables were strewn about randomly. Most had clothing draped over them and dirty dishes were on several of the cushions. A few empty glasses and bottles were scattered on the hardwood floor, leaving puddles and stains from various liquids.

On a paint-spattered easel in a corner of the apartment rested a large canvas painted in bright colors but of no recognizable image. Several similar paintings hung on the dusty, moss green walls. They were all of the modern abstract style that reminded me of something a child might produce with a box of crayons—if that child had been dosed with a little too much patent medicine.

Stepping over debris, and squeezing past the furniture obstacles, we couldn't avoid making the same clatter that I'd heard through the door. Landfors cautiously led the way to a relatively tidy section near the room's one window. A threadbare velveteen daybed, with a neatly folded wool blanket and a lumpy pillow stacked on one end, served as a sofa. I recognized Landfors' scratched Underwood typewriter on a cocktail table that did double-duty as a desk. "This is my area," he said glumly.

"Nice," I lied, as I nearly tripped over a suitcase that probably served as his closet.

"Let me open this," he offered, taking the wine bottle. Landfors motioned for me to sit on the bed, navigated his way to a small kitchen area that looked even filthier than the sitting room, and washed out a couple of glasses. He filled them nearly to the brim and made the trip back. As he put the drinks on the table next to his typewriter, Landfors said, "I'm sorry. The place really isn't in a suitable condition for guests. Would you rather go out?"

"This is fine, Karl." I reached for the wine and we each took a quick swallow without the ritual of a toast.

"Interesting place," I commented.

"That it is." Landfors shuddered slightly. "A bit *too* interesting at times, to be perfectly frank."

"How so?"

Fortified with another long sip of Chianti, he answered, "There are a lot of very peculiar characters coming through here—at every hour, day and night. You know I usually have something of an affinity for outcasts and iconoclasts—"

I couldn't help but interject, "That's because you're one yourself, Karl." He'd been part of almost every new radical cause that had popped up over the past twenty years.

Landfors smiled. "I suppose you're right." He appeared thoughtful for a moment. "But I always have a purpose. I want to expose injustice and bring about change. I know I'm often tilting at windmills, but I have to try. Most of the people here want to be different merely for the sake of being different. I don't understand their strange music or their writing style or their art. I'm not a critic, but a lot of it is simply bizarre." He waved toward the mess on the floor. "And it matches the way they live. I like things organized, but the people who pass through here seem to think that cleanliness stifles creativity. Most just stop by, leave their garbage, and move on."

"Who owns the place?"

"A writer I knew from Chicago. He's out of town and I think he's extended an open invitation to all of lower Manhattan to use the place as a flophouse."

"Then why stay? You know Margie and I would be happy to have you with us. All we can offer is the sofa, but it's yours any time."

"In the *Bronx*?" He sounded as if I'd invited him to

live in Siberia. "I mean, thank you. But it's awfully far, and I have quite a bit of work to do here."

I didn't press him, and I wasn't offended by his reaction. "You said something about the Dot King murder. Are you getting anywhere with it?"

"Oh yes." He went on to give me more details about the case than I cared to know. Twenty-eight-year-old Dot King, once a Ziegfeld showgirl dubbed "The Broadway Butterfly," had been found dead in her West Fifty-seventh Street apartment. No cause was apparent, but the death was deemed suspicious—probably chloroform—and her maid claimed that thousands of dollars' worth of jewelry were missing. This had all been widely reported already, so I didn't see that Landfors had uncovered anything new. The papers, which after her death renamed King "The Broken Butterfly," had also profiled a number of King's prominent lovers and "benefactors," which kept the scandalous story fresh as each new society name appeared in print. One of them was the son of President Harding's Attorney General and another was the scion of one of Philadelphia's wealthiest families.

Landfors' account was interrupted by a shrill blast of sound through the half-open window. The initial assault on the ears was followed by a relentless barrage of squeaks and squeals. "*Every night*," Landfors groaned. He got up and slammed the window shut. "The downstairs neighbor plays his damned clarinet on the fire escape *every night*. We complain, but he says he's going to be famous some day and that we should be grateful for the free 'concert.' His name is Trenton Schacht, by the way, so if he does become famous you can say you heard him here first."

"Soprano sax," I said.

"What?"

"It's not a clarinet; it's a soprano saxophone." I'd heard the instrument played incredibly well during spring training in New Orleans. The noise from the balcony, however, was a seemingly random sequence of notes; it sounded as if Schacht was intentionally trying to avoid playing anything melodic.

With the window closed, the shrieking saxophone was still audible but not quite as disruptive. Landfors sat back down and picked up his story. "Now *I've* got something on the Broken Butterfly case that no one else has—at least not that's been printed anywhere. And you might find it rather interesting."

So far, I hadn't, but I was willing to hear more. "What is it?"

Unnecessarily dropping his voice to a confidential level, Landfors said, "You've heard of Arnold Rothstein?"

"Everyone in the country has heard of Rothstein," I replied. Although he hadn't been convicted of it, there was no doubt that the notorious gambler had fixed the 1919 World Series by bribing White Sox players to throw games to the Cincinnati Reds. The scandal had been a disaster for the national pastime. "What does *he* have to do with it?" I asked.

Landfors let the suspense build by taking a slow sip of wine. He then faced me with a satisfied smirk. "Arnold Rothstein was Dot King's landlord."

"So?"

"He was also, according to my sources, a frequent visitor to her boudoir."

"So...?" This still wasn't all that interesting to me. Why would I care whether or not Arnold Rothstein had a mistress?

Landfors appeared disappointed in my reaction. "I

don't think you know the full scope of Rothstein's activities," he said.

"He's a gambler—fixes games, fights, and horse races. Thinks of himself as a 'sportsman' but doesn't bet on anything that isn't rigged."

"You have a limited view," said Landfors smugly. "There is much more to the world than sporting events. Rothstein bankrolls criminal enterprises of *all* types and he's trained some of the city's most nefarious gangsters."

Only Landfors would use a word like "nefarious," I thought. "All right," I conceded, "so he's a worse crook than I thought."

He went on, "Among Rothstein's more lucrative rackets is the trafficking of narcotics. And, according to my sources, Dot King paid her rent by making drug deliveries for him."

"You can prove that?"

He shook his head. "Not yet. My sources aren't exactly upstanding citizens themselves, and so far none of them wants to cross Rothstein in public. But I'm working on it, and from what I've pieced together so far I believe Dot King tried to blackmail Rothstein—and *that* could have been what got her killed."

It sounded pretty tenuous to me, but I complimented Landfors on what he'd gotten so far and wished him well. Then it was my turn to report, and I filled him in on what was going on with the Spats Pollard investigation and the threat I'd received at Katie Day's night club. While I spoke, a trumpet player from another nearby balcony decided to see if he could drown out the saxophone. They dueled relentlessly, each trying to play louder than the other, as I went on to tell Landfors about the man who was recently beaten at one of the other concession stands.

"There must be a connection," Landfors said.

"That's what I figure, too," I agreed. "I'm going to look into it."

"Perhaps there's another body," Landfors said excitedly. "The stadium could be some sort of gangland graveyard!"

"*That* seems a little farfetched…"

"It's what they do," he said. "When a new building goes up, they often dispose of their victims in the concrete. That way there's little chance of the bodies ever being found." I suspected that his sources on Rothstein had been filling his ears with some wild exaggerations about gangland practices.

I suddenly remembered Ed Barrow telling me that the newspapers had gotten wind of the Spats Pollard story. "By the way," I said, "whatever I tell you is off the record, right?"

Landfors gave me an offended stare. "You know I've never written about any of your, uh, misadventures. And I know how to keep my mouth shut."

"Yeah, I know. I just had to mention it. I have a feeling this misadventure might turn out to be real trouble."

"Then get out of it. What do you care about some petty bootlegger?"

"I *don't* care about Pollard. I *do* care about playing baseball. Working on this case is job security—if I drop it, I'm off the team."

Landfors sighed. "I'll never understand why playing baseball is so important to you. It is, after all, just a game."

I had never been able to explain it to him in the past, and didn't see any point in trying again now. The wine bottle was empty and I drained what remained in my glass. "Well, I should probably be getting home. Margie might be back from the studio by now." I start to rise from the daybed.

"That reminds me," Landfors said. "When are you going to marry her?"

I abruptly sat back down. This wasn't a subject that I particularly wanted to discuss. "You know I already asked her," I answered. "She said 'no.'" Margie had turned me down because she'd already had a husband that I never knew about.

"That was last year," he said. "And she did get a divorce, so now she's free."

Landfors wouldn't understand. He had never been married, and his relationships with women were never long-lasting. He'd broken up with a girlfriend in Detroit because of some disagreement over an obscure bit of political dogma that no one else would care about. "The thing is," I said, "I thought I knew her. We were together for years and she never told me she was married."

"Oh, it wasn't even a *real* marriage," he said. "It was a weekend lark when she was in Hollywood—before you were in the picture—and she got married on a dare. No wonder she forgot about the escapade."

I knew the details, and I realized Margie really had done nothing to hurt me, but it was still a sore memory. I tried to explain, "I asked her once and she said 'no.' That makes it awfully hard to ever ask again."

"Well, you're a fool if you don't," he sniffed. "In fact, if you don't propose to her, maybe *I* will."

That gave me my first genuine laugh of the night.

Chapter Eleven

What Karl Landfors had dismissed as "just a game" was being played for blood today. Ty Cobb's Detroit Tigers were visiting the Bronx and, as usual, Cobb was on a rampage.

When he'd first come up to the big leagues in 1905, Cobb quickly established a reputation for himself as a supremely talented but surly hothead. Aggressive ball playing was one thing, but the volatile Cobb often carried this to the point of outright violence. The "Georgia Peach" ruthlessly cut the legs of opposing players with his slashing spikes, and he got into frequent fistfights with his own teammates, as well as opponents, fans, groundskeepers, and anyone else whom he felt had insulted or offended him. He unleashed punches and kicks with the same ferocity that he ran the base paths. In 1912, during a visit to New York, he even went into the stands to beat up a crippled Yankees fan who had been heckling him. To Ty Cobb there were no strangers, only enemies he hadn't met yet.

Since Cobb viewed every casual encounter as an

opportunity for a new fight, when he developed a long-term grudge against someone it could precipitate all-out warfare. For several years now, one of the most prominent targets of Ty Cobb's wrath was Babe Ruth. Cobb used an extensive array of weapons, most of them mean and petty, against the big guy.

One of the reasons Cobb despised Ruth was because the Babe had supplanted him as the game's premier player. The Tiger also hated the fact that Ruth had brought about a change in the way the game was played. Cobb, along with John McGraw and others, loved the strategy of playing for one run—place hitting, bunting, hit-and-run, stealing bases. But then the slugging Ruth came along and everyone wanted to see home runs. The ball was made livelier to help satisfy the fans' demand for homers and the tactics of "inside baseball" had fallen out of favor. All it took to score a run now was a big swing and an obliging fastball. When I was his teammate, I'd heard Cobb say more than once that "any big ape could do it."

By now, in his third year as Detroit's player-manager, the thirty-six-year-old Cobb's legs had slowed considerably but he'd lost none of his intensity and he tried to instill it in his players. As manager, he insisted that any man who played under him demonstrate the same kind of single-minded aggressiveness that he had epitomized for so many years. If a player was too easy-going or friendly for Cobb's taste, he'd get another player to harass him until he was fighting mad. My former teammate Bobby Veach was a good-natured player who'd been subjected to this tactic. Cobb ordered big Harry Heilmann to taunt his fellow outfielder and light a fire under him, with the result that the happy-go-lucky Veach played a bit harder and got some more hits but he was no longer happy and he no longer spoke to Heilmann.

Cobb used the same strategy on opposing players, which never made sense to me. He claimed it was to unsettle the other team, but if he believed that angry ballplayers tried harder, why would he provoke them? Yet that was what he was doing today to Babe Ruth.

Undoubtedly on Cobb's orders, Detroit starting pitcher Hooks Dauss threw his first two pitches directly at the Babe's head when he came to bat. Neither of them made contact, but they got under the Babe's skin. In the fourth inning, after eluding two more intended beanballs, Ruth connected on one of the sharp-breaking curves that had earned Dauss his nickname and hit a slicing liner to the opposite field. While the crowd cheered the long drive, Detroit's rookie left fielder Heinie Manush scampered to play the ball off the carom and made a strong throw just in time to hold the Babe to a double.

Ruth wasn't held for long. On Dauss's first pitch to Wally Pipp, Ruth got a good jump and stole third. The crowd cheered even louder as the grinning Babe stood and brushed clay from his uniform. It was exactly the kind of play that Ty Cobb loved—when it wasn't done against his team. From my spot in the first base coach's box, I could hear Cobb screaming at Dauss for letting Ruth get an easy stolen base. Because his home runs received so much attention, it was easy to forget that Ruth was much more than a slugger. This was already his fifth stolen base of the season, more than the aging Cobb had totaled so far. Ruth's steal promptly paid off as Pipp drove him in with a solid single up the middle. That caused Cobb to renew his ranting at Dauss. When Dauss got the ball back, he angrily threw it down on the ground; I couldn't tell if it was because of Pipp's hit, Ruth's run, or the fact that his manager was loudly berating him in front of forty thousand fans. Whatever the reason, Dauss was lucky that the umpire had called time or Pipp could have made it to second base.

In the fifth inning, with the Tigers down 2-1, Ty Cobb led off against our right-handed veteran Bullet Joe Bush. As Bush went into his windup, Cobb altered his trademark split hands grip, sliding both fists down to the knob—a slugger's grip. The fastball was on the inside part of the plate and Cobb pulled it, barely fair, past Ruth and over the right field fence. Ruth had barely taken two steps in the direction of the ball before realizing it was gone.

Cobb remained in the batter's box for a long moment, then shrugged as if to indicate anyone could hit a home run. It was one of his favorite ways to taunt Ruth. Every now and then, Cobb would demonstrate that he could hit the long ball, too, and claimed that he didn't do so more often because it required no intelligence and he found them boring. To further aggravate Ruth today, he rounded the bases in an obvious imitation of the slugger's pigeon-toed trot. Cobb succeeded in instigating catcalls from the Yankee partisans, but I saw no reaction from the Babe. He had his hands on his knees, ready for the next play, pointedly refusing to look in the direction where Cobb's hit had landed.

We went into the bottom of the sixth, tied at two runs apiece, with each team's star successfully emulating the other's style of play: Babe Ruth had scored after a stolen base, and Ty Cobb had tied the game with a home run.

Joe Dugan led off for us by hitting a feeble popup that Hooks Dauss caught for an easy out. I paced in the coach's box, wishing to get in the game myself. Whenever I saw a weak hit like that, or a strikeout, I would think to myself, "Hell, *I* could have done that."

When Ruth strode to the batter's box, I called to him, "C'mon Babe! Get it started!"

As he had in each of the Babe's previous plate appearances, Dauss threw the first one at Ruth's head. Ruth leaned back just far enough to avoid it, and I let the pitcher have a few choice words about being afraid to put one in the strike zone. He ignored me and sent another in the direction of Ruth's ear that was again barely dodged.

Having failed in his attempts to insert a baseball into Ruth's skull, the Tigers' pitcher next let loose with a hard curve. The Babe took a mighty swing. If he'd made contact, the ball would have ended up in another county, but the pitch broke sharply, Ruth missed it completely, and he was so off balance from his effort that he stumbled and nearly fell.

The big guy regained his composure and got back in the box wagging his bat menacingly. Dauss stared him down before delivering another curve in almost the same location.

Once again, Ruth took a powerful cut, this time topping the ball enough to bounce a grounder up the middle. Dauss made a desperate stab at the ball but it skittered under his glove untouched. The Babe raced for first and I was sure he had a clean single. Tigers' shortstop Topper Rigney put it in doubt, though; he raced behind second base, short-hopped the ball, and made an off-balance throw to first. Lu Blue stretched and dug the ball out of the dirt. It was a helluva a play, but too late. Ruth beat the throw by half a step.

"Out!" cried umpire Johnny Heller, jerking his thumb into the air.

"*What?*" I squawked in disbelief.

"Like hell!" bellowed Ruth.

I took a couple of steps toward the beefy Heller. "He beat the throw—he was *safe*!"

Color immediately rose in Heller's face like a thermometer dipped in boiling water. He put his hands on his hips. "He's whatever the hell I call him, and I called him *out*!" Johnny Heller was usually one of the league's more competent men in blue. From his heated reaction, I suspected that he realized he had blown the call.

"You blind sonofabitch!" I moved up to within a foot of him, the bills of our caps nearly touching, and continued to protest.

The argument grew so intense, that I only gradually became aware that Babe Ruth was pressing against my back, trying to get to Heller. Ruth's voice was deafening in my ear, as he castigated the umpire in language far less polite than mine.

I realized that I had to shift my efforts. Instead of arguing with Heller in a futile attempt to become the first player in baseball history to convince an umpire to change his call, I had to protect the Babe. Three of Ruth's suspensions last year had come from run-ins with umpires, including one in which he'd thrown dirt in the face of George Hildebrand. Back when Ruth was a pitcher, he'd gone so far as to punch plate umpire Brick Owens because he disagreed with Owens' ball-and-strike calls.

I began shuffling about, keeping myself between Ruth and Heller as they escalated their verbal broadsides. I vaguely noticed that Miller Huggins had joined the fray and was dancing around trying to grab Ruth's arm to pull him away. I was also aware that Ruth was directing some of his anger at me for acting as buffer and frustrating his attempts to get to Heller.

The Babe made another attempt at the umpire; he failed to touch him, but the force of his lunge drove me directly into Heller's body. The ump jerked his right thumb in the air again while pointing the forefinger of his left hand at my nose. "Yer outta the game!" he roared.

Huggins and I both let Heller know what we thought of him in the most ungentlemanly terms. Meanwhile, enough Yankees had come from the dugout to drag Ruth safely back to the bench.

When he saw that Ruth was out of range of Heller's wrath, Huggins nudged me with his elbow. "C'mon, Mick. Let's get on with the game."

As we walked back to the dugout, the manager gave Heller a parting shot over his shoulder, then said to me, "You did exactly right by keeping Ruth away from that blind bum. But he's pretty steamed at you for doing it, so you better keep away from him. Take your shower and get out of the clubhouse quick."

I walked glumly to the locker room. I knew that I had done the right thing; it was better for the team to lose a first base coach than to lose Babe Ruth from the lineup. But I had just been ejected from a game that I wasn't even *in*, and now I was banished from the clubhouse to boot. I don't think I ever felt more expendable.

* * *

I did as Miller Huggins told me. I showered, changed into a charcoal gray worsted suit, and was out of the clubhouse before the eighth inning had begun. I had the sense of being completely adrift. I'd certainly spent enough games on a dugout bench, but I had never been *this* far out of a game before.

I couldn't bring myself to leave the stadium while the game was still in progress, so I went up to the mezzanine level and wandered aimlessly along the concourse.

Whenever I heard a noise from the crowd, I hurried to the nearest tunnel to get a glimpse of what was happening on the field. As I walked, I passed dozens of fans on their way to lavatories and returning from refreshment stands. Not one of them recognized me.

Eventually I came to Joe Zegarra's concession stand. One of the lights in the baseball chandelier was flickering and audibly crackled. The malfunctioning light must have helped attract attention because more than a dozen customers were crowded at the counter. This seemed like an opportune time to talk to Zegarra again, so I took a spot at the rear of the pack. Few of the men ahead of me ordered food, so the line moved fairly quickly as they placed their orders and walked away carrying their bottled drinks.

When I reached the edge of the counter, a young man I recognized as one of Zegarra's musclebound nephews brusquely asked, "Beer?" He lazily mopped a small spill with a dingy rag. Behind him, the other nephew turned sausages on the grill with equal indifference.

I really didn't want a near beer but I thought Zegarra might be more inclined to be helpful if I was a paying customer. "Sure," I said.

The young man intoned in a bored voice, as if he'd given the same spiel a thousand times today, "Two bits for the usual, fifty cents for the good stuff."

Fifty cents was outrageous, even at ballpark prices, and as far as I was concerned there was no such thing as "good" near beer. Nevertheless, I placed a half dollar on the countertop. "The good stuff."

From behind the counter, he pulled out a green bottle of Fervo. When he pried off the cap, some foam sloshed out and added one more stain to his soiled apron.

I was about to ask where Joe Zegarra was, when he

waddled out of the storage room scratching at the narrow fringe of gray hair above his ear. Zegarra was attired in the same white cotton shirt and trousers as his workers, the only difference being that Zegarra's outfit was spotless and his pants sagged so much that he was almost stepping on the cuffs. When he glanced at the man working the grill, his doughy face fixed in a stern expression. "You burn any o' them sausages, an' it's comin' outta yer pay," he warned him. His nephew replied with a grunt and some indecipherable muttering.

Zegarra turned away from him and spotted me. "Hey, Rawlings," he greeted me. "What are yuh doin' up here? It's only the eighth inning—don't you got a ballgame to play?"

"One of the umps decided I was done for the day, so I figured I'd have myself a brew." I tilted up the bottle and forced myself to take a swallow.

While I drank, Zegarra seemed to be studying my reaction.

To my astonishment, it really *was* the good stuff. This was no weak "cereal beverage," but real beer as good as anything brewed before Prohibition. "That hits the spot," I said, quickly taking another long pull.

Zegarra smiled. His teeth were the same color as the fingers of a lifetime cigarette smoker.

I held up the bottle and quickly scanned the red label. Sure enough, it had the *Fervo* logo and the words "Non-Intoxicating Cereal Beverage." But as Tom Van Dusen had pointed out when I'd been served beer in a Moxie bottle at Katie Day's, it's what's on the inside that counts.

A voice from the back of the line called, "Hey buddy! We're thirsty too!"

I stepped to the side of the counter to make room for those behind me, and asked Zegarra, "Can I talk to you for a minute?"

"We're pretty busy," he said. "But for you, sure." He motioned for me to follow and we went into the small storage room, out of earshot of his customers. Peering up at me, he commented, "Yuh seem to like our product."

"It's *good*—and it's not what I was expecting."

"We don't advertise what we got here, yuh know."

I could understand his desire for discretion. But I didn't think anyone would care about selling beer at a ballpark. After all, every restaurant and night club in New York served alcohol. Why shouldn't a man be able to drink a decent beer at a baseball game? "In my book, you're providing a public service," I said.

He smiled and nodded, causing his chins to ripple. "That's exactly right. We're just satisfyin' the demands of a thirsty public."

"The reason I wanted to talk to you," I said, "is there was trouble at one of the other refreshment stands. The fellow who owned it got beat up pretty bad."

Zegarra shook his head solemnly. "Yeah, I heard about that. Damn shame."

"You have any trouble like that yourself?"

"Nah." He jerked his head toward the young men staffing the counter. "With them two around, I don't gotta worry about no trouble like that." He added with a humorless chuckle, "They ain't got half a brain between 'em, but they got muscles and they know how to use 'em."

"It's a strange coincidence," I went on, looking at the spot where Spats Pollard's corpse had been hidden. "There was the body that was found here in your place, and then a fellow almost gets killed at another stand. You think there could be a connection?"

He frowned and shook his head. He had claimed that his nephews were brainless, but now it was Zegarra who looked as if he was incapable of thought. "Was he robbed?" he finally asked.

"Not that I know of." Andrew Vey hadn't mentioned anything about robbery.

"Well, I tell yuh, it just ain't easy servin' the public," Zegarra said. "Whether yer runnin' a bar or a rest'rant or candy shop, yuh get all kinds comin' in. And here there's thousands of men at every ball game. Some of 'em are bound to be bad apples."

"I suppose so." But the coincidence still bothered me. "So business has been good for you?"

"Oh yeah. As long as attendance is good, our business is good." He smiled. "And attendance is good when you fellows are playing good. Keep it up, will yuh?"

"We'll try," I promised.

"If there ain't nothin' else," he said, "I really gotta get back to work."

"Just one thing more."

"Yeah?"

I held up my empty bottle. "Can I have another?"

* * *

It was a dream I'd had before, in which I was at home plate hitting long line drives to every field. But I could never run to first. My feet remained frozen to the ground as if the chalk line of the batter's box was an impenetrable barrier.

Then the dream developed a strange new twist. The field was on the deck of a troop ship and bells were sounding the time, like when I'd gone to France with the American Expeditionary Force. When the bells fell silent, the ballpark was on solid ground again.

I woke up to Margie gently shaking my shoulder.

"Huh?" I said drowsily.

"You have a phone call."

So that was the source of the ringing. "Who is it?"

"Says he's a friend of yours from Katie Day's." She sounded sleepy, too, but worried. "It's two in the morning. What could he want at this hour?"

"I dunno. I'll see."

I rolled out of bed while Margie crawled back under the covers. On the way to the parlor, I rammed my toe into a dresser and let out a few words normally reserved for umpires. When I got to the phone, I angrily picked up the receiver. "Who is this?"

"You really don't wanna know who I am," was the reply. I recognized the voice—it was the man who'd confronted me at Katie Day's night club.

"What do you want?" I demanded.

"I already told you what I want: For you to keep your nose out of things that ain't none of your business. But you don't seem to listen."

Trying hard not to sound as angry as I felt, I said, "I'm listening now."

"Good. Because there's something more."

"And what's that?"

"I called 'cause I want you to know I got your phone number. And I got your address." He paused. "I know exactly where you and your little lady live. So you better give some more thought to what we talked about before."

"I got the message," I said. "Now don't ever call again. And one more thing: If you decide to pay me a visit, you better be ready for a rougher greeting than you might expect." With that, I hung up.

I took a few minutes to settle down before going back to bed. Even though it was only a cowardly phone call in the middle of the night, this gangster had invaded our home. I was furious, and I was determined to defend Margie and me. But I didn't want her to see my anger.

When I was sufficiently calm, I went back to the bedroom, hoping that Margie had already fallen back asleep.

She hadn't. "Anything the matter?" she asked in a sleepy voice.

"Wrong number," I answered. Very wrong, I thought to myself.

Chapter Twelve

In the morning, before she left for work, I gave Margie the full story about the phone call and asked that she avoid being in the apartment by herself. With her athletic ability, and her experience in action movies, she could probably defend herself pretty well, but she agreed. Since she'd been putting in long hours at the studio, our daily schedules were such that we were almost always home at the same time anyway. I didn't know what to do when the team had to leave for our next road trip, but I had a few days to figure that out. I also urged Margie to keep a watchful eye for anyone who looked suspicious whenever she was outside; I assumed she'd be safe within the confines of the Griffith studio, but she might be vulnerable while coming and going.

Later, at Yankee Stadium, life was almost back to normal after my ejection the previous day. The Babe was in a good mood, having won yesterday's game in the bottom of the ninth with a single that drove in Wally Schang, and was no longer angry at me for having prevented him from dismembering umpire Johnny Heller.

The win had put us in a tie for first place; if we beat Detroit again today, we'd be alone at the top of the standings.

The only residual effect of yesterday's conflict with Heller was that Huggins thought it wise to keep me out of the umpire's view. That meant I was not only out of the line-up, but out of the coach's box. I was relegated to the bench while Charley O'Leary coached first.

That gave me nine innings to watch the game and think. What I considered most was the fact that I had too much on my mind that had nothing to do with baseball. I didn't want to split my life this way. I was just a ballplayer, not some kind of detective, and I needed to permanently free myself from the problem I'd been given. I concluded that the only way for me to get out of this crime business was to carry it through to the end. So, while our lineup went on a hitting spree that ultimately led to a 9-1 thrashing of the Tigers, I began formulating a plan.

* * *

The following evening, after the Tigers took revenge by shutting us out 6-0 in the series finale, I walked across the Macomb Dam Bridge to Upper Manhattan. The old swing bridge spanned the Harlem River, providing easy access to the Giants' Polo Grounds on the Manhattan side and to Yankee Stadium in the Bronx.

Not far from where I had once played for John McGraw, on a seedy block of Amsterdam Avenue, I came to a small restaurant. It was below street level, tucked between a pawn shop that promised *Money to Loan on Anything and Everything* and a second-hand clothing store with a large placard that simply read *Cheap* in black block letters. The sign above the restaurant was faded, but more extravagant in its language: *Silk Shaughnessy's Dining*

Emporium.

When I walked down the crumbling concrete steps, I had to step around an emaciated old man who was curled up in a fetal position and snoring violently. He was layered in several tattered coats and sweaters that would barely make up one complete garment. Inches from his colorless, creased face was a pool of fresh vomit—not a good advertisement for the restaurant, I thought.

I pushed through the door and a bell jingled to announce my entry. From what I saw inside, I doubted that it rang often. Shaughnessy's restaurant was plain enough to pass for a Wild West saloon, except that there was a lunch counter instead of a long bar and no one wore cowboy hats. The place was poorly lit, its floor was strewn with clotted sawdust, and the dining tables looked like they might have been made from old packing crates. The only decorations were a few sepia photographs of old-style pugilists and several pairs of boxing gloves hanging from the low ceiling. Only one customer occupied a stool at the counter; he was nearly as poor a physical specimen as the old man outside the door, and was sleeping with a folded newspaper for a pillow.

A mustachioed man of about fifty, whose rolled-up shirt sleeves exposed sinewy forearms, beamed at me from behind the counter. "Would you like a table, sir?" His bearing suggested that he was the proprietor.

"Thanks, but I'm meeting someone. And I see him." The man nodded agreeably and I stepped further into the restaurant.

Two of the room's six tables were taken, one of them by Andrew Vey. He was seated alone, his attention directed down at the pink pages of the *Police Gazette*. On a plate in front of him was slab of meatloaf the size of a paving stone and a heap of mashed potatoes that looked like mortar. A smaller plate held two enormous pickles and there was a full glass of milk in his fist.

Vey didn't notice me until he tilted back the glass to take a drink. When he did, he coughed up some of milk. "Rawlings?" he gasped in his thin voice, then coughed again. Vey's little bow tie was crooked and looked like the propeller of an airplane about to take off. Bits of potato flecked his chin.

"Hope you don't mind me showing up like this." I put a hand on the chair opposite his. "Can I join you?"

His eyes betrayed his puzzlement but he answered, "Sure." He slid the *Gazette* to the edge of the table.

I sat down and studied him for a moment. Vey's wild red hair poked in every direction and the freckles across his nose appeared about to jump off his face. "There's a couple of things I want to talk to you about," I began.

"Why not talk to me at the ballpark? How'd you find me *here?*"

"It wasn't hard. I asked around, and found out this is where you go for dinner Thursday nights." Lately, it seemed that everybody had been able to find me, and I wanted Vey to know that I could track people down, too.

"But why?" he asked.

"I wanted a private talk, just you and me."

The man with the rolled shirtsleeves came by, and Vey introduced us. He was indeed the owner, Silk Shaughnessy. When he asked what I'd have, I ordered coffee and he went off, his mustache drooping with disappointment.

"Talk about what?" Vey asked guardedly.

"About this mess I'm in with Spats Pollard, and about that fellow getting beat up at the concession stand, and about me getting threats from some goon. You see, it occurs to me that you're in the middle of just about

167

everything that's been going on."

"You think so?" He took a sip of his milk.

"No doubt about it." A mug of black coffee was put before me; I shook off Shaughnessy's offer of cream or sugar and waited until he left before continuing. "When Pollard's body was found, *you* showed up at the concessions stand; when the newspapers got wind of the story, it was *you* who got them to drop it; when that fellow at the other refreshment stand got beat up, it was *you* who talked him into keeping quiet about it. *You* know that I'm investigating Pollard's murder, and I'm supposed to report to *you* on whatever I learn." I paused. "So yeah, I'd say that *you're* in the middle of everything."

There was a hint of a smile on Vey's face. "It sounds like you think I'm *behind* everything." He calmly hacked off a chunk of meatloaf and pushed it to the side of his plate near me. "Try some—you won't find none better."

It did look tempting, and I was hungry. "I honestly don't know what you're behind, or who's side you're really on, but I'm sure you know a whole lot more than you let on. And I need answers."

"I don't know if I can give you any answers," he said. Motioning again at the piece of meat, he added, "But I'll share my dinner with you."

I picked it up with my fingers, tasted it, and waved for Shaughnessy. "Changed my mind," I said to him. "I'll have the same thing."

"Comes with potatoes," he replied. "Pickles is a nickel extra."

"No pickles, but you got ketchup for the meatloaf? And some gravy for the potatoes?"

"Of course." He smiled, causing the waxed tips of his handlebar mustache to perk up. "I keep telling Andy that meatloaf without ketchup is like pretzels without mustard, but won't never try it." He looked at Vey and let out an exaggerated sigh. "I just can't teach this boy nothing." To me, he said, "Your dinner will be right up."

Vey mumbled, "Ketchup looks too much like blood for me."

"You're squeamish about *ketchup*?"

"I seen so much blood in the ring, I don't even like the color red."

"You boxed?"

He held out his hands, displaying the mangled fingers that I'd noticed before. "Sure did, and wasn't half bad." He nodded toward Shaughnessy, who was checking on a quiet couple who were the restaurant's only other diners. "That's how I come to know Silk. He was one of the best middleweights in the business before he retired to open up this joint. Still goes to the gym and helps the young fighters. He taught me most of what I know— especially how to keep my guard up." Vey shoveled a heap of mashed potato into his mouth. Silk Shaughnessy might have taught him how to box, but it appeared that he'd learned to eat from Babe Ruth. "And boxing is how I come to work for Mr. Barrow."

"I saw the picture in his office—him and John L. Sullivan."

"Mr. Barrow was quite a good fighter." Vey put down his fork and knife. "And as far as I'm concerned he's a good man. I'm telling you right now that I'll never say or do anything against him."

"*Is* there something to say about him?"

"Maybe, maybe not. But I won't break any confidence of his, so if you're looking for information that I'm not at liberty to give you—well, then all you'll be getting tonight is a mighty good dinner."

That dinner was placed in front of me. I noticed Vey

avert his eyes when I dosed my meatloaf with ketchup. While we both hungrily dug into our food, I asked, "How exactly did you get to know Mr. Barrow?"

"I was supposed to throw a fight and I didn't do it. I was never asked, and never agreed; the men who ran those things just told me what round I was supposed to take a dive in and expected me to follow orders. The gambler who tried to fix the bout lost a wad of cash on it, so he had me beaten up bad enough to end my career." Vey examined his knuckles. "But I put a couple of his boys down for the count before the rest of them got the better of me. Anyway, Ed Barrow was friends with my manager; he heard what happened, and he gave me a job. I was just an errand boy for him at first, but I worked hard and he kept moving me up." Vey smiled with pride. "Now look at me: A kid from the street going to work for the New York Yankees in a suit and tie." He dug a finger into his collar as if he didn't like the tie part of it at all. "I owe everything to Mr. Barrow."

"I won't ask you to betray him, or betray any confidence," I promised. "But if there's something you *can* tell me, will you help me out?" I recalled some of the looks I'd seen on his face and some of the things he'd said to me. "Sometimes I've had the feeling you're on my side."

"Wouldn't say I'm on your side, exactly. But I believe in a fair fight, and it seems to me you ain't in one. The Yankees want you to do a job for them—a dangerous job—but they're not giving you all you need to do it. They're sending you into a fight with one hand tied behind your back."

"What else do I need?"

"Information."

"Yeah, that's what I've been saying. And I expect you

have some."

"I do."

"What are you able to tell me?"

"I'm not sure." He bit into a pickle.

"How about this?" I persisted. "If I tell *you* a few things, could you keep them just between us for now?" He pondered that and agreed.

While we continued to eat, I filled him in on what I'd learned, what I suspected, and of the new telephone threat from the hoodlum I'd met at Katie Day's. When I told him about the phone call, he shook his head sadly and said, "That ain't right," sounding genuinely surprised that somebody would do such a thing.

We finished our discussion at the same time that we'd cleaned our plates. I said, "You can see I'm not getting along as fast as I need to on my own. If you can help me, I'd really appreciate it."

"I'll see what I can do."

I still wasn't entirely certain that I could trust Andrew Vey, or if it was wise to confide in him, but now and then you have to make a judgment call and hope it leads to the best. I had the feeling that if he *was* on my side, Vey could be quite an ally.

* * *

I had to wonder if Detective Jim Luntz ever did any actual detecting. When I went to see him again at the Forty-fourth Precinct stationhouse, he was leaning back in his chair with a fedora over his face and his feet propped on his desk. Instead of the khaki suit I'd seen him in previously, he was wearing a dark brown one that made the tobacco burns on his lapels less visible. His thick-soled shoes were scuffed and his socks were different colors.

I cleared my throat after standing patiently for a

minute and said tentatively, "Excuse me…" I got no response and repeated it louder.

Luntz started abruptly, almost falling from his chair. "Huh? What is it?" He swung his feet down, kicking a small stack of papers as he did so, and removed his hat to reveal puffy red eyes. It took him a moment before he was awake enough to recognize me. "Oh, Rawlings. Did we have an appointment?" He tossed the fedora on top of a file cabinet behind him and frowned at the papers that were now in disarray on his desk.

"No, do I need one?"

"Nah." Luntz reached for a canning jar filled with dark tobacco. He undid the wire bale, removed a thick wad of the stuff, and tamped it into his pipe with a thumb. "What can I do for you now?" He lit up and puffed vigorously to get it burning.

"It's about the Spats Pollard murder," I said.

"Are you still on that?"

"Aren't you?"

Luntz smiled blandly. "Oh, his file is still on my 'open' stack—but it's nowhere near the top."

"Have you found out anything more?"

His pipe answered with a horizontal back-and-forth swing: No.

I was starting to gag on the acrid smoke. "Have you tried?"

The detective didn't appear to like that question, but he answered, "I explained it to you before: My interest is protecting law-abiding citizens, not two-bit hoods. And I don't see what it matters to you."

"It doesn't—except that I need to get this whole thing over with. And the only way I can do that is to solve it."

"There's nothing to solve." Luntz plucked the pipe from his mouth and pointed the stem at me like a teacher using a pointer to instruct a particularly dull student. "Spats Pollard was a minor crook trying to get a share of the illegal booze business. Now he's dead, and some other bum will take his place. That bum won't last long, either—none of them ever do—and then there'll be a new one. They're all fighting for little slices of the same pie, and no matter how many of them come and go, there will always be more to take their place."

It sounded as if Luntz accepted murdered gangsters as part of a natural cycle of criminal life. I tried another tack. "Last time I was here, you told me you want to keep the Bronx safe for honest citizens. How about that concession owner who got beat up in Yankee Stadium a week or so ago—are you looking into *that*?" I still thought the attack on the vendor could be connected to Pollard's murder.

Luntz appeared genuinely mystified. "I never got any report about that."

Andrew Vey had mentioned that he'd convinced the victim to say he'd been beaten outside the stadium, not inside, but perhaps the man was too scared to report it at all. Since that seemed to be a dead end, I went on to the one tangible thing that I did want from Luntz. "I'd like that list Pollard had. I could really use the names of his customers."

He clamped the pipe between his teeth as firmly as if he was locking up a safe, and it again made a horizontal, negative swing.

"Mr. Ruppert would like for me to have it, too." Bluffing, I went on, "If you need some kind of formal request, I could ask Mr. Barrow, then he could ask Mr. Ruppert, then Mr. Ruppert could call your captain. It's up to you."

Luntz casually leaned back and puffed a few smoke

rings into the air. Finally, he said, "Listen, you just caught me on a bad morning. I was up half the night chasing a lead on an armed robbery in Hunt's Point. I still haven't had enough coffee. You want some?"

"No, thank you."

The detective sat upright. "Here's what I'm going to do. First, I'm going to the toilet to get rid of the last cup of coffee I had. Then I'm going to get a fresh one. When I'm back, we'll talk some more." As he spoke, he maneuvered papers around on his desk, sliding several of them toward me along with a couple of blank sheets. He stood up, put a pencil on top of the papers, and said, "Make yourself comfortable. I'll be a little while. But I can *not* give you the list." He grabbed his empty coffee mug and walked away.

When I looked at the papers, I saw that he'd put the list I was seeking right in front of me. I scanned it quickly, barely able to contain my excitement as I read some of the names. Then I began scribbling frantically to get down as many names, addresses, and phone numbers as I could.

I didn't get all of them, but enough to keep me busy for a while. At least I should be able to determine if Pollard's customer list was a recent one.

When Luntz returned, he had a steaming mug of black coffee in his hand. "Was there much more we needed to talk about?" he asked.

"I've taken enough of your time today," I said. "But if anything else comes up, I'll be back."

He uttered a sound that indicated he was not looking forward to that prospect.

Chapter Thirteen

The next morning, Margie and I were seated in a crowded train traveling northeast out of the Bronx. We'd first taken a Westchester Avenue street car, then transferred to the New Haven Railroad. Mamaroneck was only about fifteen miles away, but the stops were frequent and the progress slow.

Neither of us was in a hurry; the view was scenic, with occasional glimpses of Long Island Sound, and we were happy to be able spend some extra time together. The Yankees were soon leaving on a two-city swing through Philadelphia and Washington, and in a couple of weeks we'd making the first extended road trip of the year to the Midwest.

As the train carried us along the electrified rails, we breakfasted on molasses cookies and sweet apple cider. Margie pointed out sights and landmarks that she passed on her daily commute. She seemed excited about my first visit to the studio and I was happy to see where she worked, even though it wasn't the sole reason I'd come with her today.

We were among the few passengers to disembark at the charming little Larchmont station. A couple of attractive women stepped down from the train with us. Margie exchanged greetings and introduced them to me as two of the Griffith studio's production staff; one was a costume designer and the other a set decorator. "We usually ride together," Margie said. "But today I wanted you all to myself for a while."

Like Margie, the women were dressed in starched white shirtwaists and plain dark skirts. From their attire, there was nothing to indicate that working in the movies was a glamorous business; they might have been stenographers from a Midtown business office or seamstresses in the Garment District. Even when Margie was one of the screen's most famous stars, she dressed simply, shunned makeup, and never put on airs.

"It's still a couple of miles," Margie said. "The studio sends a car to pick us up." She'd barely finished the sentence when a gleaming Overland touring car pulled to the curb. It was driven by a dignified man of about seventy; Margie later told me that he had been an actor for Mr. Griffith in his early days at Biograph and was kept on the payroll as a part-time chauffeur and occasional extra. The courtly old man held the door for the ladies as they squeezed together in the back while I took the passenger's seat up front. The top was down and we were bathed in bright sunshine as the driver cautiously navigated a narrow, bumpy road to Orienta Point.

When we pulled up at the impressive grounds of the D. W. Griffith Studio, I was immediately struck by the contrast between this site and the Vitagraph studio in Brooklyn where I'd first met Margie. The Vitagraph facility was a brick factory complex designed for the rapid production of one- and two-reel moving pictures. This coastal location that Griffith had chosen was magnificent, with landscaped grounds and buildings that looked like they were part of an English country manor.

"I'm going to show Mickey around," Margie told the others. She took my hand and led the way to a foot path bordered by cherry trees and flowering dogwoods. The air was rich with the sweet, fragrant scent of springtime. She said to me as we started down the path, "Mr. Griffith is still out of town, so nobody's going to check to see when I start work."

"What about Tom Van Dusen?" I asked. "Wasn't he left in charge?" Van Dusen was the main reason I'd come today.

"Oh, Tom's writing a scenario now—some hokum about King Arthur and the Knights of the Round Table. He's leaving the rest of us to do pretty much whatever we please."

"Doesn't Griffith keep track of what's happening at his studio?"

Margie laughed. "Not very well—and that probably explains the company's finances. He sends a cable now and then telling us to prepare for some kind of scene that he's planning, but then he usually changes his mind and we have to scrap whatever work we did. Mr. Griffith has always spent a lot of time traveling—Lillian Gish had to direct the first movie made here because he was off on a trip somewhere."

As we toured the sprawling grounds, Margie told me that Griffith had bought the land from the Henry Flagler estate three years ago for $375,000—a bargain price for such a grand property. Its twenty-eight acres included a mansion, a number of cottages, stables, a dock, a sandy beach, and a small forest. Many of the site's natural features had already been used in Griffith's motion pictures.

There had also been numerous additions to the existing property. While we walked, we often had to tread carefully over electrical cables running from the generator Griffith had installed. Open spaces on the grounds had been used for the construction of movie sets too large for indoor filming. I recognized the Bastille, Notre Dame, and the royal palace that had appeared in Griffith's French Revolution epic *Orphans of the Storm*. These sets had yet to be torn down, but most of them were starting to deteriorate badly. Margie mentioned that one of the advantages of having the studio outside of New York City was because the building codes were less stringent and safety inspections were rare.

After seeing the grounds, including a thriving vegetable garden that provided food for the studio commissary, we headed up a flagstone walkway toward the main house, a stately mansion complete with turrets and towers. We passed smaller cottages nearby, and Margie pointed out the ones that were used as living quarters. One of these was reserved for Griffith and his current romantic interest Carol Dempster, an actress who only got roles in films that he directed.

Inside the mansion, Margie showed me the changes that had been made to turn this vacation home into a working movie studio. The ground floor ballroom had been converted to an enormous stage, and the upstairs bedrooms were used as dressing rooms, offices, and storage space. A glass-walled studio, like a giant greenhouse, had been built adjacent to the mansion to take advantage of natural light. The camera department was in the basement and a specially-built laboratory for developing film was housed in another addition.

It was an impressive place, and I'd been a fan of

Griffith's movies years before he achieved world-wide fame with *The Birth of a Nation*, but I couldn't stay long. "I'll need to catch the 11:15 back to the city," I reminded Margie. That would get me to the ballpark in time for batting practice. "I'd like to see what *you* do here."

There was a happy glow in Margie's eyes when she took my arm and led us up a curved staircase to the second floor. What had once been a bedroom was now crammed with racks of clothes, bolts of material, dressmaker's dummies, and several drawing tables. The only person working in the room was one of the women from the train, a petite blonde of about thirty who gave the impression of a schoolmarm. Her hair was pulled in a high, tight bun and gold-rimmed spectacles were halfway down her nose. She was drawing on a sketchpad, and judging by the scowl on her face was not satisfied with the results.

"This is Debra Hewitt," Margie reminded me. "She's the best costume designer in the business."

Hewitt looked at me over her spectacles. "And you're Mickey Rawlings the *Yankee*." She nearly spat the last word.

"Yes, I am." I forced a smile.

"I'm a Red Sox fan," Hewitt snapped.

"I used to be one, too," I replied. "In fact, until February I hated the Yankees."

"Well, perhaps you'll come to your senses again." She chuckled in a way that I knew she'd only been teasing me.

Margie proceeded to show me some designs that she and Hewitt had come up with for women's costumes. "Mr. Griffith is awfully old-fashioned," Margie said. "If it was up to him, we'd all still be wearing bustles and hoop skirts. But it's impossible to do stunts in such clothes. Debra and I are working on ways to keep the outside appearance the same, but making some modifications to the underclothes so that women can move more easily and do the stunts safely."

I looked over the drawings and made sounds of approval. I was impressed with their work, but didn't understand any of it. After years of living with Margie, I still couldn't figure out all the kinds of garments women wore.

Margie and Hewitt began going into greater and greater detail, explaining every stitch and every button. I began to squirm, trying to be attentive, but I couldn't focus on the minutia of fashion design. I nodded and smiled without knowing if my responses were appropriate to what they were saying.

Eventually Margie burst out laughing. "I think we've tortured him enough," she said to Hewitt, who joined in the laughter. To me, she said, "We just wanted to see how long you would try to stay interested. And you did very well—you're sweet. Now come along and I'll take you out of here."

After I said goodbye to Hewitt, we left the main building and walked to one of the smaller cottages. "This is Tom Van Dusen's," Margie said when we reached the door. "He should be inside working on his scenario." She gave me a kiss. "I know you'll need to get right to the ballpark after you talk with him. Tom will get you a ride to the train station, and I'll see you tonight. I'm thinking of making spaghetti."

"Sound good to me. And believe me, I'd rather spend more time with you than talk to…" I tilted my head toward the door.

"Me too. But go ahead and do your investigating." Margie walked back to the main house and I paused to watch her for a moment. It occurred to me that I really did want to spend more time with her.

From within the cottage, I heard the slow irregular clack of a typewriter. When I knocked on the door, I was greeted with an angry, "What is it now, dammit?"

"It's Mickey Rawlings," I answered calmly. "I was hoping I could speak with you."

Shuffling footsteps approached the door and Van Dusen opened it. "I wasn't expecting you, Rawlings." He flashed a toothy smile. "I thought it was one of the studio idiots. Seems no one can do anything without me, and I can hardly get any work done." It looked as if he *had* been working. Instead of dressing like a fashion plate from a moving picture magazine, Van Dusen wore a wrinkled soft-collar shirt and baggy trousers supported by olive drab suspenders. He needed a shave and his sandy hair had yet to be pomaded into place.

The director stepped aside for me to enter. As I did, I took a quick look around. The one-room cottage appeared to function as an office rather than as living quarters and was sparsely appointed in dark, mission style furniture. The clean designs were almost smothered by the clutter that surrounded them, however. The walls of the place were crowded with publicity stills, lobby cards, and sketches for set designs; they seemed randomly tacked up, with many of them overlapping. The pigeonholes of Van Dusen's writing desk were crammed and the stack of paper next to his typewriter was precariously high.

"Say, I don't mean to press you," Van Dusen said. "But have you spoken to Babe Ruth again about making our picture? I've called his hotel a few times but he hasn't gotten back to me." He pressed his lips together in a pout.

"Not yet," I answered. "Actually, I came here to ask

you about another matter."

"Oh." The pout became more firmly fixed.

"But I'll be happy to talk to the Babe about your movie after today's game," I promised. "I'm sure he just needs a reminder."

"I'd appreciate that," he said, mollified. He walked to a rolling service cart that was laden with bottles and glasses. "Drink?" he offered.

"No, thank you." As he began to pour one for himself, I added, "But that's what I want to talk to you about."

Van Dusen laughed. "You want to talk to me about *drinking?*"

"About your supplier: Spats Pollard."

The laughter turned into a cough. "Pollard?"

"Yes. I believe you knew him."

Van Dusen turned to me and took a swallow from his glass. Adopting the tone of a politician, he said, "Well, as you know, the buying and selling of liquor isn't legal at present. I would prefer not to discuss any such dealings I might have."

"Your name is on Pollard's customer list. And don't worry about revealing he's a bootlegger—he's a dead bootlegger now, and won't mind anything you say about him."

"*Dead?*" Van Dusen was either genuinely surprised at the news or he was a better actor than a director.

"Yes. Did you know him well?"

"No, not really. To be honest, I didn't particularly want to know him."

A sudden, ragged snore rumbled from the direction of the sofa. I hadn't noticed before, but Natalie Brockman was curled up under an afghan, her pale head almost invisible on a white throw pillow.

Van Dusen said, "She had a little too much of the hootch herself last night." He quickly added, "Not anything from Pollard." Brockman rolled over, her mouth agape, and the snoring became more regular.

I turned my attention back to the director. "What did you mean you didn't *want* to know Pollard?"

"I didn't care for his sales manner," Van Dusen answered. "He bragged about famous customers, claimed that he could provide the best quality products, and implied that he had some rather powerful underworld connections. It was all supposed to impress me, but to be honest it worried me a bit—there are some kinds of people I don't want to get involved with." He sat down at his desk, swiveled the chair to face me, and asked, "What's your interest in Pollard?"

"We were on the Cubs together five years ago. He pretty much dropped out of sight after that, and I was wondering what became of him. After he turned up dead, I just got curious and found out that he'd become a bootlegger."

"I see… You were friends?"

"Not really, just teammates. But teammates do tend to stick together."

He took another slug of his drink. "It's your *current* teammate I'm interested in," he reminded me.

"I promised I'll talk to him, and I will." I paused. "Would you mind a few more questions while I'm here?"

Van Dusen nodded to go ahead. He understood that the more he helped me, the more I was likely to help him with Babe Ruth.

"When were you in contact with Pollard?"

"Oh, around the holidays. December… January… something like that."

"Any time since then?"

"No. I only met him a few times and he always initiated the meetings. I never bought from him, and eventually he must have caught on that I wasn't going to." He took another sip. "I didn't need him—I have a good supplier in the city and another who makes deliveries here."

"How did he take your refusal to buy from him?"

"I never out-and-out refused. I simply kept putting him off until he gave up." His brow creased and he said, "You didn't mention how Pollard died."

"He was murdered."

Van Dusen appeared frozen for a moment. Then he gulped down the rest of his drink.

Chapter Fourteen

I met Karl Landfors Thursday morning at a busy coffee shop on Seventy-seventh Street, across from the American Museum of Natural History. The aroma of hot buttered toast and fresh coffee, and the sound of sizzling bacon and frying eggs, were enticing, but I had already eaten an early breakfast with Margie. I ordered a cup of coffee at the counter and brought it to a small table near the window where Landfors was already seated.

A half-empty mug and the remnants of his meal were in front of him. I removed his black derby from the chair he'd saved for me and sat down across from him. Touching a finger to the corner of my mouth, I said, "You got a…"

"Oh, thank you." He dabbed at a drop of egg yolk with his napkin and I nodded when it was gone.

"So… Who is this fellow we'll be meeting?" I asked. When Landfors telephoned me, he had been too excited to be coherent about the details. He didn't have to convince me to meet him, though; I'd learned over the years that if he said something was important it probably was.

Landfors sat on the edge of his chair. His eyes were bright and he was fighting not to smile. He looked altogether like a little kid with a secret he was bursting to tell. "Remember I told you that I'm looking into an Arnold Rothstein connection with the Dot King murder?"

"Yes. How's that going?"

His eager expression faltered. "Well, to be perfectly frank, I'm not making as much progress on that as I would like. But I now have an excellent source within Rothstein's organization and he's starting to provide me with some very useful information." Landfors paused to clean his spectacles with a handkerchief, letting the suspense build before coming to the point. "What's more, he has some information for *you*."

"What kind of information?" I wasn't eager to meet someone who worked for Arnold Rothstein. Simply being seen with an associate of the notorious gambler could end a ballplayer's career.

"I'll let him tell you." Landfors checked his pocket watch. "We meet him in twenty minutes." Tucking the watch back in his vest pocket, he asked, "Have you come up with anything new on that dead pitcher?"

I proceeded to fill him in on what I'd learned since we'd last spoken. When I recounted my meeting with Andrew Vey, Landfors agreed that Vey seemed to be smack in the middle of everything and he warned me not to trust him.

"Vey seems more trustworthy than the cops," I said. "I went to see Detective Luntz again, and either he's the laziest cop on the force or there's a reason he won't investigate anything."

"Do you think he's on the take?" Landfors asked.

"I can't imagine any other reason why a New York City police detective would be so indifferent about a murder. He says that one dead gangster will only be replaced by another anyway, and he isn't doing any kind of investigation. I'm wondering if whoever killed Spats Pollard is paying Luntz to look the other way."

"It's possible," Landfors said. "Bootlegging is big business in this city, and the people running it can afford to buy anything and anyone."

I next told him of my meeting with Tom Van Dusen at the Griffith studio. If the director was telling the truth, Spats Pollard had been trying to build up his liquor business as recently as December or January. Unfortunately, I didn't feel I could take Van Dusen at his word, so I would have to continue working with Pollard's customer list.

"You know," I said, "one of the toughest things about this case is I don't know who to believe or who to trust. Sometimes it seems the only people I can ever trust completely are you and Margie."

Landfors beamed at the unexpected compliment. "You can always count on me," he said.

I went on, "Even that fellow who runs the concession stand where Pollard was found—Joe Zegarra's his name—I found out he isn't completely honest, either."

"He lied about something?"

"His bottles did. The labels are for near beer but he's selling the real stuff. Doing a booming business with it, too, from what I could see."

Landfors' skull-like head suddenly brightened into a lifelike expression and he blinked rapidly. "A bootlegger is found dead in a place that's selling bootleg beer? That can't be a coincidence! Maybe Zegarra's behind it."

I'd already considered the possibility that Pollard and

Zegarra had been competitors. "Possible," I acknowledged, "But it doesn't make sense to me. If Zegarra killed Pollard, would he stash the body in his own place? I don't think so."

Landfors frowned in response and pulled out his watch. "Time to go meet my contact," he said.

"He isn't coming here?"

"No, he doesn't want to be seen with us."

The feeling was entirely mutual. "Where then?"

"Across the street." Landfors smiled. "In a most unlikely place to find a gangster. Or a baseball player, for that matter."

Minutes later, we were inside the venerable American Museum of Natural History, climbing a series of stairs to the fourth floor. When we reached it, we passed through the bone-filled Hall of Fossil Invertebrates and went into one of the museum's newest exhibits, The Hall of the Age of Man.

The cool, high-ceilinged room featured exhibits showing what the world was like when cave men populated the earth. There were murals depicting the landscapes, display cases containing the skulls of human ancestors, and frightening full-scale models of the animals they hunted. The first section we entered was identified as "Pleistocene of North America" and included the fossilized skeletons of a saber-toothed tiger and an American lion.

Landfors nudged me and pointed at a gangly young man in a double-breasted wool overcoat that was a couple of sizes too big for him. His hat was also large, a black wide-brimmed fedora with a maroon band. The man was slowly pacing around a giant ground sloth, and seemed to be appraising it as if wondering which of them would win in a fight.

Landfors and I casually drifted in the direction of the sloth. As we did, I glanced back and forth from a diorama of a prehistoric North American landscape to the young man whose face was barely visible between his upturned coat collar and the turned down brim of his hat. I saw that he somewhat resembled Landfors, with pale skin and gaunt features. His cheeks were pockmarked and a long fringe of blonde hair almost as light as Natalie Brockman's poked from the edge of his fedora. I guessed his age to be about twenty-five, but the way he wore his oversized clothes, like a boy trying to wear his father's suit, made him look younger.

When we were next to him, pretending to share an interest in the giant sloth, he muttered to Landfors, "This your friend?"

Landfors confirmed that I was.

"Let's walk," the man said.

The three of us fell into step, wandering around the displays as if we were simply touring the museum. I thought the caution might be a bit excessive, but was certainly willing to go along with it. Being seen together could cause us both a lot of trouble.

Landfors made an attempt at introductions, but was cut off by the young man, who said to me, "Call me 'Whitey.' And I know who you are." He hunched his shoulders as if trying to puff himself up. There was no need to make himself look bigger; the hard expression on his sharp face was sufficiently intimidating. He continued, "I hear you're interested in Spats Pollard."

"Did you know him?"

"Yup. Not real well, and I didn't much like him, but we were acquainted."

If there was one thing that was consistent throughout this strange case, it was that those who knew Spats

Pollard didn't care for him. I said, "If you didn't like him, then I guess you won't be sorry to hear that he's dead."

Whitey's penetrating eyes darted to mine and briefly fixed me in an icy stare. "You think that's news to me?"

"It wasn't in the newspapers," I said. "And it's been kept pretty quiet."

"I don't need no papers to know what's going on. But I'll tell *you* something that might be news."

"What's that?"

"Pollard getting killed was two years overdue."

That certainly *was* news to me. "What do you mean?" I asked.

The three of us were working our way past an exhibit on "The Evolution of Man," with individual display cases labeled "Neanderthal," "Cro-Magnon," and "Piltdown Man." Whitey answered, "Pollard got too friendly with my boss's mistress, a showgirl named Jenny Reece— good-lookin' blonde who used to dance in *George White's Scandals*."

"Your boss is Arnold Rothstein," I said.

Landfors gave me a bony elbow to the ribs. "We don't mention his name," he whispered.

Whitey didn't seem to notice. He had stopped to look at a reconstruction of a Neanderthal woman's head. "Sure glad I didn't live back then," he said. "Them dames was *ugly*." The bright light of the exhibit hall was harsh on his pockmarked face, and I thought she might feel the same about him.

I said, "So Pollard was seeing this showgirl, and I take it your boss didn't like that."

"We got rules," Whitey replied. "And that's a bad one to break. Stupid, too—there's a million chorus girls in this city, so why the hell should Pollard go after one who's off limits?" He shook his head in disapproval of

Pollard's poor judgment.

"What did your boss do when he found out about it?"

Whitey had stopped to examine a full-sized model of a Cro-Magnon man. "Hey, I think I know this guy—he's a bookie with the Kid Dropper gang." Chuckling at his own joke, he answered my question as if it was equally amusing. "What the hell do you think he did? He gave an order. Pollard was supposed to be taken for a ride— the kind you don't come back from." Whitey started walking again and we moved along with him. He continued his story, "When Pollard disappeared, we all thought the job was done. Then a few months ago, Pollard turns up alive, running around and trying to get a cut of the liquor business."

"Why wasn't he killed as soon as Roth— I mean, as soon as your boss found out he was still alive?"

"Because it ain't that simple. Pollard being alive means there's a lot of questions we got to get answers to. Why wasn't the job done two years ago? Where's he been all that time? Does he got partners? Is he tied in with another gang?" Whitey shrugged. "If we killed him as soon as he come out of hiding, we might never find out what all he's been up to."

Whitey had raised a number of questions that I hadn't thought of and didn't want to investigate myself. For a moment, I was dejected that I might have to look into many more things than I had anticipated. I wanted this over with soon. Then it occurred to me that Rothstein might have already done the work for me. "Did you find any answers to those questions?" I asked.

"Not as far as I know." Whitey fidgeted in his bulky coat. "Tell you the truth, we was disappointed that Pollard got killed when he did—we wanted to know a lot more." He looked around, at nothing in particular, then back at me. "Anyway, that's about all I know about Spats Pollard. That help you any?"

"I think it does. Thank you." We'd reached the end of the exhibit hall and were standing next to a wooly mammoth that dwarfed the three of us. "One more question, though, if you don't mind."

"Shoot," he said, not even cracking a smile at his choice of word.

"Why are you helping me? What's in it for you?"

Whitey's slow smile was even more frightening than his cold eyes. "Same reason I'm helping your writer friend here. Two reasons, really. One is that he's gonna owe me a favor—maybe somebody he'll write something that helps me, or leaves my name outta something that might hurt me." He glanced at Landfors, who promptly nodded in agreement. "The other reason," he continued, "is if somebody else in our business takes a fall, maybe it opens up a spot for me. I'm always looking to move up."

It sounded rather cannibalistic. "You don't have any loyalty to your friends?" I asked.

The smile turned to one of genuine amusement. "There's a big difference between us, Mickey Rawlings: *You* got teammates, *I* got rivals. There ain't one guy in our gang who wouldn't stick a knife in my back if it meant he got a little something out of it. And I'd do the same to him. Forget what you hear about criminal 'organizations.' In my business, it's every man for himself. Ain't no such thing as loyalty."

I had to give him credit for bluntness. Although I had the impression that he could kill a man with no more conscience than swatting a mosquito, I also had the feeling that he was one of the few people I'd spoken to about the case who was telling me the truth.

* * *

Back when I'd played for the Giants, Sunday baseball was still illegal in New York and some managers, including John McGraw, had occasionally been arrested for violating the old blue laws. Now, we rarely had a Sunday off, and most other breaks in the schedule were for travel. This Friday was to be our last off day for some time, so Margie and I decided to spend it enjoying springtime in the Bronx.

Of course with only one day to do as we wished, we thought of a dozen different ways to use the time. Margie telephoned the studio to say that she wouldn't be in, and we settled down to eat a pancake breakfast and go over the options. By the time we cooked up a second stack, Margie was making a case for visiting the New York Botanical Garden in Bronx Park, while I was expressing my preference for a boat ride in Crotona Park. For me, looking at flowers wasn't any more interesting than looking at pictures of flowers. But I realized that it never really mattered where Margie and I went, since we enjoyed almost anything we did together.

I had just agreed to the botanical garden when I noticed the kids on the street choosing up sides for a ballgame. No doubt they should have been in school, but today's weather was much better suited to baseball than a classroom.

The kids had some new equipment laid out next to a fire hydrant. New for them, anyway. I'd recently brought them several baseballs that had been used in Yankees batting practice and a couple of bats. One of the bats was a Bob Meusel Louisville Slugger that had a chipped knob; the other was a barely-used Mickey Rawlings model that the equipment manager insisted I would have to pay for.

The boys chose sides, half a dozen on a team, and the game quickly got under way. Home plate was a manhole cover, first base was the left rear fender of a rusted Studebaker that hadn't budged from the curb in months, and second and third bases were yellow bricks that had once been part of the crumbling front stoop of the apartment house on the corner.

As I watched the boys play, it was clear that their joy in the game was in no way diminished by the poor quality of their "field." Although the action was often interrupted by passing traffic, and they were subjected to a brief tirade by a shopkeeper across the street who feared for his windows, they seemed to have just as much of a thrill in a solid hit or a good catch as my teammates and I did. The essence of baseball was the same whether played on the asphalt of a city street, on a cow pasture in Indiana, in a textile league in South Carolina, or in the steel and concrete expanse of Yankee Stadium.

Did I really need to stay with the Yankees to enjoy the game? I wondered. If I dropped the Spats Pollard mess, the Yankees might drop me, but I would find another team someplace and I would still be able to play the game I loved.

Turning away from the window, I stared at Margie for a long moment. "Do you ever miss acting?" I asked.

She paused with the pitcher of syrup hovering over her plate and gave me a quizzical look. "Why do you ask?"

"I was wondering… People saw your movies all over the world, the newspapers and movie magazines were full of stories about you, you had millions of fans… Everybody knew Marguerite Turner. Don't you miss that?"

"Not really," she answered thoughtfully. "I acted in those movies because it was fun, not because I wanted to be famous. I miss those days, sometimes, because the picture business was more fun and free back then. No one thought movies would last, so we didn't take ourselves seriously. But I don't miss acting. I enjoy what I'm doing now." She cut a piece of syrup-sodden pancake with her fork. "And besides, if I ever do get the acting bug again I can always go back into it. Of course, I'll probably be cast in matron roles at this point…"

"I was just wondering." I stabbed at my own pancake. "Oh, and you're still much too young to be a 'matron.' "

Margie smiled teasingly. "You were a little slow on that, but I'll attribute it to the fact that you're thinking about something else."

"I am?"

"Yes. What you're really wondering is if *you* would miss baseball if you couldn't play." She sipped her coffee and touched a napkin to her full lips. "Why are you even worrying about that?"

"Miller Huggins is using me as a coach more than a player. He says he thinks I could be a manager myself someday."

" 'Someday' is a long way off," Margie said, with a confidence I myself wasn't feeling.

I continued poking at the pancake, turning it into a shredded mess. "Sometimes I think playing baseball is the most important thing in the world to me. Other times—like when I have to get involved in crimes—it doesn't seem worth it. I could go back to playing for a mill league like I did before I made it to organized ball. Or I could work with kids like those." I nodded toward the window, where the exuberant sound of their game was coming through. "I might like managing."

"You need to do whatever you feel is right for you," she said firmly. "When you have something you're burning to do, you need to do it. And if you ask me, I think you're still burning to play baseball." After a moment, she added, "I hope you know that whatever you decide to do, I'll go with you."

Baseball suddenly evaporated from my thoughts. "There's something else important to me," I said.

"What's that?"

"It's not a 'what.' It's *you*—and I want you to be safe."

She smiled. "You silly. I feel perfectly safe."

"We have this road trip coming up, and I'd feel better if you weren't alone."

"You want somebody to come stay with me?"

"No, not here. I was thinking maybe you could stay in one of those bungalows at the studio. It'll only be for about a week. You wouldn't have to travel, and there'll be other people living there, right?"

She nodded.

Before I could continue making my case, the telephone rang. "Speaking of the studio," Margie said, hopping up to take the call, "that might be Natalie. She and Tom have been having some problems and I told her she could call me if she needed anything." Margie put the receiver to her ear, listened for a few seconds, and said into the mouthpiece, "He's right here."

I quickly went to the phone and took the receiver from her, hoping it wasn't another threatening call. "Yes?"

"Mickey, it's Andrew Vey. I think I can help you out."

We spoke for a few minutes. When I hung up, I said to Margie, "I hate to do this, but I have to meet someone—it might be important. Can we go out tonight instead of to the park?"

She agreed, although her eyes betrayed some disappointment.

* * *

I felt badly for putting a damper on the day we had planned, but, as she had been so many times before, Margie was completely understanding. Since I worried about her being home alone, I was relieved that she decided to go the botanical garden anyway. She'd recently bought a new Brownie camera and promised to take photographs for me.

About the time that I had expected to be on a romantic outing with Margie in Bronx Park, I was instead walking into a dingy shoe repair shop a few blocks from the Polo Grounds. The shop, in the same rundown neighborhood as Silk Shaughnessy's Dining Emporium, reeked of tanned leather, neatsfoot oil, and old sweat.

The only occupant was a gnarled man at a messy workbench with a bare bulb hanging above it. He was hammering a nail into the heel of a woman's lace-up boot. The man looked at me just long enough to ascertain that I wasn't a customer and muttered through a mouthful of nails, "They're in the back."

I walked across a dusty floor littered with scraps of leather, bits of thread, and bent nails to the open door of a small room behind the workshop. It was set up as a sort of office, and might have been furnished with rejects from the Forty-fourth precinct. The one desk consisted of a battered pine table with a rubber heel wedged under a short leg, a file cabinet in the corner was missing the handles from two drawers, and the only feature that the room's three wooden chairs had in common was that they were all missing either a rail or a spindle.

Seated on two of the chairs, their backs to the door, were a couple of men hunched in front of a radio that was on a workbench similar to the cobbler's. I'd seen a few of the devices before; according to the label on the cabinet, this one was a "Radiola" manufactured by the

Radio Corporation of America. Glowing tubes from the back of the radio emitted an eerie light and I could hear loud static like a bad telephone connection.

Andrew Vey was listening to the headset that the other man held up to his ear. They were both trying to turn one of the radio's knobs and arguing over which way it should be rotated.

"Mr. Vey?" I said to get his attention.

He turned. "Ah, Rawlings. Cooper here was just showing me his new wireless." To the other man, he said, "I don't know how you can listen to this noise. I'd get a headache in ten minutes."

"Radio is only going to get better—you'll see." The man swung around and cheerfully announced, "I'm Vern Cooper."

The name meant nothing to me. "Good to meet you," I said.

Cooper put his feet up on the desk; considering where we were, I was surprised to see that the shoes needed new soles. His overall appearance was as unremarkable as his nondescript gray suit. Cooper was probably in his late forties, with undistinguished features and a bland expression. He would probably make a good criminal since no one would ever be able to give the police a description other than "average looking." The only thing at all noticeable was that his medium brown hair was cut somewhat lopsided; it looked like he and Andrew Vey might frequent the same blind barber.

Vey stood, tugged down the bottom of his vest, and shook my hand. "Glad you could come." He gestured at Cooper, who had reached into a bowl of walnuts on his desk. "I believe Mr. Cooper can help you with at least part of this puzzle you've been working on."

"I could certainly use the help," I said. Although I

wasn't sure how a cobbler could help me.

Vey sat back down, causing his vest to ride back up. It was nearly as undersized as his little bow tie and had no chance of covering his muscular torso. As he pulled at it again, I wondered if he ever wore an outfit in which every article of clothing actually fit him.

Cooper smashed open a walnut with a small claw hammer. He said in a mild voice that was devoid of regional accent, "That fellow who threatened you at Katie Day's night club. His name is Leo Kessler. Low level hood in Arnold Rothstein's merry band." He popped a piece of freshly shelled walnut in his mouth.

Questions flashed through my head faster than I could articulate them. The first one I could get out was, "How do you know that?"

Vey spoke up. "Mr. Cooper is a private detective. He works for the Yankees."

I looked around the room and Cooper guessed the cause of my bewilderment. "The shop out front belongs to my brother-in-law," he said. "I rent this room from him. Gives him a little extra income, and provides me with an inconspicuous place to run my business."

I still wasn't quite following. "And your business is doing detective work for the Yankees?" If the Yankees already had a detective on their payroll, why the hell was *I* the one looking into Spats Pollard's murder?

Cooper looked to Vey, who explained, "Mr. Cooper's sole assignment for the Yankees is to keep tabs on Babe Ruth. This is no secret, by the way, which is why I feel at liberty to tell you. After the Babe's difficulties last year, Mr. Ruppert and Mr. Barrow decided to protect the team's investment by hiring Mr. Cooper to keep an eye on him."

"Does Ruth know?"

"Of course," answered Vey. "The goal is to keep him from getting into trouble, not to catch him at it. If the Babe knows he's being watched, he's less likely to do anything harmful or embarrassing to the team."

I recalled coach Charlie O'Leary coming into Miller Huggins' office with a report on Ruth's doings. The only way O'Leary could have known was if someone was keeping tabs on him.

After smashing and consuming another walnut, Cooper spoke up again. "Of course, now and then the Babe likes to give me the slip—like you did in Boston. Since he had a car waiting for him, I assumed you went to his place in Sudbury." The detective gave me a look that expected an answer. When I said nothing, he shrugged and went on, "I was following him the night he met you at Katie Day's. I saw the two of you together, and I spotted Kessler."

"What made you notice him?"

"What I noticed was *you*. I didn't remember you and Ruth palling around before, so when I saw you drinking with him in a night club, I thought maybe he was getting you into his bad habits. I believe the Yankees were hoping you could be a good influence on him, instead of the other way around."

Vey uttered a confirming noise.

"How do you know it was this fellow Kessler who confronted me? We were the only ones in the men's room, and when I left he was gone. How did you see him?"

"I get paid to notice things," Cooper replied with a small smile. "I was keeping an eye on your party because that's where the Babe was. When you left the table, I noticed Leo Kessler along with a couple of his cohorts get up and follow you. Kessler's been around a while and

I recognized him easy. I thought it strange when he posted his goons outside the men's room. Sometimes a gangster will do that for protection—he wants the place to himself so no rival gangster catches him at a time when he's vulnerable. But you were already in there, so I thought it odd."

"Can you tell me anything more about Kessler?"

"He used to run crooked dice games years ago, but lately he's building up a liquor business—that's where the money is right now. Doesn't have the brains to be a big-time operator, but he is dangerous. He's done some muscle work for Rothstein, collecting bets and late payments."

A disquieting thought occurred to me. "Did you say anything to Mr. Barrow about me talking to Kessler?" Meeting with an associate of Arnold Rothstein could doom my baseball career.

Through a mouthful of partially chewed nuts, Cooper answered, "Never said a word about it until Vey here came to me and asked if I noticed anything that night. For one thing, finding gangsters in a night club is about as unusual as discovering that they serve booze. For another, like you said, I never *saw* you talk to him—as far as I know, you could have just been using the facility at the same time."

"And you won't say anything?"

"No reason to," answered Cooper.

Vey spoke up. "Just as I hope *you'll* be quiet about our meeting here today. Like I said, I don't feel I'm betraying Mr. Barrow's confidence, but I don't know that he would see it the same way."

"You have my word," I promised.

Cooper said, "That's about all I can tell you, but if anything else comes up we can get in touch through Mr.

Vey."

"Thank you," I said, getting a benevolent nod in reply. Turning to Vey, I said, "And thank *you*."

I left the shop more confident that Andrew Vey was on my side. But I also had a new puzzle to figure out. There were now two of Arnold Rothstein's gang mixed up in this: Karl Landfors' source Whitey, who was purportedly helping me, and Leo Kessler who was threatening me. Which side were they really on? And was Rothstein himself involved?

*   *   *

Instead of a picnic, or a boat ride, or a stroll through the gardens in Bronx Park, Margie and I went on a very different outing later that night. After a trolley ride to Manhattan, we got off at Broadway, a block south of Central Park. This area of Midtown, with all the theaters and speakeasies, reminded me of New Orleans during spring training. The evenings here were perpetually festive, with well-dressed people moving from one show or club or party to another.

Margie and I walked to 232 West Fifty-eighth Street, where the sign above the door read *Club Durant*. It had recently opened as one of the city's more exclusive night clubs.

I discovered how exclusive when we walked inside and were stopped by a massive host in a tailored tuxedo. He looked strong enough to give Andrew Vey a thrashing and mean enough to do it just for the pleasure. "Name?" he demanded.

"Mickey Rawlings."

"Never heard of yuh." His stolid face and dull eyes could have been carved from granite and he had no discernable neck.

"We're just here to have a couple of drinks and do

some dancing," I said.

"Not if I don't let you in, you ain't." Speakeasies often required code words or membership cards to keep out the authorities, but it should have been obvious that we were not Revenue agents. This fellow simply enjoyed his job a little too much.

Margie said to me in a hushed voice, "Let's go someplace else."

There was a particular reason I wanted to get into the Club Durant, and I wasn't going to let this bruiser stop me. "I play for the Yankees," I said. "And if I like this place, maybe I'll tell my teammates."

"I follow the ponies," the man said, unmoved. "Baseball don't interest me. If you was a horse, I might let you in." He called to another man near the coat check room, who was similarly attired. "Hey, Frankie! Come here, wouldja?"

Frankie strode over. Although slightly smaller, this man looked even more intimidating. He was horse-faced, with short-cropped hair and a five o'clock shadow. "Got a problem, Dutch?" he asked the host.

"This guy wants in and I don't know him from Adam. Claims he's with the Yankees. You know baseball, you ever heard o'— What you say your name was again?"

When I repeated my name to Frankie he said, "Yeah, I know who you are. You were with the Browns last year, weren't you?"

"That's right," I said. "So can we get in?"

"Yeah, of course. The cover's five bucks each."

As I pulled out a ten, a couple of men in sharp suits, each with a flashy woman on his arm, tried to go past us. "Whoa," said Frankie, putting a firm hand on the chest of one man. "You gents know the drill. Hardware stays with me."

Without protest, each of the men pulled a gun from inside his jacket and handed it over. One of them offered up a second weapon tucked in his pants. "Collect them when you leave," said Frankie, carrying the firearms to the coat check room.

Margie was starting to look apprehensive. I calmly paid the cover charge and we went into the club. From behind, I heard Frankie reprimanding Dutch, "We don't make money by keeping customers *out*, you idiot! Besides, if some guy claims to play for the Yankees you think he's gonna give his name as *'Mickey Rawlings'* unless he's telling the truth? Use your head, dammit!"

We were escorted to a small table near one of the black velvet walls. The place was well-appointed and fairly large, accommodating a couple of hundred customers. Although it was still early, more than half the tables were already taken. When a waiter came by, I ordered a bottle of champagne. It was overpriced, but I wanted to do something special for Margie.

On stage was the reason I'd chosen this particular speakeasy. Jimmy Durante's Jazz Band was filling the air with some of the best music I'd heard in a long time. A few couples were dancing, but most of the customers were listening, drinking, and quietly talking. It was difficult to sustain a dance when Durante played because he would frequently pause in mid-song to regale the audience with quips and stories. His voice was funny in itself, a gravely tone with a broad New York accent, and his prominent nose was the butt of many of his own jokes. I had seen him several times over the years with the Original New Orleans Jazz Band; Durante was the only member not from New Orleans, but his skills at ragtime piano were such that he fit right in musically. Even then, though, he had a propensity for making jokes in a voice that betrayed his New York origins.

When the band took a break, I slipped a couple of dollars to our waiter to give Durante a message.

Minutes later, Jimmy Durante arrived at our table. "Well, if it ain't Mickey Rawlings," he rasped in his distinctive voice, the words coming out staccato. "Put 'er dere, pal." We shook hands and he pulled up a chair to join us. He looked at Margie, his eyes twinkling with good humor. "Ha-cha-cha-chaaa... Who's dis lovely lady?"

I introduced him to Margie, who seemed immediately charmed by the entertainer. "Do you two know each other?" she asked with surprise. I had never mentioned Durante to her before.

"Oh, sure," said Durante. "Dere was some lean times durin' de war when de band outnumbered de audience. Mickey was a regular when he was in town, and we got to talkin' now and den."

"It doesn't look like you're having lean times anymore," I observed.

"It's been good," he replied. "Dere's nights when de place is so populated, every time I turn my head I knock over five or six dancers wit' my Schnozzola."

Margie laughed brightly.

"But dat's been a recent eventuality," he said. "Wasn't even sure de jernt would open for a while. You seen de sign—Club *Durant*?"

"It's missing an 'e,' isn't it?" I said.

"Dat's on accounta we couldn't afford it. De sign painter left it off unless we paid him more money."

The club had only been open for a couple of months and I wondered how his fortunes had changed so fast. "You must have turned things around quickly," I said. "I mean, I know people will want to come see you perform, but doesn't it usually take time for a club to start attracting customers?"

"To tell yuh da trut'," he said in a confidential tone. "I got myself some investors. Dey helped me get da place resurrected off da ground."

"Are your investors the kind of men at the front door?"

"Dem's de gents dat's got the moohla," he replied. "And dey keep de place respec'able. Frankie knows every hood in de city by sight, and he alleviates 'em o' dere weapons before they can set a foot in de jernt." Durante flagged a waiter and ordered us another bottle of champagne on the house and a beer for himself.

"Can I ask you about one of them hoods?" I asked.

"It's usually best not to talk about 'em," he demurred.

"This particular one won't mind," I said. "His name's Spats Pollard and he was a bootlegger. Your club was on his customer list. Did you buy from him?" Since Club Durant had opened so recently, I figured I might learn something about Pollard's business dealings shortly before he was killed.

"Dat ain't my department," he answered. "I play de music an' make wit' de jokes. I don't know de business end too much."

"Do you know who would?"

The waiter had arrived with our drinks and Durante instructed him to get Frankie to our table. By the time we'd finished making a toast to Durante's continued success with the club, the horse-faced strongman had arrived. "You want me, boss?" he asked.

Durante said, "My friend Mickey was makin' a inquisition about a fellah name o' Spats Pollard. Yuh know 'im?"

"I did," Frankie answered. I noticed his use of the

past tense. To me, he said, "What's your interest in Pollard?"

"Since you know baseball," I said, "you probably know Pollard pitched for the Cubs one year—1918. We were teammates that season, and I was wondering how he was doing. Last I heard, he got into the liquor business in New York."

"He didn't do so good at that," Frankie answered flatly. "He came by, offered us some product he claimed was better than anything else on the market, but no sale."

"Why not?"

"We already had a supplier lined up. Pollard was trying to cut into somebody else's business."

"You ever hear anything more about him?"

"Nah, he's been real quiet lately." To Durante, he said, "If there ain't nothing else, I better get back to the door."

Durante told him to go ahead and said to us, "I gotta go, too. It's been a pleasure, but I gotta proceed wit' de musicalities."

Margie and I slowly drank our champagne, thoroughly enjoyed the music, and after she thought I was sufficiently intoxicated she took me onto the floor to teach me a new dance called the Charleston. I had no more luck with it than I had with any other kind of dance, but we had a wonderful evening.

Chapter Fifteen

I wanted to yell at Miller Huggins, "I'm at the wrong base!" What on earth was he thinking when he put me in at *first* base?

But I didn't need to scream it. Huggins had clearly seen my confusion when he'd told me to go in to play first at the top of the seventh inning. I was so stunned, that he'd had to repeat the order, adding "Now get your ass out there," before I ran out of the dugout to assume the strange new position. As trotted to the bag, I realized I didn't even have a first basemen's mitt, just my usual fielder's glove.

I understood why Wally Pipp needed a defensive replacement. He had been spiked by Ken Williams in a collision during the fourth inning, and had been hobbling in pain until he finally had to come out of the game. But Pipp was over six feet tall, practically a requirement for a first baseman, and I was more than a few inches shy of that mark. If I went into a stretch to take a throw, my overall reach would probably be a foot shorter than Pipp's.

As I threw warm-up grounders to the other fielders, I told myself not to waste time questioning why I was put in this position, but to prepare myself to succeed with the opportunity. It was, after all, a chance to shine in front of my former teammates, the St. Louis Browns, in our final home game before the road trip.

When Sad Sam Jones got ready to throw his first pitch to the Browns' left-handed hitter Gene Robertson, I had trouble figuring out where to place myself. Second base was where I played best, and I was comfortable at shortstop or third, although my arm wasn't strong enough to make long throws on a regular basis. First base, however, was alien territory. I decided to play it as a mirror image of third base, and positioned myself off the bag accordingly.

Jones, a right-hander with a curveball that dropped like a falling rock, worked Robertson to a 2-2 count. On the next pitch, another sharp curve, the Browns' third baseman pulled a hard chopper up the first base line. I barely had to move to field the ball, but hesitated a moment after snagging it in my mitt. My instinct was to throw to first after fielding a grounder; on this play, I had to remind myself that I *was* the first baseman. I simply ran a few feet to step on the bag for the out.

Next up was the bottom of the Browns' batting order, pitcher Hub Pruett. I had gotten to know Pruett pretty well during his rookie season last year. The crafty left-hander had three unusual traits for a big-league pitcher: He was an aspiring medical doctor, the strongest language he ever used was "shucks," and he practically owned Babe Ruth when the Babe came to bat against him. Pruett's season record was only seven wins and seven losses, but he chalked up one statistic that any other American League pitcher would envy: Pruett struck out

Ruth ten of the first thirteen times he faced the slugger.

Although Hub Pruett had some pitching success against the Babe, he rarely succeeded as a hitter against anyone. Pruett was even more hopeless at the plate than most pitchers, and demonstrated that on his first swing against Jones. He dribbled a weak roller that was little more than a bunt up the first base line. I raced in, scooped up the ball, and got Pruett out on a swipe tag as he ran past me.

With two out, and nobody on, hard-hitting lead-off man Jack Tobin came up—another left-handed hitter. I caught on to what Miller Huggins had had in mind. Three lefties in a row were batting against a right-handed pitcher with a sharp-breaking curveball. They were likely to be pulling the ball to first. Huggins didn't need a tall first basemen to stretch for throws; he needed a good glove man—and he'd chosen me.

Huggins' strategy was nearly blown when Jones offered up a fastball for his first pitch. Tobin certainly pulled it, lifting a towering drive that seemed destined for the right field bleachers. Fortunately, the ball hooked into foul territory for a long, loud strike. Having learned his lesson, Jones went back to the curveball that he'd been throwing so well. Tobin got around solidly on this one, too, but he launched it on a lower trajectory—right at my head. Purely by reflex I got my glove up in time to snag it for the final out of the inning.

I loped to the dugout, savoring the cheers of the fans. I was pleased that I had handled my chances well and delighted that, after all these years, I could still learn something about the game. As I went to the bench, Aaron Ward jokingly called, "Hey, Rawlings! You mind letting us play a little baseball, too?"

Huggins, with some amusement in his eyes, said,

"Good going out there, Rawlings. You learned how to play first base awful quick."

I wanted to say, "Good managing," but simply nodded my thanks. He knew that I'd caught on to what he'd been thinking. Miller Huggins had just given me another lesson on baseball strategy. Or maybe it was tactics—I never was sure of the difference.

* * *

After the game, a 4-2 win that put us three and a half games ahead of the Athletics in the standings, I walked home feeling taller than any first baseman in baseball. On Webster Avenue, only a few blocks from our apartment, my elation plummeted.

A gruff voice behind me said, "You just don't listen to me, do you, Rawlings?" It was Leo Kessler; I didn't need to see his brooding dark eyes or the teardrop-shaped scar to recognize him.

I turned to face the hoodlum. "Is there some reason I should?"

"I already gave you one." Kessler patted his hip; I knew what the baggy pin-striped suit was concealing. "But I'll give you another, since you seem to need more convincing." He glowered at me from under a white Panama hat.

"What's that?"

He gestured toward the door of the Faris Pharmacy, only a few feet from where we stood. "Let's step inside and talk."

I glanced around. This stretch of Webster Avenue was a mix of small businesses and modest apartment buildings. There were people socializing on front stoops, shoppers going in and out of the stores, and half a block away several girls were playing a noisy game of jump rope. I didn't think Kessler would try anything out in the open. "I'm not going anywhere with you," I said firmly.

He bared his teeth in that wolf-like leer of his. "What—you afraid you're gonna get jumped? I don't need to set you up like that. I told you: I can get to you anytime, anyplace."

"Following me from the ballpark is no great accomplishment." I didn't know what he was up to, but I knew it wasn't going to be good. I figured if I failed to cooperate, it might at least throw him off his game a little.

Kessler's smile, fake as it was, vanished. "Hey! I got tipsters all over the five boroughs. There ain't a ballplayer or a jockey or a fighter does anything in this city that I don't know about."

That explained how he knew I'd be at Katie Day's, I thought. With Rothstein's penchant for fixing every kind of sporting event, it made sense that he kept tabs on anyone he might be able to bribe or blackmail into helping him.

I crossed my arms and stood my ground. "If you have something to say to me, you can say it right here. But make it quick."

Kessler was clearly taken aback. This encounter was not going at all as he had planned. "Look," he said. "You're misunderstanding me. See, we thought you could be scared off the Pollard thing, but we was wrong. So I got a little something for you from my boss." He reached into his jacket and I prepared to spring at him if a gun emerged. With two fingers, he pulled a thick manila envelope partway out of an inside pocket, just enough for me to see. "Your salary ain't much," he went on. "We figure we could help you out with that—give you a little bonus, you might say. And all you need to do to earn it is nothin'." He eyed me meaningfully. "And I mean absolutely *nothin'*. If you take this, and go poking into

Spats Pollard again, we'll take a refund outta your dead hide." Baring his teeth again, he added, "I don't expect you want me to hand this over to you in front of the whole world to see. You pick a place, we'll step inside, and you'll find yourself with a nice chunk of pocket money."

I didn't budge. "You tell Arnold Rothstein I don't need his money. And if anything does happen to me, friends of mine are going to come looking for *you*, Leo Kessler."

Mentioning those names was like a one-two punch to Kessler's gut. He stammered, "Have it your way... I was just relaying the offer... But if you don't want..." Kessler made sure the envelope was tucked back securely in his pocket and began inching backwards. "We'll be seeing each other again." He tugged down his hat, turned, and strutted away.

I had no doubt that we would meet again, but I figured it wouldn't be for a while. Kessler would want to find out how I knew his name and of his connection to Rothstein. Before he could do anything more, he'd have to find out how much I really knew and if I really had the "friends" that I'd mentioned. That should buy me some time—and I didn't think I'd need much more of it, because I felt I was close to a solution.

Chapter Sixteen

The one-week road trip was something of a respite for me. Away from New York, I thought over everything that had been going on this year, from my role on the Yankees, to the Spats Pollard murder, to my life with Margie.

While I was away, I telephoned Margie every day. During my absence she stayed in a bungalow at the Griffith studio, as we'd discussed, and she had seen nothing of Leo Kessler. I didn't expect that she would, since it would probably take him some time to sort through what I had said to him, but I was reassured to know she was safe.

In Washington, I not only had time to think, I had a quiet hotel room in which to do it. During our stay in the nation's capital, Babe Ruth barely spent a minute in the team's quarters. Miller Huggins could hardly punish him for breaking curfew, though, because on two of those nights Ruth stayed at the White House as a guest of the president. Ruth later told me about the poker game he'd played in the Yellow Oval Room. The card players included President Harding, Secretary of the Navy Edwin Denby, Attorney General Harry Daugherty, whose son Draper had briefly been named as a suspect in the Dot King murder, and several senators whose names Ruth couldn't remember. As they played cards and smoked cigars, Mrs. Harding mixed cocktails for the men. It was no secret that Harding liked his whiskey, and the Babe told me that some of the president's best booze was confiscated bootleg liquor that had been diverted to the White House by the Treasury Department's Prohibition Unit.

During our three-game series against the Athletics, I did have to share a hotel room with Ruth. He never made it in exactly by curfew, but only missed it enough to irritate Huggins. He always arrived in time to get a good night's sleep, and he always came in sober. The Babe was keeping to his promise that he would devote himself to baseball this season. His batting average topped .350, he'd slammed ten home runs, and no one was telling him to change a thing. The two of us had a number of conversations in Philadelphia, mostly about baseball and how we were going to demolish the rest of the American League this year.

I also asked Ruth again about making the movie for Tom Van Dusen. He agreed that he would sign a contract with the Griffith Studio but wouldn't do any filming until the baseball season was over. His overriding priority was to lead the New York Yankees to the team's first world's championship. I was delighted to hear him so optimistic and so dedicated.

I let Margie know about the Babe's answer so that she could relay it to Van Dusen. She was happy at the news and grateful that I'd spoken to him. There was more that I had to tell her, and I hoped it would make her even happier, but it would have to wait until the team returned to New York.

By the time the Yankees did pull into Pennsylvania Station again, the entire ball club was riding high. We had extended our lead in the standings, and confidence was growing that we would make it to the World Series. It seemed to me that everything was going as well as could be—except for that nagging problem of the dead Spats Pollard and the live Leo Kessler.

Early in the morning of my first full day back home, Karl Landfors telephoned and said he thought he could help with my predicament. "I want you to meet somebody," he said. "He might be able to provide some information."

"Another gangster?" I asked.

"Oh, much better than that," Landfors replied smugly. "A writer!"

* * *

In the afternoon, with no game scheduled, I walked beside Karl Landfors through a light, chilly drizzle down Broadway toward the southern tip of Manhattan. Both of us were in good moods, although I worked hard not to reveal the reason for mine. As much as I wanted to share my news with Landfors, I knew I should wait for another time.

Landfors, for his part, was as exuberant as a little boy on his way to a county fair. The writer we were about to meet was evidently a hero to him, the kind of muckraking journalist Landfors himself aspired to be. According to Landfors, the man had been writing exposes since the 1890s, most notably a series in *Harper's Weekly* that uncovered election fraud by Tammany Hall and rampant police corruption. Those articles helped lead to an investigation by the state senate, the election of a reform mayor, and a house-cleaning of the New York City Police Department. It also led to a number of death threats directed at the man who revealed the extortion, bribery, and graft by which the city had been operating. Undaunted, he had continued to monitor the activities of police, politicians, and criminals over the years, and Landfors believed he could help me unravel a few matters with the Pollard case.

When Landfors had told me we were going to meet a writer, I'd initially wondered if we'd be visiting the squalid type of place where he'd been staying in Greenwich Village. It was a pleasant surprise when we arrived at a well-maintained home on Pearl Street in the Battery. The architecture of the house was of such an antiquated style that it might have been built by one of the more affluent of the early Dutch settlers who'd come to the island in the 1600s. The three-story structure was topped by a hipped roof with sloping sides and a railing around the top. Its yellow brick exterior featured subtle embellishments of granite and marble, with freshly painted black ironwork.

We were greeted at the door by a middle-aged housekeeper with a cheerful face and a welcoming demeanor. She led us through a wide hallway to a library at the rear of the home. From all that I could see, the furnishings were elegant but not ostentatious. Everything appeared comfortable, orderly, and meticulously clean.

When we reached the open door to the library, it occurred to me that Landfors had never mentioned the name of the man we'd come to see. He had been so busy regaling me with the famous writer's accomplishments, that he had omitted that piece of information.

The library was of modest size, its Sheraton style furniture was minimal, and the room was completely lacking in feminine touches. Floor-to-ceiling bookcases were built into three of its walls. Even that wasn't enough shelf space, for many volumes had to be wedged in horizontally atop other books. These weren't gilt-and-leather volumes displayed for decoration or to impress visitors; these had the used appearance of books that had been read and studied.

Seated at a mahogany desk was a silver-haired man writing in a journal with a fat fountain pen. He had thick, old-fashioned Franz Josef whiskers that swooped down from his sideburns and over his lip. When he saw us, he removed a pair of small, wire-rimmed spectacles from his face and stood. His clothes were as quaint as his facial hair; he wore a pearl gray cutaway suit with a high stiff collar and a Windsor tie.

"You must be Mickey Rawlings," he said with an easy smile. "It's a pleasure to meet you. I'm Marshall Webb." He was in his seventies, a good six feet tall, trim, and had a strong handshake. Except for the regal whiskers, he reminded me a bit of Connie Mack.

Like the room itself, Webb's manner was gracious if a bit formal. He greeted Karl Landfors like an old friend and asked the housekeeper to bring us coffee and tea. When she left, Landfors and I took chairs and Webb sat back down at his desk.

Looking directly at me with clear, intelligent eyes, Webb said, "Karl has explained your situation to me. I hope you don't mind him confiding in me; I assure you I can be discrete." When I said I'd be grateful for his advice, he asked, "What can I help you with?"

"Well, I think I'm getting close to figuring this out. But I'm not sure who I can go to about it. I'd like to pass it on to the police, but the detective who's supposed to be working the case seems determined to do absolutely nothing. That has me stymied, and it makes me suspicious. I can't imagine a police officer intentionally letting a murder go unsolved unless he's getting paid to look the other way."

Webb mulled that over for a moment before answering. "He could be an honest cop who's simply handcuffed, so to speak."

"How so?"

"The murdered man was a bootlegger, correct? With underworld ties?"

"Yes," I answered. "There's no doubt about that."

"Illegal liquor is a big business in New York—and everyone gets a share." Webb toyed with the fountain pen as he proceeded to explain. "In order to avoid police raids and remain in operation, a speakeasy in this city typically pays a hundred dollars a week to the local precinct captain. Bootlegging is considered a service instead of a real crime, so the police generally have no qualms about taking their cut—after all, bootleggers have 'customers,' not 'victims.' " He laid the fountain pen on the journal. "The problem comes when there's a disagreement between bootleggers. Since their business is illegal, they can't take their disputes to court. So they settle their problems with guns and knives and bombs. Investigating the violence can present a quandary for the police: How do they go after someone who is paying them graft? Even if a particular officer isn't the recipient, his superiors might be, so he's stymied."

The housekeeper brought us the drinks and a plate of scones. Webb and I opted for coffee, while Landfors accepted a cup of tea.

When we were left alone again, Webb asked me, "What's the name of this detective?"

"Jim Luntz, Forty-fourth precinct."

He jotted a note. "I'll make some inquiries. I still have some connections."

Landfors gushed like a baseball fan talking about his favorite ballplayer's heroics, "There's nothing Marshall Webb can't find out—especially when it comes to police corruption. After his *Harper's Weekly* series was published, so many police were under indictment that the city had to cancel the annual police parade!"

Webb smiled, laugh lines crinkling the corners of his eyes. "To be fair, Teddy Roosevelt was responsible for canceling that parade—1895, it was, the year he became police commissioner." With an approving nod, he added, "T. R. did a fine job cleaning up the department." He spread his long-fingered hands. "But, of course, corruption is an evil that's never kept in check for very long."

"Speaking of evil," I said, "another question I have is whether or not Arnold Rothstein is involved. A couple of the men I've encountered in this case have connections to him."

"*Rothstein*," repeated Webb, almost choking on the name. He ran a finger over his whiskers as if trying to comb Arnold Rothstein out of them. "If there's a major crime in this city, there's a good chance he's involved—but never at the street level. Rothstein is a financier and a mentor to up-and-coming criminals. They call him 'The Brain.' Part of his genius is that his connections go far beyond the usual gangs, who limit their memberships to their own ethnic groups. Rothstein takes in Jews, Italians, Irish—anybody who can make money for him. The only color he sees is green. He'll provide financing for all sorts of enterprises, and he'll give orders for his henchman to carry out, but you won't see him directly involved in street crimes."

Landfors put his tea cup on the saucer he'd been balancing on his knee. "I have a theory," he said. "What about Jacob Ruppert? With Prohibition in effect, Ruppert no longer has an outlet for his brewery. Perhaps he went into partnership with some bootleggers—they're selling the beer right in his ballpark."

It didn't sound like a particularly well-considered theory to me. Landfors simply had a natural suspicion of any wealthy boss or owner. On the other hand, the idea wasn't impossible.

Webb gave Landfors the courtesy of appearing to consider the notion carefully. "Jacob Ruppert was quite active campaigning against Prohibition," he said. "And then he lobbied for increasing the permitted alcohol content in near beer. But as far as I know, he was open and aboveboard in all those efforts—and when they failed, he complied with the new law. Besides, the breweries have converted to making malt syrup now, and they're doing quite a good business with the new product." Malt syrup, perfectly legal, was used to make homebrewed beer.

Landfors appeared disappointed. He comforted himself with a scone and a sip of tea.

A hallway clock chimed the hour. Webb smiled and said, "I'm sorry I can't speak with you longer. I promised my wife I'd help her at Colden House—it's a shelter she runs not far from here. There's always something that needs attention." He didn't sound at all reluctant to go, and he spoke lovingly of his wife as he briefly told us about her work at the women's shelter.

Landfors and I stood and thanked him for his time.

"I promise I'll look into these matters," Webb said to me. "Can I contact you through Karl?"

"That would be best," I said. "I have to go on the

road again soon."

"Well, gentlemen," said Webb, adjusting the perfectly tied knot of his tie. "Feel free to stay and enjoy your tea and coffee. But I'm off to see Rebecca."

I noticed there was an eager glint in his eyes like a young suitor courting his first sweetheart. It was touching to see someone of his age so obviously still in love. I hoped Margie and I would be like that.

* * *

That night, I put into action the plan I'd been concocting for more than a week. I'd gone over it a hundred times, and revised it a hundred more. By now, I had every detail worked out to perfection—in my imagination, at least.

The evening started well. When Margie got home from work, I surprised her by telling her that we were going to have a night out. It would be our first since we'd been to the Club Durant. She dressed for the occasion in a stylish golden frock with white embroidery and a scoop collar that I knew would be a distraction for me. I donned a suit that I knew she liked; it took several attempts to knot the tie, however, since my fingers were feeling about as nimble as stone.

I kept our destination a secret, even whispering it to the taxi cab driver so she wouldn't hear. The trip took more than an hour, and the taxi meter ticked off quite a fare, but this was a special night and well worth the cost.

When the cab turned into the sandy drive of the Sea Dip Hotel on Coney Island, Margie exclaimed, "What a sweet idea!"

"I thought you might like it," I said, my voice trailing as I saw the condition of the place. The hotel hadn't aged well over the past decade, and hardly looked as I remembered. Several windows were boarded over, there was little paint remaining on the weathered exterior, and a flag flying from a rooftop turret was in tatters.

Margie went on, "The place where we first met. Well, not 'met' because we met at the Vitagraph. But where we first had dinner. And danced." She laughed. "*Tried* to dance." For some reason, she sounded as flustered as I felt. Was my nervousness contagious, or did she suspect something?

After paying the cab driver, we went up the creaking porch and found that the rundown lobby was nearly empty. I began to wonder if the place was still in operation, and was disappointed that the evening I had envisioned wasn't taken shape as I had hoped. The Sea Dip Hotel had once been one of the jewels of Coney Island, with a sumptuous dining room and first-rate service. Now it had deteriorated to just another seaside ghost of a place that had once been full of life. I was considering a change of venue, but Margie remained enthusiastic, so we went inside. An elderly clerk, incongruously dressed in a formal morning coat with striped trousers, was absorbed in a newspaper. I asked him if the dining room was still serving dinner.

He seemed surprised at the question. "Oh, yes sir. Finest food on the island."

I doubted that claim, but we let him show us to a table. The dining hall was large, which made the lack of customers all the more noticeable—and depressing. Only four other tables were occupied in a place that could fit a hundred diners. Where a full dance band had once played, there was now a just a sleepy-eyed violinist scratching out a mournful tune for a couple who tipped him to go away. The chandelier that had once sparkled with light was swathed in cobwebs and there was a rancid smell of spoiled food that mingled unpleasantly with smell of the ocean outside the open windows.

We were about to sit down when I noticed our tablecloth had a large red wine stain and crumbs from a previous meal. "Maybe we should go someplace else," I suggested. I did not want this night to be anything less than perfect.

"This will do fine," Margie insisted. "We'll have a lovely evening here. It's always going to be a special place for me."

The clerk, who doubled as a waiter, moved to hold Margie's chair but I edged him out of the way to do it myself. He lit a wilted candle, which did add a romantic touch, and said, "I'll be right back with your menus."

"No need," I answered. "We know what we want."

"Our fare might be a bit limited, I'm afraid," he said. "We don't have much of a kitchen staff on duty tonight."

"They won't have to do any cooking," I replied. "All we want is fresh oysters and a bottle of your best champagne."

Margie smiled with delight.

The waiter promised to see what he could do, but cautioned that their wine supply was as limited as their dinner selections.

When he left, Margie and I tried to make small talk, but we kept stumbling over our words. I tried to remember my script and replay it in my mind like a movie reel, but it was more like a single frame that had gotten stuck in the projector and melted away. I did the best I could, but was pretty sure I said some things that made no sense at all. And I wasn't certain what Margie was saying. All I knew was that she looked radiant and had a contented expression on her face.

The waiter returned with a dusty bottle. "Veuve Clicquot," he announced proudly. "Pre-war. Our very best, and we only have a few bottles left in the cellar. But it *is* a bit pricey, sir. If you—"

"It will do nicely," I said. Tonight, money didn't matter.

With a tremulous hand, he filled two champagne flutes and left.

When I lifted my glass to make a toast, I noticed that my hand was shaking a bit, too. "To us," I said, my voice cracking slightly.

"To us," Margie responded in little more than a whisper. We clinked glasses and each took a sip. The champagne was no disappointment; it tasted better than any I'd ever had.

I quickly reviewed in my mind what I had planned to say and took a deep breath. My mouth suddenly went dry and I drank a little more champagne to wet it. Margie sat quiet and expectant.

Just as I was about to speak, the strolling violinist appeared at my elbow. He began playing something classical and out of tune. I gave him a generous tip, hoping he'd leave. I must have tipped too well, for he began working the bow with additional energy. He seemed determined to give us a complete concert. I began trying to indicate with my eyes, then my head, for him to go away. Eventually he finished, bowed low, and went to sit in a chair near a broken window.

Margie and I smiled at each other, took another sip from our glasses, and I again prepared to speak. As soon as I opened mouth, the waiter came by with our oysters. Were we never to be left alone?

I squirmed impatiently as he told us how fine the oysters were and where they had been harvested. He refilled our glasses and made suggestions for dessert afterward. I was tempted to stab him with my fork to drive him away.

As soon as he left, I quickly glanced about to be sure no one else might interrupt us and blurted to Margie, "There's something I wanted to tell you. *Ask* you, I mean."

"What is it?" Margie murmured invitingly.

Now that I had my chance to speak, I couldn't remember the words that I'd so carefully composed. "Well, it's like this…" I halted when I realized those weren't the words I had planned to open with. What the hell, I decided. I would just have to tell her what was on my mind.

"Yes?" Margie prompted in a soft voice.

I took one more quick gulp of champagne, then forced myself to speak as best I could. "You see, I've been very wrong about something: I've always thought that baseball was the most important thing in the world to me. But it isn't. *You're* the most important thing in my life." I had a pang of worry that I shouldn't have referred to her as a "thing," but quickly went on, "I love you, and I want to keep you in my life forever."

Margie's eyes welled with tears, and I don't think I'd ever seen so much happiness in her smile.

On impulse, I slid out of my chair and got on one knee next to hers. I took Margie's hand in mine and discovered that we were both trembling. It was a long moment before I could say the rest. I'd phrased it so many ways, so poetically, but none of those compositions came to mind. All I could do was come right to the point. "Would you marry me?"

She didn't keep me in suspense. "You know I will." There was a mix of laughter and sobbing in her voice.

I stood, and Margie got to her feet with me. We embraced and kissed, oblivious to anyone else in the room.

The violinist was soon a few feet from us again. He began to play an easy waltz with every note in tune. Margie and I started to sway, then the swaying turned into dancing. We waltzed across the floor together in perfect step.

Chapter Seventeen

It was strange, but now that I had a whole new future ahead of me with Margie, other matters seemed considerably less important and not nearly as exhilarating. Even baseball, my lifelong love, was no longer uppermost in my heart.

Prior to the first game after Margie accepted my proposal, it was something of a struggle for me to get through batting practice. This was a pregame ritual that I'd always looked forward to, especially since I so seldom had a chance to hit once the umpire called "Play ball!" Now I had difficulty hitting the easy pitches offered up by Carl Bilancione. My mind was elsewhere and my insides were roiling with a joy that threw off my timing and had me swinging wildly.

At least I knew that baseball would come back to me. In time, I would settle down and again be able to concentrate on playing to the best of my ability. One thing that I did *not* want to coming back to me was the problem of Spats Pollard's murder. The threat from Leo Kessler hung over both Margie and me, and I wasn't going to live with that. I needed to get the entire situation resolved. Fortunately, I felt I was close to doing so.

Immediately after the game, a 2-0 shutout of Cleveland that I watched from the bench, I met with Andrew Vey. Ed Barrow was away from the stadium, scouting some hot new prospect, so Vey and I had his office to ourselves. A lot of assistants would probably make themselves comfortable in their bosses' chairs, and maybe put their feet up on the desks, but Vey had too much respect for Barrow to do that. The two of us instead sat at a side table under a portrait of Ulysses S. Grant, in whose honor Barrow had been given the middle name "Grant."

I had several reasons for speaking with Vey, not the least of which was to demonstrate that I was still working on the case. I hadn't been playing much lately, so this task might be the only thing that was keeping me on the team's roster.

I first filled him in on my most recent encounter with Leo Kessler on Webster Avenue. I wanted to be completely upfront about Kessler's attempt to bribe me. That way, if it ever came up later, the Yankees would realize I hadn't been concealing anything from them. I also wanted them to know that I had emphatically turned it down.

As I told him about Kessler, Vey kneaded his big misshapen hands and had a look in his eyes that indicated he would like to get those hands around Leo Kessler's neck someday. It occurred to me that Vey hadn't been fidgeting in his clothes as I'd seen him do in the past. I finally noticed that he was wearing a suit of blue seersucker that fit him perfectly and a butterfly bowtie that was an appropriate size for his thick neck. A triangle of white silk handkerchief poked up from his jacket pocket.

Vey realized that I'd been studying his sartorial transformation. "My fiancée," he explained sheepishly. "She took me shopping and picked out these clothes for me—said I needed to dress better."

"Looks great," I said. "I didn't know you were engaged. Congratulations." He nodded his thanks, and I added impulsively, "I have one, too."

"One what?"

"A fiancée." It was the first time I'd used the word to describe Margie. I wouldn't be able to use it for long, since we'd agreed to be married as soon as possible.

"Congratulations to you, too! When's the wedding?"

"No date yet. We just got engaged." The only other person I'd told was Karl Landfors. I didn't know why I had just made Andrew Vey the second recipient of the news, other than I was bursting to share it.

I then went on to where matters stood on the Spats Pollard murder. "So far," I said, "I don't think there's anything that can reflect badly on the Yankees. Pollard was *trying* to line up customers for his bootleg booze, but didn't seem to have any success. I think he was working from somebody else's customer list, maybe trying to steal them away. I'd say Pollard had no connection to Babe Ruth at all." I was sure that was the club's main concern, since Ruth got most of the team's publicity.

"Good," said Vey, nodding. "Mr. Barrow will be happy to hear that. But why was Pollard killed? Who put him in that wall?"

"I'm getting close to answers on those," I said with a confidence that I truly felt. "And I think you can help— if you're willing."

He frowned slightly. "How?"

"There are six concession stands, right?"

"Yes. And the main restaurant downstairs."

"But it's only the stands that are rented out. Can you find out who has the concession on each one of them?"

Vey considered my request. I was sure he was debating whether or not Barrow would approve. "Yes," he decided. "You know, we don't really control them. They rent the space and run their own businesses. You think it's important?"

With a man found dead in one stand, and another concessionaire nearly beaten to death, how could it not be?

* * *

Tillinghast L'Hommedieu Huston grew up badly in need of a nickname. As a young man, he earned one— "Cap"—by serving as a Captain of Engineers in the war with Spain. Huston remained in Cuba for several years after the war, building the fortune that enabled him to purchase the Yankees with Jacob Ruppert in 1915. During the Great War, Huston served his country again, this time with the Sixteenth Engineers; he achieved the rank of Lieutenant Colonel, but was still popularly known as "Cap."

Cap Huston's engineering experience made him the logical choice to direct the construction of Yankee Stadium, and he went about it as if launching another military campaign. He coordinated the architects, engineers, and construction workers, and completed the ballpark in a timeframe that most thought impossible. Huston's drive and dedication got the stadium built in less than a year. His success in constructing the team's new home did nothing, however, to repair his rift with Ruppert. The relationship between the two Colonels had deteriorated to the point where one of them had to go—

and it was no secret that Huston was the one who'd be leaving.

I knew that Jacob Ruppert was unlikely to approve of me meeting with his partner and enemy, but I needed information on the ballpark's construction. To save time, I decided to start with the man who was in charge. When I contacted him, Cap Huston agreed to meet with me at his favorite watering hole, the lobby of the Commodore Hotel.

The palatial hotel, named for "Commodore" Cornelius Vanderbilt, was part of Terminal City, a complex of luxurious hotels and offices connected to Grand Central Terminal. The Commodore had opened only a few years earlier, boasting a capacity of more than two thousand rooms and "The Most Beautiful Lobby in the World."

I was convinced of the truth of that claim when I walked into the lobby for the first time. It was a clean, open space with a glass roof and elegant archways. The lobby was designed to look like a Mediterranean courtyard, with a tile floor, hanging plants, wrought iron furniture, and alabaster urns. There was even a waterfall along one wall.

It was difficult to believe that such a tranquil place could be found in the busiest part of downtown Manhattan. It was also hard to imagine that this peaceful room had been the scene of a notorious temper tantrum by Cap Huston last October. After the Yankees lost the World Series to the Giants for the second year in a row, Huston went into a rage in this lobby, knocking glassware and bottles onto the floor and screaming that Miller Huggins had managed his last game for the club.

When told of the incident, Jacob Ruppert overruled his partner, stating that he would not fire a man who had led the team to two straight pennants. After this public disagreement, the partnership was doomed and all that remained was to finalize the details for severing the relationship. The two men were so different in personality and background that perhaps it was inevitable they would have to part.

The aristocratic Jacob Ruppert was born into wealth and high society, and was attended by a retinue of servants. His political connections helped him to win four elections to the United States Congress. A lifelong bachelor, Ruppert collected oil paintings and Chinese porcelain, and maintained an exotic menagerie at his country estate in Garrison, New York. He owned a yacht, dabbled in horses, drank little except his own beer, and generally led a life free from scandal.

Cap Huston was a gregarious self-made man who had served in two wars, enjoyed hunting at his lodge in Georgia, and had a number drinking companions that included Babe Ruth, Brooklyn manager Wilbert Robinson, Red Sox owner Harry Frazee, and most of the newspaper writers in New York. He was as slovenly in appearance as Ruppert was fastidious, often wearing the same suit several days a week. His simple tastes included food and beer, and lots of both, making him considerably overweight.

I found Huston sitting near one of the lobby's archways, in a massive chair of carved walnut and tooled leather. A whiskey glass and a half-filled crystal decanter were on a side table next to him, and he was speaking to a bellman about getting a sandwich. When Huston dismissed the bellman, he noticed my presence, flashed a ready smile, and heaved his bulk off the chair, staggering a little as he did so.

"Rawlings," he said, slurring the "s" and pumping my hand. "Good to finally meet you." His tie was stained, the lenses of his gold-rimmed spectacles were smudged, and it looked as if he'd slept in his sack suit. The fifty-five-year-old Huston had a face that could have been formed of putty and his hair had receded almost halfway up his head.

"I appreciate you seeing me, Colonel."

" 'Cap' will do," he said, lowering himself into the seat again. He motioned for me to pull up one of the nearby wrought iron chairs, and said, "You were in the war, too, weren't you?"

I removed my straw boater and sat down. "Yes, sir, but only for a few months before the Armistice."

"It doesn't matter for how long. You served your country, and I respect that." He drank a slug of whiskey. "Say, I just ordered lunch, and I'd be happy to get you some, too."

"That's very kind of you, but I'll have to be getting to the ballpark soon, and don't want to take up any more of your time than I have to." I also figured that since the man was already a little tipsy, I'd better talk to him while he was still relatively clear-headed.

He nodded and took another swallow from his glass. Before I could ask anything of him, Huston suddenly turned to me and demanded, "What do you think of Miller Huggins?"

I answered without reservation. "He's about the best manager I've ever played for."

Huston raised an eyebrow. "Are you aware that I never liked him?"

"Yes, I've heard that." Huston and Ruppert had feuded over the manager for years and the World Series quarrel was merely the latest.

"You want some kind of favor from me, don't you?" he asked.

"Yes…"

"Then don't you think you'd stand a better chance if you agreed with me about Huggins?"

"Maybe. But you asked me a question and I gave you my honest opinion. If that means you won't help me, I'm sorry, but I told you the truth."

"Hmm. At least you have the guts to disagree with me to my face." He shifted in his seat. "Ruppert stabbed me in the back when he hired Huggins. I wanted Wilbert Robinson for the job, so Ruppert waited until I was overseas in the war. Then he went and signed that little runt." Robinson was a pretty good manager, I thought, but it was common knowledge that his main qualification as far as Huston was concerned was that the two men were buddies.

I didn't want to debate the merits of Miller Huggins with Huston, so I moved on to my reason for meeting with him. "I understand you oversaw construction of the new ballpark," I said.

"I did," he answered proudly. "You know, I do believe Yankee Stadium is going to last as a monument for the ages."

"It's an incredible accomplishment," I said. "Not only what you built, but how fast you got it done."

Huston's sandwich arrived, served on a silver tray along with fried potatoes and a pile of cole slaw. He again offered to buy me lunch, too. When I politely declined, he forked some potatoes in his mouth before answering. "Well, I knew my time with the team was almost over, so I wanted to make a contribution that people would remember me by. Players and managers will come and go, and there'll be good years and bad, but through it all, Yankee Stadium will stand—and people will remember that I'm the man who built it."

"They will," I agreed. "But something happened in the stadium at the start of the season—and if people found out, it might give the stadium some bad publicity."

"What is it?" he demanded, his eyes wide.

"They found the body of a bootlegger walled in one of the refreshment stands."

From the shocked expression on his face, I was sure this was the first he'd heard of it. It didn't surprise me that he had been kept in the dark; Jacob Ruppert rarely communicated anything to his partner any more. "I don't believe it!" Huston finally gasped.

I gave him a quick rundown on what had happened, and went on, "The body was supposedly found because some repairs had to be made to the plumbing. I'd like to check if that was true—if there were really repairs scheduled."

Huston was still in a fog over the news. He reached for his whiskey glass before answering, "It's possible. Everything was on a tight schedule and some things had to be fixed or altered."

"Could you tell me who I might check with to see if that's what really happened?"

"Certainly. White Construction was the general contractor. I'll make a couple of phone calls and tell them to give you any information you need. You go to their office tomorrow morning and I'm sure they'll cooperate with you." He shook his head. "I can't believe something like this could happen in my ballpark."

I thanked him for seeing me and got up to leave.

He frowned and nodded a goodbye. When I was a few steps away, he called after me, "What do your teammates think—will the Yankees finally go all the way this year?"

"We're sure of it," I answered. Nothing was "sure" in

baseball, but that was how we all felt.

"I'll look forward to seeing it happen." Huston smiled wanly. "But by then I'll probably have to buy a ticket."

* * *

Cap Huston might have been on his way out as far as running the ball club, but the construction workers who had worked for him in putting up Yankee Stadium still considered him the boss. They also clearly held him in high esteem.

I met with three men in the downtown office of the White Construction Company the next morning, and they all spoke with admiration of Huston's engineering skills and hands-on leadership. We sat around a large work table covered with blueprints and building plans. One of the men was some kind of foreman, dressed in a soft-collar shirt and serge trousers. The other two were a plumber and a plasterer, both of them in faded denim pants and flannel shirts. Prior to discussing the reason I had come, all three gave testimonials as to what a "regular guy" and "helluva leader" Cap Huston was.

Huston had already given them a brief account of my interest in the concession stand, and I elaborated while the men paid close attention. "I was told," I said, "that plumbing repairs had to be done and that's why you had to break into the wall."

The foreman shook his head. "I don't understand. We didn't have *any* repairs scheduled in that area. Look, here's the log." Thanks to Cap Huston's telephone calls, the men had come prepared with all the relevant paperwork for me to review.

I looked over a thick book filled with work orders and job descriptions as if it made sense to me. "Well, I was told that was why you had to break into the wall," I said again. I didn't mention that it was Joe Zegarra who had given me that story.

The foreman opened another ledger. "No, there was a report of a leak in the stand's storage room. By"—he struggled to read the name—"somebody named *Zeegar*, it looks like."

"Zegarra," I said, "He's the one leasing the stand."

The plumber said in a gravelly voice, "I'm the one who checked it out. I knew it was nonsense—the pipes don't even run through that wall. There was a pool of water on the floor, but it wasn't from no leak. To me, it looked like a spill so I mopped it up. The plaster job was pretty bad, though, and Zegarra insisted it was from water damage."

"I told you I didn't do that job," the plasterer said defensively. "I'll put my work up against anybody in this city."

"We all know you do good work," said the foreman in a placating tone. "Nobody's saying you don't."

The plumber went on, "Anyway, Zegarra said the pipes had to be leaking from someplace, and then he went on a rant about how it could ruin his business if we didn't fix the problem. Like I said, I knew it was a crock, but I busted through the wall just to shut him up. I figured the wall had to be replastered anyway, since it was so sloppy. That's when I found the body."

"And look at the job I did fixing it," said the plasterer. "That wall is going to last a thousand years!" He folded his arms across his chest and looked at each one of us as if daring anyone to contradict him."

I asked the plumber, "Did Zegarra say anything any more about the leak? Did he have you check the pipes?"

"No," he answered. "Come to think of it, as soon as we broke into the wall, he shut up. At first he was all agitated saying water damage would ruin his place. Then he wasn't worried anymore. In fact, he walked away like he didn't have a care in the world." He frowned. "Why do you think he did that?"

I had a pretty good idea, but I didn't share it with them.

Chapter Eighteen

I found the rotund Joe Zegarra, dressed in his clean white concessionaire's uniform, at a refreshment stand on the first base side of the park a couple of hours before game time. He stood, arms akimbo, watching his nephews lug boxes of candy and popcorn, what Zegarra had dismissed as "the nickel stuff," out of the stand's storage room.

This concession stand was equipped the same as the others in the stadium, with an enameled refrigerator, sink, and grill. It was also built on the same design, with a baseball chandelier hanging above a long wooden counter. Behind that counter was where the stand's previous owner had been found beaten nearly to death. Piled on top of it now were several cases of *Fervo*, the falsely labeled "cereal beverage" that actually contained Joe Zegarra's beer.

"I see you got yourself another place," I said to Zegarra. Andrew Vey had checked into the concessions for me and found that Zegarra now had the leases on half of the stadium's refreshment stands.

The pudgy old man looked at me with surprise evident on his face. "Business has been good," he said. "And when business is good, yuh expand." He scratched at his bald dome, probably trying to figure out what I was doing here.

"What if you want to expand and no place is available?" I asked.

Zegarra hiked up his droopy pants and leaned against the counter. "Yuh negotiate," he answered with a sly smile, revealing his dark yellow teeth.

"And if that doesn't work, you beat up the competition?"

Still smiling, but with no humor in it, he said, "There's all kinds of ways to negotiate."

"Sure hope you don't find any bodies in *this* place."

Zegarra glanced at his laboring nephews. "How 'bout we move away from here if yuh wanna talk," he suggested.

When I agreed, he yelled a warning to them that they had better keep working, and the two of us began walking slowly together along the concourse. Although I strongly suspected that Zegarra was behind some of the violence that had occurred, I had no fear of him doing anything himself. The way he wheezed and wobbled with every step, I was sure he lacked the energy to attack me.

Once we were away from the stand, Zegarra said, "I dunno what to make of yuh. Yer a nosy fellah, but I know it's on account of Mr. Barrow wantin' yuh to do this investigatin'."

"That's true," I replied. "If it was up to me, I'd just as soon forget about it and play baseball. I really don't care a damn about Spats Pollard or who owns what concession stand or what they did to get it."

"That's kinda what I figure," said Zegarra. "So I think

the question is: How do we get yuh to forget about it?" He scratched his big nose. "Maybe if I give yuh a little... let's call it a 'present.' Like I said, my business has been good and I'll bet the Yankees ain't payin' you nothin' like what Ruth gets."

That was certainly true, but I wasn't at all tempted by Zegarra's offer. "Hell, I'd drop this for free," I said. "But what Mr. Ruppert and Mr. Barrow want from me is to find out what happened to Spats Pollard. Until I can give them an answer on that, I'm stuck with it. And you're stuck with me poking into your business."

Our conversation ceased briefly while a couple of delivery men passed near us. They were pushing carts loaded with programs, pennants, and other merchandise that vendors would soon be selling to thousands of fans throughout the stadium.

When the delivery men were out of earshot, Zegarra demanded with some irritation, "So how's this *my* problem anyways? I didn't have nothin' to do with Pollard gettin' killed. He just happened to turn up in my place."

"Oh, you had something to do with it," I said. "But you didn't actually kill him."

Zegarra's deep-set eyes turned on me sharply and his chins quivered. "You think you know somethin', smart guy?"

"You told me Pollard was found because they had to do some repairs to the plumbing. That's not what happened—I checked. You're the one who got them to break into the wall, claiming a leak that didn't exist. You *wanted* the body to be discovered."

"And why would I want somethin' like that?" He was studying me closely.

"Maybe Pollard's killer was some kind of threat to you,

too."

"Ain't nobody a threat to *me*," he said.

I went on, "Since you wanted Pollard's body found, I figure you didn't kill him—if you did, you'd have kept him sealed up. So I think you know who *did* kill him and you wanted him caught—either by the police or by the guys he works for."

"Huh?"

"Spats Pollard was supposed to have been killed two years ago, but the man who got the assignment let him get away. When Pollard came back to New York, the fellow who was supposed to kill him finally had to do it—otherwise he's in trouble himself."

"Why didn't he do the job the first time?"

"I don't know," I admitted. "Maybe they were friends. Or maybe he took a payoff from Pollard in exchange for letting him skip town." From what I'd been learning about gangsters, I had the impression that the primary motive for anything they did was money.

"Still don't see how *I* figure in all this," Zegarra grumbled. "I'm just a merchant."

"Yes, but your merchandise is illegal."

"Hey, it's what the people want."

"I agree," I said. "The problem is you need certain connections to run your kind of business. And partners. You have any partners, Joe?"

"Partners cut into the profits," he said.

"That's what it's all about, isn't it? Every one of you guys is trying to get everything you can for yourself while cutting out—or killing—anybody in your way."

Zegarra said, "I need to head back and keep an eye on the boys. Any time I ain't watchin', they go on break and start drinkin' the stock." We turned and began the return trip to his new concession stand.

I continued, "Spats Pollard was back in New York for a few months trying to get into the booze business, claiming he had a good source. But no one was buying. He needed a partner to distribute the booze. Somebody like you."

"You think Pollard and I was partners?" Zegarra chuckled. "Hell, he was just a dead man in a wall."

"There's a reason he was stashed in your place—so that you could control what happened afterward. Maybe the fellow who killed Pollard made himself another partner. That's a three-way split. After he kills Pollard, it's fifty-fifty. Then if he takes the fall for Pollard's murder, you have the whole business for yourself. It would be awful smart—you get rid of two partners without having to do any killing yourself."

We walked in silence for a while before Zegarra spoke again. "You say yer only interested in who killed Pollard, right? Not about my business?"

"That's right. I don't care what you sell, or who your partners are. As soon as I can satisfy Mr. Barrow, my job is done."

"And yuh got any ideas on who Pollard's killer might be?"

"Yes." I looked at him to gauge his reaction. "Leo Kessler. You know him?"

Zegarra's soft fleshly face turned hard. "Heard of 'im. Why Kessler?"

I didn't want to reveal to Zegarra everything that I knew or suspected. "I believe Kessler had the assignment two years ago to kill Pollard," I said. I'd also noticed that Kessler had contacted me after my previous meetings with Zegarra.

"So once you get this Kessler fellah, yer done?"

"That's it. Then it's all over." I hoped.

Chapter Nineteen

I had done all that I could for now. I hoped that I had successfully given Joe Zegarra the impression that if he gave up Leo Kessler, he would be free to continue his business without further interference. I simply had to wait and let Zegarra make his decision. Considering the cutthroat business practices of those in his profession, I was pretty sure it would be an easy one for him to reach.

Meanwhile, I had a much happier matter to occupy me. In the late afternoon, I visited the Bronx Office of the City Clerk in Borough Hall. Margie and I had decided to get married in a civil ceremony before I had to leave on the long road trip. Although we'd been together for years, we were now so eager to be married that we didn't want to wait one more hour than necessary. I was discouraged to learn at the City Clerk's office that we would have to wait a full twenty-four hours from the time we got the license until we could return to be legally wed.

I walked home along Third Avenue, imagining the wedding and thinking how pleased Margie would be that I'd gotten all the forms we needed to become husband

and wife. There were few pedestrians on this stretch of the street, but fairly heavy automobile traffic, and trains rumbled on the Third Avenue el overhead.

Lost in a reverie about my upcoming marriage, I was barely aware of the dark green Packard that pulled to the curb ahead of me. I didn't notice it until three men hopped out of the car. One of them was Leo Kessler, who quickly positioned himself a few feet in front of me. He wore an outfit similar to the one I'd seen him in last time, a baggy pin-striped suit with the same white Panama hat crowning his dark hair.

The other two men moved into place, one further up the sidewalk and one behind me, to block any attempt I might make to flee. They were also dressed in the standard gangster uniform, except with oversized woolen flat caps. From their less flashy attire, I took them to be of lower rank than Kessler, and from their physiques I assumed their job was to provide additional muscle.

Kessler took a step closer to me. He fixed me in a deadly glare; even the scar below his left eye looked angry. He smiled his malevolent grin and mumbled so that only I could hear, "You shoulda took the money, you stupid sonofabitch."

"What do you want?" I tried to sound defiant, but was shaken by the realization that Joe Zegarra had shattered my plan. I had expected that Zegarra would give up Leo Kessler. Apparently he'd decided to let Kessler get rid of me instead.

The hoodlum answered smoothly, "I want you to come for a ride with me."

"I'm not going anywhere with you." I glanced at Kessler's accomplices. Each of them already had a hand inside his jacket, and I knew what they were carrying. If I tried to run, they wouldn't have to bother trying to catch me—a bullet would bring me down quite effectively."

Kessler shook his head. "You're mistaken there. See, you don't got a choice in the matter. You had your chances, but you wouldn't stay out of it. I just got to give the word to my boys and you're in the car whether you wanna be or not."

"You think you can grab somebody off the street with nobody noticing? Or shoot me and not have the cops come running?"

"I *know* we can. Look around." He craned his own neck, making a show of looking here and there. "You see somebody who's gonna come save you?" He shook his head again. "Hell, we'll be driving away with you before anyone notices. Besides, this is New York—anybody who *does* notice is gonna look the other way."

I glanced around. We were in the shadow of the el, with few people nearby and noisy automobiles moving quickly past. The gangster was right; the only people interested in me were Kessler and the two men blocking my escape.

The thought flashed through my mind that if I couldn't make it past them, maybe I had a chance by running directly at Kessler; his "boys" would be unlikely to shoot with him in the line of fire. Then once by Kessler, I could hop on the running board of a passing car or truck. It wasn't much of a plan, but seemed my only chance. If I got into Kessler's Packard, I was pretty sure I'd never been seen again—until perhaps decades from now when a building would be torn down and I'd be found embedded in the concrete.

Kessler said, "You gonna get in the car peaceful now? Or do I gotta tell my boys to put you in the hard way?"

Keep him talking, I told myself, and be ready for a chance to rush him. "Where are we going?" I asked.

"Still asking questions, huh? That's what got you in trouble in the first place."

I was watching him like a base runner studying a pitcher's pick-off motion to see when he could steal. "You mean because I was asking about Spats Pollard?" I tensed, poised to make my move as soon as Kessler dropped his guard a little.

Leo Kessler didn't answer my last question and I noticed he was looking past me. I looked back to see Whitey and a smaller, craggy-faced man coming toward us. A Model T was idling at the curb while its driver remained behind the wheel.

Although the weather was warm, Whitey wore the same large overcoat that he had in the Museum of Natural History. I'd seen enough gangsters in the past couple of months to realize that they wore loose-fitting suits in order to conceal their firearms; Whitey's billowing coat was so big that he could hide an entire arsenal under it.

"Whitey," Kessler said, his wolfish smile broadening. "Glad you're here."

"There a problem?" Whitey asked. Although his pasty, pitted face was in the shade of his black fedora, there was no hiding its ugliness.

"This saphead might need a little persuasion to get in the car with us."

"The three of you can't handle him on your own?" Whitey chortled.

"Hey!" barked Kessler. "You remember who you're talking to. You work *under* me and don't you forget it!"

Smirking, Whitey answered, "Whatever you say, Leo."

"Good," said Kessler, ignoring the lack of sincerity in Whitey's reply. "Let's get him in the car."

Whitey repeated the order to the others, "Put him in

the car."

The two big men who'd arrived with Kessler slowly approached me. I thought I might be able to squeeze between them and make a break for it.

I sprang sideways, where the gap seemed largest. One of the men flung out an arm the size of a tree truck; it caught me in the throat and brought me up short. I gasped for breath as the thugs grabbed hold of my arms.

All I could do now was fight. I managed to break one arm free and drove an elbow hard into the stomach of the man to my right. It barely fazed him. I was about to launch a punch at the other hood, when my arm was back in a tight grip, pulled painfully behind me.

"Not him," said Whitey. He jerked his head toward Kessler.

The man next to Whitey spoke for the first time. "That comes straight from the boss," he said in a deep voice. With his rough-hewn face, he looked like he might be a veteran of quite a few street battles.

At hearing his words, I was immediately released and Leo Kessler was in their grasp. He struggled briefly, his pristine hat falling to the sidewalk. "Hey—what the hell—" he squawked.

"Been a change of plans," said Whitey. "Your services are no longer needed."

The men hustled the protesting Kessler into the back of the Packard. One of them picked up the fallen Panama hat and put it over Kessler's face to muffle his cries. In seconds, the car was around a corner and out of view. Kessler had been right, I realized; nobody had come to help him.

Until now, neither Whitey nor I had given any indication that we'd met before. After a long moment, I looked at him and asked, "What's going on?"

"My boss decided Kessler needed to go." Whitey had a smug grin. I recalled what he had said in the museum about always seeking a chance to move up. It looked like he'd gotten his promotion.

"Why?"

Whitey ordered his companion back to the Model T and waited until the two of us were alone before answering. "Let's call it 'dereliction of duty.' "

"Kessler is the one who was supposed to get rid of Spats Pollard two years ago, wasn't he?"

"You got it." Whitey nodded. "But Kessler got greedy. Turns out he let Pollard skip town in exchange for giving him every cent he had and everything he owned." That came as no great surprise; greed seemed to be what drove most of these men.

I was wondering where I stood in all this now, but was reluctant to ask. Instead, I said, "So when Pollard showed up in New York again, Kessler killed him to keep your boss from finding out he hadn't done the job the first time."

"That was part of it." Whitey hesitated. "We were trying to learn some more, but when we heard Kessler was gonna make a move on you today, we decided his time was up. There's some questions we just might not get any answers to now."

"You came here to save me?" I asked in disbelief.

"We ain't the cavalry," he said with a smile. "We came to make a deal. Under the circumstances, I'm expectin' you're agreeable."

"What deal?"

"Here's how it is," Whitey said. "After all that bad press my boss got over the 1919 World Series—completely unfounded, by the way—he don't want no more trouble over baseball players. So the deal is that I tell you what happened, and then you drop it."

"Go ahead," I said.

Whitey jammed his hands deep in his pockets. "Spats Pollard had the idea to sell beer in the ballpark. Joe Zegarra had a concession stand, so they became partners. Then Kessler cut himself in as a third partner figuring Pollard owed him. The thing is, with three partners, each one only gets a third of the profits. Zegarra convinced Kessler he couldn't risk letting Pollard live since he was supposed to have bumped him off two years ago. He also convinced Kessler the new park was the best place to hide the stiff—it wouldn't be found 'til everyone was long dead. So Kessler did the job on Pollard, and that was one partner down. But Zegarra double-crossed Kessler—he made sure the body was found. It was only a matter of time before Kessler would be nailed by the cops or by us, and that leaves Zegarra the sole owner." He gave me a look. "*You* getting into the middle of things just made it come to an end sooner."

His story was pretty much along the lines of what I had put together myself. "And it *is* the end for Kessler?"

Whitey shrugged. "When my boss gives an order it's supposed to be carried out. Kessler didn't do that, so…" After a moment, he continued, "So here's where it stands: Leo Kessler won't ever bother you no more, and you can tell your bosses what happened to Pollard. Of course, my boss's name stays out of it. And then everybody should be happy and life goes on."

I pondered the deal for only a second. Looking down at the marriage forms crumpled in my hand, I knew there were other things I wanted to do. It was case closed, as far as I was concerned.

I nodded my agreement. Whitey touched the tip of his fedora and ambled back to the waiting Model T.

*   *   *

The following day, I reported to Ed Barrow's office. Except for the improvement to the room's décor, the scene was almost identical to the one I'd first walked into back in April, and the same men were present. Jacob Ruppert was there, impeccably dressed by his valet in an outfit that made him look like some kind of an ambassador. Detective Jim Luntz was slumped in an arm chair, his attention focused primarily on the unlit pipe in his hand.

Andrew Vey stood near Barrow's desk, wearing another well-tailored suit. He caught my eye and ran a finger over the lapel of his jacket. I gave him a small nod of approval; his fiancée was having quite a positive impact on his wardrobe.

Addressing the team's business manager, I gave a concise account of my investigation. I hit the points that I thought were of most concern to the Yankees organization, and omitted details that I didn't think they would care about—as well as a few that I simply didn't care to discuss. I told them that Spats Pollard had been killed in a feud between rival bootleggers and that it was not due to any conspiracy against the ball club. Most importantly, I stressed, the dispute between the gangsters was over and there would be no further violence in the stadium.

When I mentioned that real beer was being sold in the ballpark's concession stands, Ruppert appeared livid. His thin mustache twitched violently and he muttered words that I couldn't quite make out in a guttural accent. I had assumed that he tacitly approved of sale of beer, since it would help attract patrons, but he seemed genuinely outraged.

Throughout the meeting, Jim Luntz maintained an

expression of complete indifference. He might as well have been taking a nap.

At the conclusion of my report, Barrow said, "Well, I believe that settles the matter." His thick brows bobbed high on his head. "I'm sure I speak for everyone here when I say the New York Yankees are indebted to you." He looked to Ruppert who gave an imperious nod.

"So now I can just play baseball?" I asked eagerly.

"Yes."

"Great!" I paused for a moment. "I hate to ask this, but I do have a request."

Barrow immediately adopted a defensive expression on his bulldog face. It was the standard one used by baseball management during contract negotiations, when the front office men pretend to be surprised and saddened that ballplayers actually want to be paid for their services. "If it's reasonable," he said. "After all, we do owe you something."

"We're leaving for the road trip on Monday. Is it okay if I travel on my own to Cleveland and meet the team there? I promise to be in time for the game—I won't even miss batting practice."

Barrow's brows knitted together, making a single hedge row. "I don't understand. Why wouldn't you want to travel with the club?"

"I'm getting married tomorrow. We'd like a little time for our honeymoon."

"Married! Well, congratulations. But why didn't you tell us? We could have arranged something special for you."

"Thank you, but we wanted to keep it quiet." I had seen a couple of "special" baseball weddings before; each time, the team had used the event for publicity purposes, with the couple getting married on the field and then walking through an archway of baseball bats held aloft by other players. I wanted our wedding day to be about Margie and me, not baseball.

"As you wish," Barrow said. "But let us contribute something: We will pay the cost of your train fare to Cleveland—get yourself a first-class berth, eat well, and the Yankees will pick up the tab."

Jacob Ruppert spoke up. "That is from the team. There will also be a little present from me. You have done me a favor, Rawlings, and I am grateful."

I thanked both men for their generous offers, and I truly appreciated their kindness. But all I really wanted from them was to keep me on the team through the World Series.

Chapter Twenty

The ceremony was simple and brief, performed at Borough Hall by a harried city clerk. He spoke in a rapid monotone, almost like an auctioneer, and had to correct himself when he initially referred to me as "Michael" Rawlings. Our only guest in attendance was my oldest friend, Karl Landfors, who served as best man and as the legally required witness.

Although not elaborate, the wedding seemed perfect to Margie and me. Its memory remained vividly with me throughout the road trip west—although for some reason I was fuzzy on the details. All I could remember for sure was how gorgeous Margie looked in an embroidered dress of pale yellow silk, holding a small bouquet. For the life of me, I couldn't recall a word that was spoken other than "I do" and "I now pronounce you man and wife."

When the team returned from the road trip, I thought life couldn't get any better. I was a married man, eager to resume our abbreviated honeymoon, and I was on a team that was six games ahead of the nearest competition and on its way to the World Series.

While the Yankees were out of town, Jacob Ruppert had been busy in New York. He canceled his leases with all the concessionaires, and took control of the refreshment stands, stocking them with perfectly legal, and thoroughly unpalatable, near beer. He'd also severed his eight-year partnership with Cap Huston, buying Huston's share of the ball club for one and a quarter million dollars.

On my second morning back in the Bronx, Detective Jim Luntz unexpectedly telephoned and asked if he could come to our home and talk. I agreed reluctantly—when would I finally be able to put the Spats Pollard murder behind me?

I knew that Margie wouldn't want our flat reeking of Luntz's noxious pipe smoke, so the detective and I sat on the front stoop of our apartment building. The day was warm, and we watched the neighborhood boys play ball in the street while we spoke.

"I thought maybe we should share some information," Luntz said. He sucked at his pipe like a baby nursing on a bottle.

Landfors had relayed a message to me from Marshall Webb that Luntz appeared to be a clean cop, so I had no qualms about speaking with him. But I was surprised that he was interested in talking now, considering how completely he had ignored Pollard's murder up to this point. "I thought it was all over," I said.

"It's never over," he sighed. "I told you: When one hood goes down, it only makes room for another."

"It's over for me," I insisted.

"That *might* be true," Luntz replied. "Unless, of course, somebody wants to get some kind of revenge on you."

"Like who?"

He drew on his pipe. "Because of you, some guys are gone now—and they probably had friends. You never know who's going to feel obligated to launch a vendetta."

"Has Leo Kessler turned up anywhere?" He was the one I had most reason to fear.

"Oh yeah. We found him in the East River—enough of him to identify, anyway."

"Geez." I didn't like the idea of anyone being killed. I doubted I would lose any sleep over the loss of Kessler, though.

"Joe Zegarra's gone, too."

"Yeah, I know. Ruppert took over all the refreshment stands."

"No. I mean he's *gone*." The detective looked at me meaningfully. "Hasn't been seen for more than a week, and his nephews have taken over his business."

"You think—?"

"I sure as hell don't think he retired." Luntz blew out a cloud of smoke. "You should have listened to me, Rawlings. There's no sense going after these guys and maybe getting yourself hurt. Just stay out of the way and let them kill each other off."

"I'll be staying out of their way from now on," I promised.

"Good." He tapped the pipe stem on his teeth. "But tell me: How did you figure out what was going on?"

"It started with something you said to me."

"What's that?"

"You said these gangsters are all fighting for a slice of the same pie," I reminded him. "Yankee Stadium was a great big new pie. A place that seats thousands of thirsty men every day is better than ten speakeasies that hold a hundred each—it's simple math." Even I could figure that out, and I could barely do enough arithmetic to calculate a batting average. "Once I realized the Yankee Stadium concessions were what they were after, I just had to sort out the connections between Pollard, Zegarra, and Kessler."

"Huh." Luntz hit the pipe on the heel of his shoe to knock out the loose ash and stood up. "So what are you going to do now?" he asked.

I rose, too. "We got a ballgame and Aaron Ward has a bruised knee. So I'm gonna play baseball."

* * *

We routed the Red Sox, which was always a cause for joy in the Yankees' locker room. On top of the victory, there were a number of individual achievements to celebrate: Babe Ruth had hit two colossal home runs, one of them nearly clearing the right field façade; Herb Pennock had struck out ten Boston batters in pitching a 8-0 shutout; and I'd gone two-for-four while playing errorless ball at second base.

Although my accomplishment was more modest than Ruth's or Pennock's, I found it every bit as satisfying and was eager to tell Margie every detail. I'd showered and was almost dressed in my street clothes when Charley O'Leary came over to me. "Hug wants to see you," the coach said. "In his office."

"Thanks, Charley." I assumed Huggins was going to compliment me on my playing today, and maybe tell that I'd be starting for Ward again tomorrow.

When I stepped into the manager's office and saw the somber expression on his face, I immediately knew he wouldn't be giving me news that I wanted to hear. Huggins nodded me toward a chair and I almost slumped into it. He hesitated, and the bags under his eyes seemed to sag a little lower.

"This is tough for me," Huggins began. "I *like* you,

and I want you on my ball club. The problem is… we can only have so many on the roster."

I nodded that I was aware of that fact. I'd been through this kind of speech before, and knew where it was leading.

"The front office is hot on some college kid," Huggins continued. "Helluva a hitter, maybe as strong as Ruth. He could add a lot of punch to the lineup and we need to make room for him…"

"And that means I got to go," I said. No matter how badly I hurt inside at the news, I was determined to go gracefully and not show the pain.

"I'm afraid so. But I want to give you a choice."

"A choice?"

"Yes. As I told you before, I believe you have the makings of a good manager. And I happen to know of some clubs that could use one. It's only the low minors, but that's where you start. I'll put in a word for you, if you like."

"I wouldn't be a player anymore?"

"At some point, we all have to hang up our spikes. You got some years left in you as a player, but this might be a good time to start thinking of the future. But it's up to you—if you don't want to manage yet, I'm sure another big league club will pick you up right away." He chuckled wryly. "In fact, I'm hoping you go for the managing job because I don't want you playing against us."

I wanted to shout, *I'm a player! I'm not hanging anything up yet!* Instead, I said, "I appreciate that, Hug. And someday I do hope to manage. When I do, I know I'll owe an awful lot to what I learned from you. But can I have a little time?"

Huggins shook his head sadly. "I'm afraid we have to

let you go now."

"I mean time to decide about a managing job."

"Oh, certainly."

"I want to talk to my, uh, my wife about it." I was still getting used to referring to Margie as my "wife."

Huggins smiled. "You *are* smart. And you'll probably have a successful marriage if you to talk to your wife about things like this. Let me know in a day or two. In the meantime…"

"Yeah, I know. I'll clean out my locker." I stood, we shook hands, and I walked to the office door. Looking back at him, I asked, "Who's the kid taking my place?"

"Gehrig." He checked a piece of paper on his desk. "Lou Gehrig. A local boy, plays for Columbia."

"Tell him I hope he makes it." Hell, if I'm going to be cut I want it to be for somebody good.

I went back into the clubhouse and quietly finished dressing. Most of the players had left, the steam from the showers had cleared, and I decided to come back early in the morning to clear out my locker when no one was around.

Babe Ruth, who'd gotten a rub down from the team trainer, was now dressed and enjoying his postgame cigar. I'd just finished knotting my necktie when he walked over to me. "Hey, kid," he said. "Charley told me you're leaving. It's a damned rotten deal, if you ask me."

"It's alright, Babe. I've been around, and I know how it goes."

He shook his big head. "Damn. I wish we could keep you."

"Me too," I said. I felt privileged to have been a part of this team, and grateful that I'd gotten to know Babe Ruth.

He punched me playfully on the shoulder and offered

me a cigar. I took it and walked to the clubhouse door.

Ruth called after me, "Hey, kid!" When I turned around, he gave me a broad wink. "I'm gonna miss you, *Mickey*."

THE END

ALSO BY TROY SOOS

Mickey Rawlings
Historical Baseball Mysteries:

Murder at Fenway Park
Murder at Ebbets Field
Murder at Wrigley Field
Hunting a Detroit Tiger
The Cincinnati Red Stalkings
Hanging Curve
The Tomb That Ruth Built

Marshall Webb – Rebecca Davies
Gilded Age Mysteries:

Island of Tears
The Gilded Cage
Burning Bridges
Streets of Fire

Nonfiction Baseball History:

Before the Curse: The Glory Days of New England Baseball

Mystery Short Stories:

Decision of the Umpire
Pick-Off Play (Mickey Rawlings)

Made in the USA
Lexington, KY
09 June 2015